Romance Unbound Publishing

The Gypsy & The Rogue
BDSM Connections - Book 4

Claire Thompson

Edited by
Donna Fisk, Jae Ashley

Cover Art - Mayhem Cover Creations
Fine Line Edit - Gabriella Wolek

Print ISBN 9781723964268

CHAPTER 1

"Holy heartthrob, Batman, who is that yummy piece of eye candy?" Ruby Beckett asked her old friend, Allie.

He was tall—maybe six foot two. Ruby could easily imagine nestling her head against his broad chest as he brought those strong arms around her. She'd been an avid reader of historical romance in her teen years, and this guy was like one of her fourteenth century Scottish warlords come to life. His auburn hair was streaked with gold, his face angular and proud, with a Roman nose and a mouth that curved slightly upward at the corners, as if he knew a dark but amusing secret.

She mentally replaced his black, sleeveless T-shirt, jeans and square-toed boots with leather and fur, a jewel-encrusted sword sheathed on his hip. Without a by-your-leave, he'd hoist her onto his steed and leap up behind her, his hard body pressed against hers as he spurred the horse away.

"That's Evan Stewart," Allie replied, pulling Ruby out of her fantasy. "He's a BDSM event coordinator. He's been helping Bob get this whole thing going."

He stood near the small group of BDSM scene players decked out in the usual assortment of leather and chain. Thirty or so people were seated on folding chairs in front of a portable tripod suspension rig, waiting for the show to begin.

Allie gave Ruby a teasing nudge with her elbow, adding, "And he's single, Ruby. Just like you."

"Hey, I've been here half a day and you're already trying to match me up?" Ruby laughed. She had arrived in Portland that morning, and Allie had enlisted her to help get her vendor booth organized for the upcoming grand opening of the BDSM Connections Event Center. "Anyway, I'm just admiring the view. I avoid the pretty boys as a rule. They tend to be full of themselves."

"Rules are made to be broken," Rylee, Allie's friend, quipped. "Seriously, though, Taggart knows him from some of the BDSM conventions where he's sold his leather gear. Says he's definitely popular with the ladies, but he's a standup guy." She turned to Allie. "When we were at dinner, I didn't get the impression he's one of those dudes who thinks he's god's gift to women. Did you?"

"Not at all," Allie agreed. "Bob took all of us to dinner last night as a kind of welcome aboard thing for vendors," she told Ruby. "Evan was very down to earth. He organizes BDSM conventions and events all over the world. Knows his way around a dungeon, too."

"And he's a wanderer, like you, Ruby," Rylee added.

"Okay, okay." Ruby flashed a grin. "I'll admit I'm interested, but there's time right? I'm here for two whole weeks."

"Two whole weeks," Allie repeated in a teasingly sarcastic tone. "Can't you ever stay put?"

"I can if I have a reason," Ruby said, glancing again at the handsome man.

Their conversation was interrupted by a booming voice. "Greetings and welcome to the soft opening of the BDSM Connections Event Center. My name is Bob Benson, though most of your know me as

Master Bob." There was scattered applause from the gathered audience. Bob had thinning blond hair fading to gray, deep-set blue eyes and a goatee that didn't quite hide his softening jaw. He was wearing a black leather vest that was a little too tight around his middle-age paunch, an ostentatiously large gold watch on his left wrist. He held a beautiful leather flogger in his hands.

"Each of you received a special invitation based on your gold status with BDSM Connections online or your experience and contribution to the BDSM scene here in Portland. Starting next week, we'll have full dungeon facilities available to rent, along with space for munches and conventions and whatever else your kinky and creative minds can come up with. This isn't a regular BDSM play club that just anyone can show up at to play. We won't have set hours or limits as to the intensity of your play, assuming it's safe, consensual and reasonably sane," he added with a guffaw. "You'll be able to rent the space, by the day or by the hour, for your parties, or for individual play."

As he spoke, the reincarnated Scottish lord stepped over to stand beside him

"As you all know," Bob continued, "the grand opening is still a week away, but I wanted to give you a taste of some of the terrific gear that will be available for sale. To that end, I'd like to introduce Evan Stewart." He gestured toward the sexy guy, who flashed a dazzling smile at the group.

"He's going to give you a quick whipping demo to provide you with a firsthand view of this beautiful impact device, just one of the many fine pieces designed by local artist, Taggart Fitzgerald." Bob held up the flogger, which was indeed lovely, with an intricately braided handle and multiple tresses that looked soft as butter. "Taggart is one of the most talented whip makers on the planet."

Ruby glanced at Rylee, who beamed at the praise for her significant other.

Allie nudged Ruby. "Whipping demo," she whispered. "I bet he'll want a volunteer."

The exact thought had just occurred to Ruby.

"Go on," Allie urged. "You know you want to."

As if her body had already decided for her, Ruby walked out of the three-sided booth and toward the audience, where there was an empty seat on the end of the front row. She took the seat as Bob handed the flogger to Evan and stepped away.

Up close, she could see laugh lines radiating from the corners of Evan's gray-green eyes, which were fringed with thick reddish blond lashes beneath straight brows. He had a tattooed ring of black barbed wire around his right biceps, and a small silver and black triskelion emblem on his left deltoid, identical to the smaller one on Ruby's right inner wrist.

To the vanilla community, it might look like a silver and black yin-yang symbol, though instead of two partitions within the circle, there were three. But the symbol, similar to the iron rings in the *Story of O*, was like a secret handshake to those in the know. The colors were significant, with the black indicating the darker side of BDSM, while some claimed the silver represented chains.

Ruby preferred to think of the silver ink on her wrist as quicksilver—a liquid metal mercury that was quick to change and couldn't be held in one place, just like her. She loved the intensity of a BDSM exchange of power, along with the excitement and unpredictability of new places, new people, new Masters.

"I need a volunteer for the flogging demo," Evan said, his eyes moving over the group. "You'll need to be comfortable with nudity and able to handle erotic pain." His voice was pleasingly husky, like a cat's warm, rough tongue stroking her senses. Ruby's entire body was alert with desire and anticipation. Pretty boy or not, she was dying to feel the stinging kiss of his flogger against her skin.

Several hands shot up, a couple of people shouting out, "Pick me!"

Ruby rose to her feet, her eyes fixed on the handsome Master. He turned his gaze to her, a slow, sexy smile lifting the corners of his mouth. "You," he said, pointing the flogger in her direction. "I choose you."

~*~

Large, almond-shaped eyes so dark he couldn't distinguish the pupils from the irises, long, loose wavy black hair, olive skin, a tiny diamond glittering in her elegant nose, the nostrils slightly flared over lush, red lips and a strong, dimpled chin. Not there a moment before, she'd appeared like a vision, momentarily distracting Evan from his patter.

Unlike the rest of the crowd, decked out in leather, boots and stilettos, this girl was wearing a red tank top over full, high breasts that clearly weren't fettered by a bra. Her flat midriff was bare above a flowing cotton skirt with swirls of silver set against a red batik background. Her feet were shod in flat leather sandals.

The woman walked over and stood beside Evan, lifting her pretty face to meet his eyes. She wasn't tall—maybe only five three or four, but she was perfectly proportioned, slender and voluptuous at the same time.

Evan rarely spent more than a month in any one location. Because his job entailed working with folks in the BDSM scene, he met lots of female submissives and sexual masochists, many of them ready and eager for casual play.

Choosing only one or two lovely ladies per venue, he would give them his full attention for the brief duration of their time together. The underlying awareness that he'd be gone in a week or a month freed him up to tumble headlong into intensity. But he always made it clear at the outset that he was only passing through, and whatever they shared was finite by definition.

Something in this young woman's gaze both thrilled and slightly unnerved him. Intrigued, he silently promised himself to get to know her better during his brief stay in Portland.

"Take off your clothing, please," he directed. "Then stand under the rig so I can secure your arms." Cuffs had been hung from the apex of the tripod on adjustable chains. The rig was set up so both the volunteer and he would be in profile to the audience as he conducted the demonstration.

He tried not to stare as she gracefully lifted the hem of her tiny shirt and pulled it over her head. Her breasts were full, the nipples dark red against smooth, tan skin. She stepped out of her sandals and hooked the elastic waistband of her skirt, dragging it down her bare legs, along with a pair of lacy black panties.

After folding her clothing in a neat pile near the rig and then stood beneath it as he'd instructed. There was a small, intricately inked red rose tattoo on her left hip, a tiny drop of blood suspended from one of the thorns on its stem. Her mons was covered in a small triangle of dark curls. Evan, used to the current fad of women shaving off their pubic hair, was oddly excited by this bold statement of feminine individuality. This, clearly, was not a woman swayed by what others did or expected.

He was vaguely aware of the excitement and sexual tension in the group of onlookers on their folding chairs, and didn't doubt every straight man there was sporting an erection at the sight of such feminine perfection, but he no longer cared about giving them a demonstration. All he wanted to do was flog this beauty, and then take her back to a room somewhere so he could fuck her.

"What's your name?" he asked.

"Ruby," she replied in a low, smooth voice.

"And you have experience in the scene?"

"I do." She turned her right arm to show him the small circular tattoo on her inner wrist.

He smiled. "And your safeword?"

"Quicksilver."

"Quicksilver," he repeated, though it was highly unlikely she would need to use it. This demo was more about giving the crowd a show and creating buzz for Taggart's gear than it was taking a submissive to the edge of her limits. He needed to remember that. This Ruby wasn't his lover, though if he had his way, he'd soon change that.

But first things first. "Stand with your back to me and lift your arms so I can cuff your wrists."

She turned her back and lifted her arms, which, while slim, were muscular and firm. Standing behind her, so close her full, round ass brushed the denim of his fly, Evan closed the Velcro cuffs around her wrists and reached up to adjust the chains to pull her arms taut.

Forcing his eyes away from the naked beauty, he addressed the group, many of whom were leaning forward in their chairs, the Doms no doubt wishing they could be the ones with the whip, the subs aching for the sting of its tresses.

"Taggart Fitzgerald makes these superior pieces by hand," Evan said, pulling his fingers through the soft strands of leather. "You won't find finer workmanship anywhere in the world." Evan wasn't lying. He had rarely seen such beautiful craftsmanship as the Leather Master brought to his BDSM implements. The leathers were first class, the handles perfectly weighted, the designs both functional and artistic. The price tags were hefty, but they were worth every penny.

He started slowly, warming Ruby's supple skin with the leather tresses, aiming carefully so as not to inadvertently curl the tips around her hips. He shifted his stance slightly and aimed for her shoulders, his balls tightening as the flogger rippled over her skin.

Though she didn't move, she reacted to the impact on thinner skin with a sudden intake of breath. Pleased, Evan struck her back and shoulders in a steady rain of leather before moving again down to her ass, which reddened nicely as he focused there.

As he whipped her, he managed to talk to the audience about the merits of the flogger, and about correct flogging technique and protocol, having done it so many times in the past that he could put his brain on autopilot. That was a good thing, because all he could concentrate on was how the rich, soft leather looked as it struck her body, and her increasingly evident reaction to its kiss.

Standing to her side, he could see her profile. Her cheeks were flushed, her lips parted. She was breathing rapidly now, her chest rising and falling, her red nipples erect, a sheen of perspiration on her glowing skin.

He wanted to take her further—to push her past her pain threshold and up into that wild sub stratosphere he knew from personal experience was like nothing in this world. But he forced himself to rein it in. For all he knew, she might shout out her safeword at any moment and totally ruin the mood.

He eased off the flogging and finally lowered his arm. Giving her a pat on that luscious ass, he said, "I hope I wasn't too rough on you."

She turned to him, her eyes sparkling. "The warm-up was great, thanks," she said in a bantering tone. "But when are you going to get to the actual flogging?"

~*~

"You are so full of shit, Ruby," Allie said with a laugh as Ruby returned to the booth, dressed once more. "Evan gave you more than just a warm-up and you know it."

Ruby shrugged. "He deserved the smartass remark. He quit right when I was really getting into it. A little more and he'd have sent me to the moon."

"His expression was priceless when you sassed him," Rylee added. "He was probably expecting you to fall to your knees and kiss his feet."

Ruby glanced back to find Evan staring in her direction. When she met his gaze, he flashed a roguish grin that melted her insides, before turning away to address the audience.

"Maybe you should have." Allie nudged Ruby. "I wouldn't let that one get away if I were you."

Allie and Ruby had first met over a decade before at a small arts college in Boston, and they'd been fast friends ever since. While Allie had focused on gemstone and rare metal jewelry, Ruby had worked with wood and textile design. Even after leaving the program, she'd continued to earn money at art fairs all over the world with her small wooden sculptures, primarily of nudes, and her painted and woven textile designs.

Along with their passion for art, the two of them had discovered their shared love of BDSM, and had spent their free time roaming the city, seeking out the BDSM underground dungeons and clubs. Ruby, wanderlust getting the better of her, ended up leaving the arts program after two years. She'd headed off to Nepal to study textile-painting techniques with an incredible artist she'd heard about online, supporting herself by teaching English at a community college in Kathmandu. Somehow a decade had got behind her, and she'd never stopped traveling.

"Do you like the way I've set this up?" Rylee asked, pulling their attention to the glass display where she'd arranged some of the finer pieces.

"It looks really good, Rylee," Allie said. "Thank you."

"It's all so gorgeous. I could just dump this stuff in a pile and it would sell," Rylee said with a grin.

"Your work is truly inspired, Allie," Ruby agreed. She continued to glance outside the booth, trying to catch a glimpse of Evan Stewart, but he had disappeared. Tuning back to Allie, she asked, "How will you have time for this retail stuff when you're so busy with the online site and the actual business of creating the jewelry?"

"We'll only sell on specific days when there are events planned. Bob's already got some things lined up. I can opt in, or not. If the place takes off, maybe I'll be in a position to hire someone to run my booth. It might become a significant secondary revenue stream."

"Listen to you, with talk of secondary revenue streams," Ruby said, impressed and horrified in equal measure. "Next thing you'll be talking about stock options and going public."

"Not hardly," Allie laughed. "But it is pretty cool to think there's a market for my BDSM pieces."

"Of course there's a market. Your work is beautiful."

Allie had created fine quality jewelry, all with a BDSM theme, including tiny handcuff earrings with pretty gemstones in place of chain, necklaces that could also be worn as slave collars, and an assortment of bracelets in silver, gold and leather that could also serve as restraining cuffs.

"Did you check these out?" Rylee said to Ruby, reaching for what looked like a walking cane set in a wicker umbrella stand by the counter. The piece was made of polished wood with a crystal knob wrapped in delicate silver filigree on top for the handle.

"But I thought you were showing just your BDSM wares in this storefront?" she asked, perplexed.

Rylee handed Ruby the cane. "See that little seam, right there?" She pointed to a barely noticeable break in the wood.

Ruby examined the cane more closely, understanding dawning. "Ah. It's hollow. I once saw a guy arrested at the airport in Mumbai, trying to get one of these things through customs. He'd hidden like a pound of hashish in there."

"Mine have something even better inside," Allie said. "Open it and see."

Curious, Ruby twisted the two halves of joined wood. They slid easily apart. She pulled out the long, thin bamboo cane, the handle end bound in leather. She whipped it in the air with a laugh. "Sweet."

She slid the cane back into its groove and returned the walking stick to its incognito status before placing it carefully back into the stand with the other four offerings, each with a unique handle grip. "I bet you'll sell out of these the first day."

"About that," Allie said with a lift of her eyebrows. "You do such beautiful woodwork, Ruby. Would you be interested in helping me with these canes while you're here? I'm more of a metal and fine gem girl, myself, as you know. I'd split the proceeds down the middle and provide the materials, if you wanted a little something to do while you're house-sitting?"

Frank and Janice Martin, friends of Ruby's parents, had picked her up from the airport that morning. She had been back in the States only a few weeks when the opportunity had presented itself to cat sit for the couple while they traveled to Canada. Ruby, already chafing from the stifling hospitality of her chronically disapproving parents, had leaped at the chance.

"Sure," Ruby agreed, picking up another of the canes. "These are made from maple, right?" As Allie nodded, Ruby continued, "We could try other woods too, like black cherry and walnut. I learned a cool polishing technique in Chile that really brings out the grain. It's been a while since I did any woodwork. I'd love to tackle the project."

"Great. I've got a nice workshop at home, and I have a good wood supplier who should be able to get us whatever you need." She looked with satisfaction around the small booth. "I think we have this pretty well in hand. You guys want to come back to my place?"

"Thanks, but I have a website I need to get finished," Rylee said.

Ruby glanced again out into the warehouse, her ass still tingling pleasantly from the flogging, but there was still no sign of the handsome Dom. "I should get back to Cuddles and Binky," she said. "It's time for their afternoon walk."

"A walk?" Rylee asked. "I thought they were cats, not dogs."

"They're very special cats," Ruby said with a smile. "Mr. and Mrs. Martin spent the better part of an hour this morning detailing their daily regimen. They wrote it all out for me, too, in case I forget. I don't dare vary from the routine, or the kitty cats might freak out." She shrugged. "It's not really that onerous. It's the least I can do in exchange for the use of a car and luxury accommodations for two weeks."

"Maybe you could come over for dinner then?" Allie said.

"Yeah," Rylee added. "Taggart and I are coming too."

Ruby wavered. As eager as she was to catch up with her dear friend and meet all the new people in Allie's life, she was exhausted from the early plane flight and not yet adjusted to the three-hour time difference.

"Liam invited Evan Stewart to join us," Allie continued. "You should totally come. Seven o'clock."

The no that had been forming on Ruby's lips vanished into thin air. "Sure," she said. "I'd love to."

CHAPTER 2

Evan pulled up to the address he'd been given and cut the engine. There were already two other cars on the street in front of the house. He picked up the bouquet of flowers he'd bought along the way and climbed out of the car.

Normally he didn't accept personal invitations from the folks involved in the BDSM events he helped to coordinate, preferring to scope out the local scene on his nights off, but this group was different. He already knew and quite liked Taggart Fitzgerald, as they'd crossed paths a number of times over the years at various BDSM events. Taggart and his friends weren't the usual weekend dabblers. They were clearly dedicated to the lifestyle. Plus, Liam had mentioned his state-of-the-art personal basement dungeon, which Evan was looking forward to checking out.

He walked up the path to the front door and pressed the bell. Allie Byrne pulled open the door with a smile. "Hey there, Evan. Come on in." She gave him a quick kiss on the cheek.

He held out the bouquet. "Thanks for having me over. These are for you."

Allie beamed as she took them. "They're beautiful. Thank you." She stepped back and gestured him inside. "Come on back. Can I get you a beer or a glass of wine?"

"Sure, a beer would be great," Evan agreed.

He followed Allie into a large living room. Taggart and his partner, Rylee, were ensconced on one end of a large sofa, snuggled against each other. "Hey there, bro," Taggart said in his deep, gravelly voice.

"Hey," Evan said back, smiling at the couple. "Hi, Rylee."

Then he saw her.

His body reacted a split second before his brain, stopping mid-stride. Blood drained from his head and limbs into his core in a sudden, adrenaline-induced gush that left him lightheaded.

She had vanished from the warehouse that afternoon before he could extricate himself from his duties with the crowd. Now she sat at the other end of the sofa, a glass of red wine in her hand, her dark, wavy hair falling over her shoulders. She had changed from her earlier outfit into a red blouse that hugged those gorgeous breasts, tucked into black slacks, red slippers on her feet. If possible, she was even more beautiful than he'd remembered.

"I'm not sure if you were formally introduced," Allie said beside him. "This is my good friend, Ruby Beckett."

For a moment, Evan forgot how to speak. He just stared, mouth hanging open, cock hardening at the sight of the lovely Ruby. His hands twitched with the muscle memory of whipping that beautiful naked body.

"Yes, yes, of course," he finally managed. He cleared his throat. "You kind of disappeared after the demo. It's nice to see you again, Ruby." The momentary fog that had assailed his brain lifted, and he realized he was grinning like an idiot.

Ruby flashed him a dimpled, radiant smile, a devilish glint in her dark eyes. "Nice to see you, too, Evan," she replied in that low, pleasing voice.

He had a nearly overwhelming desire to pull her into his arms and crush her lips with his. Instead, he forced himself to settle into the chair near her. He crossed his legs to hide the sudden erection seeing her had caused.

"I'll just go put these lovely flowers in water and get you that beer," Allie said.

Evan was able to pull his gaze from Ruby. "Thanks, Allie."

"I was just telling the girls about that National Leather Association convention in LA a few years back," Taggart said. "When that guy was doing the violet wand demonstration and there was a loose electrode and he shocked the shit out his volunteer."

"Oh, yeah," Evan replied, shaking his head. "As I recall, he didn't make too many sales that day." He looked at Taggart. "That's where we first met, right? You sold out of your gear in like ten minutes."

He had met Taggart a few more times on the road, as their paths crossed at various BDSM events. They'd gone out one night for a drink, and Evan had enjoyed Taggart's easygoing manner. Though he was pretty famous within the BDSM community for his whip making talents, the guy was completely down to earth, not a conceited bone in his body.

Taggart offered a rueful grin. "Yeah. I never could keep up with demand. Even with two full-time guys working with me now, I still spend too long on every piece."

"That's because you care about the quality," Rylee said, adoration on her pretty face. "Our slogans aren't bullshit. There really is no better whip maker than the Leather Master."

Allie reappeared a moment later with Evan's beer, Liam just behind her. Evan rose to his feet and accepted the beer from Allie before turning to shake Liam's hand. "Nice to see you again. Thanks for having me."

"Glad you could make it, Evan. Dinner's just about ready. Anyone else need a refresher?" He held up the half-full bottle of red wine. "How 'bout you, Tag? Another brewsky?"

"Nah, I'm good, thanks," the big man replied.

"Okay, but this is last call. We'll need to sober up before we go down to the dungeon."

That sounded interesting.

Rylee and Ruby both held out their glasses. As Liam refilled them, Taggart leaned toward Evan. "I heard you tried out one of my floggers this afternoon. How'd you like it?"

"It's a beautiful piece. I'm surprised you can keep any inventory in stock. Your craftsmanship is phenomenal." Evan let his gaze sweep over Ruby. "Though apparently I didn't do my volunteer justice," he added, recalling her wisecrack. "We'll have to remedy that."

Ruby lifted one fine eyebrow, her mouth quirked in a half-smile that could have meant anything.

A timer dinged from what must be the kitchen. Both Allie and Liam jumped to their feet. "Come on to the table, everyone. Liam's awesome lasagna and garlic bread await you," Allie said.

Rylee and Taggart sat on one side of the table, Liam and Allie at either end. Evan pulled out Ruby's chair, though he would rather have pulled her onto his lap. As food was passed and conversation ensued, Evan almost wished he was sitting across from her, just so he could drink in the strong, graceful planes of her face and those almond-shaped dark eyes. Only almost, though, because it was better to be next to her, especially when their arms or thighs brushed accidentally on purpose. Something fizzy and electric arced between them each time they touched.

The food was delicious, and, when he was able to get his mind off Ruby for a second, he thoroughly enjoyed both it and the company.

"You and Ruby have something in common," Allie said to Evan when everyone had eaten their fill. "You've both traveled all over the world."

"Is that right?" Evan turned his head with interest to the sexy woman beside him. He wanted to hear more of that low, smooth voice.

But Ruby only said, rather cryptically, "Yep."

"Ruby doesn't just pass through, either," Allie continued. "We met in Boston, where we're both originally from. But she's lived in Mexico, Chile, Argentina, Greece, Budapest and Nepal." Allie looked at Ruby. "What am I forgetting, Ruby?"

"New York City, if that counts," Ruby said with a laugh. "That sometimes seems like a foreign country all to itself."

"Impressive," Evan said, meaning it. "I've done a lot of traveling, but mostly in the US and Canada. Plus a short stint in London."

"She's been there, too, right, Ruby?" Allie interjected, clearly proud of her friend.

"Cut it out, Allie," Ruby said, though there was affection in her tone. "Let's talk about something else, like that dungeon you told me about. I can't wait to see it."

"We can do better than talk about it," Liam said, pushing back his chair. "Come on down, and we'll give you the grand tour."

Liam wasn't kidding. The dungeon was fantastic, as well-equipped as most BDSM play clubs. There was a gorgeous St. Andrew's cross made of wood with an inlay of steel, along with a padded bondage horse, a wooden punishment beam and a woven leather sling with stirrups set in an aluminum stand.

"And check this out," Liam said, leading them toward the back of the dungeon where the floor and wall had been tiled like a bathroom. "Allie has become incredibly well trained in intense water play. She's grace personified."

His wife's face flushed a pretty pink at his words, and she smiled up at him as if he were a god. A sudden, uncharacteristic stab of jealously poked at Evan's gut, but he shook it away. The world was full of sexy submissives he had yet to meet. If he had his way, Ruby would be the next one to succumb to his charms.

"Wow, this setup is really something," he said appreciatively. They had installed a large Plexiglas water submersion tub. There were three shower hoses topped with adjustable spray nozzles neatly coiled on the wall nearby. Evan had always found water play, especially boundary-pushing immersion and breath play, quite erotic, with the right partner.

"Would you care to see a demonstration?" Liam asked, putting his arm around his wife.

Evan would have rather put Ruby into the submersion tub, but he only said, "Sure."

"Allie," Liam said. "Strip and take your place against the wall."

"Yes, Sir Liam," she said, her expression softening.

Rylee and Taggart were standing nearby, Ruby on Evan's other side. Rylee stood on tiptoe and whispered something into Taggart's ear. He nodded. "My sub would like to join Allie for the demonstration. That okay, Liam?"

"The more the merrier," Liam said with a smile. "How about you, Ruby? There's room for three."

"No, thanks," Ruby said. "I'll just watch for now."

For now.

That boded well, or at least Evan decided to assume it did. The night was still young, after all.

Allie and Rylee stripped down to bare skin. They were both extremely easy on the eyes. Allie was slender and graceful. Her nipples had been pierced, and pretty gold hoops accentuated her high, round breasts. Rylee had the broad shoulders and narrow hips of an athlete, though her breasts were large and full.

Ruby stood quietly beside Evan as Liam directed both girls to sit on stools set against the wall. The guys wrapped rope around the girls' thighs, tying it off on either side of each stool to hooks strategically placed in the wall. This position forced them to spread their legs wide.

The girls then raised their arms overhead, allowing their wrists to be cuffed and secured against the wall, further immobilizing them for the fun to come. Evan would have enjoyed using the hose to spray those pretty, bare cunts until each girl begged for mercy, but he was content to stand beside Ruby and watch—for now.

Liam turned on the spigots below each coiled hose and handed Taggart one of the hoses. Liam looked back to Evan and Ruby. "I'm a softy, so I added a thermostat feature to the hoses. Though if Allie is being punished, it's cold water all the way," he added with an evil grin.

The guys took their places in front of the bound, naked women.

"Let's stand over here so we don't miss the action." Evan put his arm around Ruby's shoulder as he guided her to a spot with a clear view. He left his hand in place as they came to a stop and was pleased when she didn't pull away. He glanced down at her. She was staring at the spectacle before them, her full lower lip caught in her teeth, her eyes wide.

The men aimed their nozzles at the girls' naked bodies and pulled the triggers, sending jets of water pulsing between their forcibly spread legs. Both girls squealed.

Ruby stiffened, drawing in a sudden, sharp intake of air.

Evan glanced down at her again. "You okay?"

She looked up at him, her dark, luminous eyes wide. "Yeah. I just"—she paused and blew out a breath—"I'm fine. Water play makes me kind of nervous. It's just so…intense."

"You act like that's a bad thing," Evan said with a grin, but he pulled her a little closer, feeling suddenly protective.

"Oh god, oh god, oh god," Allie began to chant, while Rylee just mewled like a kitten, her hands clenched tight around the ropes above her wrist cuffs.

"Not yet," Liam warned.

"Wait for permission," Taggart added.

They moved the focus from the girls' pussies to their breasts, eliciting more squeals and wriggling.

"Please," Rylee gasped as the water cascaded over her bound form. "I can't…"

"Oh god, oh god, oh god," Allie repeated, like a mantra, trembling from head to toe, her cheeks flushed, her eyes squeezed tightly shut.

Ruby put her hand on Evan's arm, momentarily distracting him with her touch.

"Don't worry," he reassured her. "It's clear they all know what they're doing."

Ruby nodded, some of the tension leaving her body.

Then, at a nod from Liam, both guys adjusted their hose nozzles so the spray narrowed to a single, pulsing stream. They aimed the water between the girls' legs, letting the spray pummel their sexes with relentless force.

"Now," Liam shouted. "Come for us."

The girls' moans and breathy cries filled the air as they shuddered and twisted beneath the water's onslaught. Ruby gripped hard on Evan's arm. His cock throbbed, his balls aching as he watched the girls climax.

Only when the guys finally eased off the triggers and moved toward the girls did Ruby release her death grip on Evan's arm. "Whoa," she breathed. "That was intense."

The men helped their women from the stools and wrapped thick, white robes around their shivering forms.

Liam was grinning, the pride evident on his face as he hugged his wife to his side. Taggart bent down and kissed Rylee on the mouth as he pulled her into a bear hug. They led the girls to the recovery couch, which was near the back wall of the dungeon. The girls collapsed side by side on the couch. Ruby rushed over and inserted herself between them, putting her arms around their shoulders.

Evan offered to help as Taggart and Liam returned to the water area to squeegee the floor and coil the ropes.

"Nah, we got this," Liam said with a shake of his head. "But you could make tea for the girls." There was a glass electric kettle on the counter near the recovery couch, already filled with water. Evan turned it on and found mugs in the cupboard above, along with tea bags and a small plastic bottle of honey shaped like a bear.

He turned to the girls still nestled together on the couch. "Honey in your tea?"

"Yes, honey for me," Allie said. She had coiled her copper-colored hair into a knot on top of her head. Her face was flushed, her smile luminous.

"Me, too," Rylee echoed, her face also flushed, her dark hair damp and tucked behind her ears.

"How about you, Ruby," Evan asked. "Would you like some tea?

"Not for me, thanks," Ruby said, getting up from the couch. "But let me help you."

Ruby put the tea bags into the mugs and squeezed in some honey as Evan poured in the boiling water. "We make a good team," she said.

"In more ways than one," Evan said, flashing his *I want you* smile at her.

They handed the tea to the girls, who accepted the hot mugs with thanks. The guys had finished cleanup and now approached the group.

"This place is really something," Evan said appreciatively. "I'd love to check out that rope suspension rig you've got set up there."

"Sure," Liam said. In the center of the space, Liam had hung thick ropes from the ceiling beams, the ends knotted around large metal rings perfect for suspending a naked sub girl. "You'll need a volunteer."

"You read my mind," Evan said, fixing his gaze on Ruby, who had followed them. "How about you, Ruby? Care to continue where we left off this afternoon?"

Her saucy smile reached her eyes. "Sure, but I think something more intense than a flogging would be fun," she suggested, to his delight. "And how about we shake things up a bit, hmm? You already had a turn to be the Dom. Now it's mine."

"I'm sorry, what?" Evan said, now confused.

"You look like a guy who enjoys a challenge," she continued in a bantering tone. "Why don't *you* strip for *me*, and we'll see what you're made of?"

Now he got it. She expected him to refuse, but she didn't know him. He hadn't pegged her for a switch, but looking at her now, with her hands on her hips and the challenge clear in her saucy expression, he didn't doubt her. Nor would he miss this chance to scene with her.

"That's quite an offer," Liam said with a laugh. "But Evan may not be hardwired to receive a whipping with as much grace as I heard you demonstrated today."

"Evan might not be up for it, but I'd be happy to volunteer," Taggart interjected, approaching the group. "After all, turnabout is fair play now and again. We should be willing to experience what we mete out." He turned back to Rylee. "That is, if it's all right with you, babe?"

Rylee lifted her tea mug in consent. "Sure, why not?"

"No, that's okay," Evan said quickly, his skin already prickling in anticipation. "I got this."

He'd play Ruby's game, but he'd raise the ante. "I'm willing to submit to you, Mistress Ruby," he said with an easy smile. "But only if I get the chance to Dom you in return."

Ruby pursed her lips as if considering the offer. Then she tossed back her thick, glossy hair, her dark eyes flashing. "Okay. You've got a deal."

Evan unbuttoned his shirt and let it fall from his shoulders. He could feel the eyes of everyone in the room, but he kept his gaze on Ruby as he kicked off his shoes, undid his belt and slipped his jeans and underwear down his legs.

He walked to stand beneath ropes that were suspended from the beams. He glanced at Ruby as he lifted his arms up to the cuffs. She was watching him with an enigmatic smile. Determined to play the game, he smiled back.

Liam and Taggart secured his wrists and then stepped back to stand beside their partners. Evan could see Ruby in his peripheral vision as she moved toward the wall that was hung with a wide variety of whips and floggers. He was vaguely aware the others were watching the unfolding scene, but his focus was on Ruby.

She returned with a short-handled single tail whip, a wicked gleam in her eyes. "Think you can handle something a little more intense than a flogging, boy?" She cracked the tail in the air near his ass.

Evan's heart kicked up a notch. Who *was* this girl? "Sure," he replied, not missing a beat. Though it had been a long time, he could still remember the sweet, stinging kiss of a single tail from his early days in the scene. "Can you?"

"Try me," she replied, her words sending a shiver of lust through him.

She appeared in front of him, eyeing his naked body as if she owned him. His cock stiffened beneath her scrutiny, and there wasn't a damn thing he could do about it. She knew her power, but what beautiful woman didn't?

"I'll warm you up first," Ruby said. "Just in case, what's your safeword? That is, if you even have one?"

"*Puta madre*," he replied, thinking of his early submissive explorations with Mistress Marta.

"Pooty whatee?" Rylee asked from behind him.

"He said *puta madre*," Ruby answered for him with a laugh. "It's Spanish for motherfucker."

"Yeah," he agreed with a chuckle. "Not quite as poetic as

quicksilver, but it gets the message across."

She moved behind him and ran her fingers lightly over his ass cheeks before smacking him lightly.

Rather than pulling away, he leaned into her, welcoming the warming slap of skin on skin as she slowly but steadily increased the intensity. Her touch was sure and firm. Though he wasn't into the spanking itself, he did like the feel of her hand on his body.

When his bottom was tingling, the blood flowing beneath the skin, she spoke from behind him. "How about ten strokes? Think you can handle that?"

"Yes, please, Mistress," he said with a smirk.

The first stroke whipped over his left buttock. He drew in a breath, but managed to remain quiet. The second one landed on the other cheek in the same spot, her aim perfect.

Again and again, the lash flicked and stung over his flesh. Sweat prickled beneath his arms as the throw snapped against him. Evan kept his lips pressed tightly together, flaring his nostrils to keep from gasping with pain. As the years had passed, he'd lost his love of masochistic play, his sensibilities shifting solidly toward the D side of the D/s equation. Though he got no erotic pleasure from the whipping, he could still appreciate her skill and grace.

"Ten," Ruby finally said as Evan sagged with relief against his cuffs.

"Good job, Evan," Taggart said heartily, coming up beside them. "I've watched you scene before at the conventions, but this is the first time I've seen you submit. You took that like a real sub. I'm impressed."

Evan shrugged, mildly embarrassed at the praise.

Ruby appeared again in front of him. "Thank me, boy." She lifted the whip to his mouth.

Evan gave the whip a cursory kiss. "I'll thank you, all right," he said with a grin. "Now it's your turn."

"You think so, huh?"

"I know so."

Liam and Taggart released him from the ropes while Ruby wiped down the whip and returned it to the rack. Rylee and Allie walked over, still in their robes, their clothing in their hands.

"I hate to break up the party," Taggart said, "but Rylee has a Jiu Jitsu competition in the morning and she needs to get her rest." He clapped Evan on the shoulder.

"And Liam and I need to clean the kitchen before bed," Allie said with a meaningful glance at Liam that made Evan wonder what was going on.

"That's right," Liam continued smoothly, picking up the theme. "But don't let us interrupt your scene. You two can stay down here and take all the time you like."

Allie smirked at Ruby, and the two couples disappeared up the stairs.

After they'd gone, Ruby grinned at Evan. "She used to do that back in college too."

"Who used to do what?" Evan asked, though he was pretty sure he knew.

"Allie. She orchestrated their group exit just now, you can be sure of it. That girl's always been an incurable matchmaker. Even back in college, she'd try to fix me up with some guy or other." Ruby laughed, affection in her tone. "It never worked out."

"Maybe it'll be different this time," Evan said, keeping his tone light. He bent down and grabbed his clothing, though he made no move to get dressed. His ass was still stinging from the whipping. "Be that as it may, I need some aftercare, *Mistress*."

"That you do." Ruby craned her head to see his ass. "You have several nice marks there. You did pretty good, for a Dom," she teased.

"Yeah? You did pretty good for a sub girl."

"Uh huh," she said with a toss of her hair. She led him back to the recovery couch. Sitting down, she patted her lap. "I'll just put Arnica on those welts and you'll be good as new."

Evan dropped his clothing in a heap by the couch. He lay across her lap, his cock instantly hardening against her thigh as she smoothed the soothing balm on his welts. When she was done, she gave him a light pat. "There you go. All better."

Evan lifted himself and sat beside her on the sofa, wincing slightly as his bottom made contact with the towel she'd spread there.

Ruby reached for one of the bottles of water that had been thoughtfully placed on the side table beside the Arnica and a small pile of hand towels. "Want some?" she asked.

Evan shook his head. "No, thanks. I'm good." He smiled. "Now it's my turn."

Ruby started to rise from the sofa. "Ten strokes? Piece of cake." She looked around the empty dungeon. "Can you handle the ropes on your own?"

Evan reached out for her arm and gently pulled her back down to the sofa. "I don't plan to whip you, Ruby."

She lifted her eyebrows in evident surprise. "You don't?"

He shook his head. "I want to spank you."

"A spanking?" She made a mock pout. "But I like a challenge."

"I'll make it a challenge. Don't worry." He pointed to his lap. "Now, get naked and present your ass, sub girl."

She stared at him a moment, her mouth working as if she were about to protest, but then she just nodded. Her eyes on his, she unbuttoned her blouse and let it fall from her shoulders, revealing her bare breasts. She stepped out of her slippers and slid her pants and underwear down her thighs while Evan tried not to gape.

"Okay," she said, kicking the pants away. "I'm all yours."

~*~

Ruby had figured Evan for a guy who could dish it out, but wouldn't be able to take it. Boy, had she been off the mark. He'd handled the single tail with considerable grace. If she hadn't experienced his flogging earlier that day or felt the power of his dominant persona that radiated like an aura from his being, she would have believed, based on their quickie scene, that he was a sub.

She couldn't recall the last time she'd been so attracted to a guy. It was as if they shared a secret, and she just needed to get closer to hear what it was.

She lay over his lap, keenly aware of his erection, which was trapped between her thigh and his flat stomach. She would have liked something more intense than a spanking, but at the same time, the thought of Evan's big, strong hands stroking and smacking her bottom would be nice foreplay for whatever else he might have in mind.

He placed one hand on her lower back and used the other to lightly smack her ass, alternating cheeks. His touch felt good, and she sighed contentedly as she relaxed against his strong thighs.

The first hard smack startled her, its warm sting spreading over her flesh. She moaned softly in appreciation as the second stroke landed, just as hard as the first. Again and again his hand crashed down, smashing her pelvis against his legs. Her skin quickly heated, the force of his hard, insistent palm dragging her down into an undertow of erotic pain that nearly threatened to engulf her. He was doing something with his palm that brought extra sting to each swat, and soon she was panting in her effort not to cry out or beg him to stop.

Unable to help herself, she wriggled against him in a vain effort to avoid the brunt of his iron palm. As she twisted, her legs parted and her sex came into direct contact with his bare thigh. The pleasant friction distracted her as his leg came up to meet her sex.

She swiveled her hips as he continued the hard spanking, her clit now making direct, intense contact with his leg. A tremor of pleasure shot through her loins with each smashing stroke on her burning ass. Her heart was thumping wildly in her chest, the blood pounding in her ears, her breathing a ragged rasp in her throat.

Still his hand came down, his other hand on her lower back, holding her in place as his thigh continued to move provocatively against her throbbing clit. She yelped in a steady, breathy staccato, unable to stop. She was either going to scream her safeword or have an orgasm, or both.

And then...

Then the alchemical transformation took over. Pleasure and pain melted together, reforming into something so powerful and intense Ruby could barely process it. A huge, cresting wave of sensation rose through her, lifting her from her body and hurtling her into an encompassing silence, as if the world had suddenly ceased to exist. She was floating in a vast, white space, her body weightless, her mind a blissful blank. Her spirit soared into a silent, breathtaking vista of the most profound peace she'd ever experienced...

~*~

Ruby lay still, her breathing deep and even, her eyes closed, a soft smile on her lips. During the spanking, she had moved from stoic endurance to panting struggle and finally into that dark, sweet place where no Dom could follow.

Evan put his mouth close to her ear. "Hey," he whispered. "You okay?"

"Yes," she breathed so softly he wasn't entirely sure she'd spoken.

He stroked the hair from her face and tucked it behind her ear. Moving carefully so as not to disturb her, he reached for the tube of Arnica she'd left on the end table by the sofa and squeezed a large dollop onto his palm.

He'd been so involved in the scene, he hadn't noticed the toll it had taken on his hand, which was nearly as red as her sweet ass, still stinging from the steady, constant impact. He rubbed the balm over his palm, and then squirted more onto his fingers, which he gently massaged into her burning skin.

His cock throbbed. It would have been simple enough to flip her over and sink his shaft into her tight, wet heat. He briefly considered it, but then dismissed the idea. When he took Ruby, he wanted her fully conscious.

Instead, he lifted her gently and turned her over, cradling her in his arms. Her eyes remained closed, though she sighed, a small smile lifting her lips. As he looked down at her pretty face, so peaceful in repose, he marveled that, though they'd only met a few hours before, on some level he felt as if he'd known her since the moment he'd been born.

He snorted softly, amused at himself. He wasn't one who went in for romantic notions or poetic thoughts. Yeah, he wanted to fuck her, but he'd wanted to fuck her since the moment he'd seen her. That didn't mean they had some kindred connection. No, it was just the scene talking. He'd been moved by her ability to fly at his hand. It made him feel tenderly toward her.

He shifted her so she was more upright, though he wasn't quite yet ready to let go of her. In fact, he would have been content to hold her forever…

~*~

Ruby lay drifting in a deep, peaceful place. As she came slowly to herself, she became aware of the thrilling, low notes and rough music in Evan's voice, though it took several more seconds for her brain to process the sound as words. She opened her eyes, taking a moment to focus on his handsome face.

His expression of concern softened into a smile. "There you are. You left the planet for a while. Everything okay?"

She smiled back, the veil of languorous peace burning away as full consciousness returned, though the lingering sense of wellbeing remained. "Everything's great," she said, beaming up at him. "What the hell did you do to me?"

He gathered her a little closer, dipping his head so that for a moment she thought he was going to kiss her. Instead, he said softly, "I gave you a pretty intense spanking, Ruby. I was waiting for a cue that you wanted me to stop, but you didn't give me one. I hope I didn't go too far."

"No, not too far. It was…" How to explain? Language so often failed when it came to flying, a state she rarely achieved, and certainly never before during a casual scene with a virtual stranger. And yet, that was what had happened, no question about it. With only his hand, this man had taken her to that secret, sacred place deep in her psyche that she'd only visited a few times in her life, and then only after extensive BDSM with a trusted partner.

"It was…?" he prompted.

"Perfect," she replied. "Absolutely perfect."

~*~

Evan lifted Ruby from his lap and set her on the sofa beside him. He reached for a bottle of water, twisted off the cap and handed her the bottle. She took a long drink and gave it back to him. As he returned it to the side table, she pushed back her hair. "Can you hand me my clothes, please?"

"I don't know. What if I want to keep you naked?" Evan replied with a grin, not entirely kidding.

"It's good to want things," Ruby said with a laugh, but she continued to hold out her hand.

With a mock sigh, Evan reached down for the small pile and handed it to her. Bending back down, he reached for his jeans and boxers.

She winced as she pulled up her underwear and pants. "Ouch," she said with a grimace. "That was quite a spanking, Master Evan."

"You're welcome," he said with a laugh. He was definitely ready to continue this party of two. "How about we thank our hosts and go back to my place? I'm staying at a bed-and-breakfast not far from here."

For a moment she looked like she was going to agree, but then she said, "That's a tempting offer, but I think I need to call it a night. I haven't stopped to take a breath since five this morning, Boston time."

Evan swallowed his disappointment. He still had a few weeks in town, and if he had his way, he'd be seeing more of this lovely submissive. A lot more.

"No worries," he said casually, getting to his feet. He retrieved his shirt from the floor and put it back on. "How about let's thank our hosts, and I'll walk you to your car?"

"Sounds like a plan."

It took another several minutes to make their thanks and goodbyes, and then Evan and Ruby were outside. The night air was cool, and Ruby wrapped her arms around her torso. "*Brrr,*" she said.

"Let me warm you up." Evan took her into his arms and dipped his head, touching his mouth to hers. Her lips parted, her hands coming up around his neck. Her tongue was warm and insistent in his mouth as she pressed her small body against his. He could feel the points of her erect nipples against his chest as he gathered her close. Everything about her felt right in his arms, and he wanted to kiss her forever.

When she finally pulled away, it was only with the greatest reluctance that he let her go. He reached into his back pocket and took out his wallet. Pulling a card from it, he handed it to her. "I'm in town for a couple of weeks. Let's stay in touch, okay?"

She took the card and smiled up at him. "Will you be at BDSM Connections tomorrow? I'm meeting Rylee in the morning to help her set up Taggart's booth. Maybe I'll see you there?"

Evan had planned to do some internet networking for Bob's site back at the B&B the next morning and not go in until the afternoon. But he instantly replied, "You bet. See you in the morning."

CHAPTER 3

"Hey there, Evan," Bob Benson called out from the front of the warehouse as Evan entered via the back entrance. "You read my mind. I was just about to text you to see if you could come in." Bob stood just outside the doublewide mesh booth that would house the items they'd ordered for retail sale for the grand opening weekend. He was surrounded by a stack of boxes, a box cutter in his hand.

Evan had parked in the side lot, passing a UPS delivery truck on its way out. He'd seen a pickup truck alongside Bob's Lexus, but he hadn't seen Ruby's car. He glanced around the warehouse as he approached Bob, but no one else appeared to be there.

Evan was pleased with how the space was coming together. The ten thousand square foot warehouse had high ceilings, the ductwork and beams exposed. Banks of windows on either side of the space let in the light, but were high enough no one passing by could see in. The concrete floor had been covered with laminate flooring that mimicked hardwood. Vendor booths were set up on either side of the front entrance.

They had already cordoned off a large section near the back of the warehouse for the dungeon. They were expecting delivery shortly of some St. Andrew's crosses, bondage tables and spanking benches for use in the main area for public play, and they planned to set up portable, enclosed booths along the perimeters of the dungeon for private play. BDSM groups would be able to rent the entire space for their private events, and individuals could rent single scene stations and privacy booths.

When he reached Bob, Evan said, "It's Sunday. I thought we weren't getting this stuff until tomorrow."

"We weren't," Bob agreed. "Lucky I was here when the delivery guy showed up. Apparently they work seven days a week now, just like us," he added with a rueful grin.

"Say, have you seen Rylee and Ruby?" Evan asked, looking around again as if they might suddenly appear. "I thought they were going to be here this morning setting up Taggart's booth."

"You just missed them. They went out to grab some breakfast about ten minutes ago. They went in one car, though, so they should be back. Anyway, I had this great idea that involves you, if you're up for it."

"I'm listening."

"When we're reselling the gear at the grand opening, I was thinking it'd be fun to add a twist."

"And that would be...?" Evan willed himself to stay patient. Bob often took a while to get to the point.

"Well," Bob said eagerly. "What if we do live demos for the grand opening? We can have a floor model set up of the more elaborate equipment. Letting folks try them out on the spot will add some pizazz to opening day, and should be a definite boost to sales."

"It's a great idea if it's handled right," Evan agreed. "But as I recall, these are all extreme restraint devices. You could be opening yourself up to liability if someone got hurt testing out the gear."

"We're on the same wavelength, buddy," Bob said. "That's where you come in. I want you to put together floor models of the equipment that needs assembly and then round up a volunteer, today if possible, to try them out yourself. That way, you can oversee folks if they want to use the equipment before buying. You can make sure they're not doing something dangerous."

Just to be sure he understood, Evan said, "So, you want me not only to build the floor models, but try them out in advance with a partner?" A certain petite, dark-eyed girl leaped instantly to mind.

"Yeah. I'd do it myself, but something's come up today. I know a great lady who will be happy to volunteer," Bob said. "She's a little older than you, but she's always ready, willing and able, if you catch my drift."

"Thanks," Evan said, keeping his expression neutral. "I have someone else in mind, but if that doesn't pan out, I'll shoot you a text."

"No problemo, stud man." Bob handed the box cutters to Evan. "I better skedaddle if I'm going to make it up to Seattle and back."

"Seattle?"

"Yeah," Bob said, rubbing his hands together. "It's a terrific opportunity that could save me a bundle. A guy I know up there is closing down his BDSM club and wants to get rid of some of his bigger pieces of equipment. If it's up to par, I could cancel some of the new order we're expecting later this week. If this pans out, I'll rent a U-Haul and be back this evening."

"That's terrific," Evan said. "Let me know when you're back and I'll help you unload the stuff."

"Thanks, buddy. You're the best."

~*~

"No kidding. A purple belt in Jiu Jitsu? That's awesome," Ruby enthused. She nodded as the waiter appeared, a pot of coffee in his hand. He topped off her cup and melted away.

Rylee shrugged, a bashful smile on her face. "I've been training for years. It's a great workout. My trainer, Marco, is the best. He's into the scene, too, he and his husband, Jordan."

"That's cool. How did you meet Taggart?"

Rylee's face softened, her eyes shining. "Jordan is a documentary film maker. He let me come along on a shoot for the BDSM Connections website featuring the Leather Master—that's how Taggart's known in the scene. It was love at first sight, at least on my side." She grinned, adding, "We had a few bumps in the road at first, but I've never been happier in my life. Taggart is my dream Master."

"You girls and your Masters," Ruby said with a laugh.

"Not for you, huh? I guess you're more the Mistress type, am I right?"

For a moment, Ruby was confused. Then she remembered the scene Rylee had witnessed the night before. "Oh, you mean because of me whipping Evan?"

"You seemed to get a kick out of it."

Ruby shrugged. "It was mainly to give Evan a hard time." She leaned forward. "To tell you the truth, I didn't expect him to agree to it."

"He was into it, though," Rylee said. "I didn't have him pegged for a sub at all. When he did the flogging demo with you at the warehouse, I could feel his mastery from across the room."

"Oh, he's a Master, all right, and then some," Ruby said fervently, delicious memories of the night before moving through her mind. "In retrospect, I think he was humoring me by letting me use that single tail. Either that, or he was just showing off," she added with a grin.

"He could do that just by getting naked," Rylee said with a laugh.

"That guy has a killer bod."

"That he does," Ruby agreed. "After you guys left, we shared an incredibly intense scene. He sent me flying with just a spanking. It was, pardon my French, fucking amazing."

"That's one thing I love about the BDSM scene. You can skip all the dating foreplay and dancing around and cut right to the chase."

"Agreed. There's something about the shared hardwiring that allows you to get right down to business, if the connection is right. Too bad he didn't follow through."

"How so?" Rylee asked.

"He said he'd be at the warehouse this morning." Ruby frowned. "Maybe the connection wasn't as intense for him as it was for me."

"Or maybe we just missed him," Rylee said, lifting her hand to signal to the waiter. "Let's head back and see."

When Ruby pulled into the warehouse parking lot, her heart skipped several beats. Bob's car was gone, but there was a second car now in the lot.

"Yay, that's his car, I'm pretty sure," Rylee said. "Ye of little faith."

"Sweet," Ruby said. "Now that I think about it, we didn't really settle on a time." She smiled at her new friend. "You coming in?"

"No," Rylee said, her keys already in hand. "I have to get back to work. I have a deadline for a client." She glanced again at Evan's car. "Have fun, lucky girl."

"Jealous?" Ruby teased.

Rylee flashed a grin. "Maybe just a little." Then she shook her head.

"Not really, though. I have the Master of my dreams at home. He gives me everything I need and then some."

Taggart was a pretty cool guy, Ruby had to admit. She experienced a sudden, unexpected twinge of longing. What would it be like to settle down with just one guy? Especially a wonderful, steady, sexy guy like Taggart Fitzgerald? Or, for that matter, Evan Stewart?

She shook away the crazy idea. Evan was a wanderer like her. This infatuation would no doubt run its course by the time they both said their goodbyes, and that was fine with Ruby. Still, she couldn't deny the rush of pleasure at the thought of seeing him again.

She and Rylee exchanged a quick hug. "Thanks for breakfast. Catch ya later."

Ruby entered the warehouse through the front door. There he was by the vendor booths, looking as gorgeous as he had the night before. "Hey there," he said, getting to his feet. He'd been in the process of assembling some kind of equipment. His smiled zipped directly to her nipples. "Thought I'd missed you."

She came toward him. "Glad you finally decided to show up," she said in a teasing voice.

"Nice of you to come back," Evan retorted with a grin. Then he stepped forward, opening his arms, and she moved into them. She was expecting a cursory peck on the cheek, but he enfolded her in a strong embrace, his lips instantly seeking hers.

Ruby melted into their kiss, her body going limp as his tongue entered her mouth and his hands roamed over her back and ass. Heat whooshed through her core, like a furnace igniting inside her. Her entire body tingled with desire.

When he finally let her go, her brain, which had temporarily short-circuited, took a moment to get back online. She blew out a breath as she tried to regain her composure.

"What've you got there?" She waved her hand toward a restraining device made up of a vertical metal pole about an inch around and maybe eight feet high, attached to a base plate, wrist cuffs dangling near the top, a leather collar secured midway down, and a horizontal spreader bar attached just above the base.

"New toys. We got these wholesale and we're going to sell them at the grand opening next weekend." Evan put his hand on the piece he had just assembled. "This beauty is called the Total Lockdown System. It's pretty cool, actually, because it can be modified into several configurations so you can put your partner right where you want them. It comes with a lot of extra toys, like a breast crusher, an anal impaler and a dildo holder. "

"Yikes," Ruby said with a laugh, hugging herself. "Sounds awesome." She moved closer, looking at the add-on toys still in bubble wrap on the table. "Kind of complicated though—all those extras and attachments."

"Exactly," Evan agreed. "That's why I'm putting all this stuff together in advance. Bob asked me to build a floor model of each one. He's going to let folks try out the toys on the spot."

He moved closer to her, his husky voice suddenly softer. "That's where you come in, Ruby."

He placed his hand around her throat, the gesture so unexpected that Ruby drew in a sharp, startled breath as she stared up at the handsome man. Her nipples hardened instantly, her pussy moistening. Her hands moved instinctively toward the hand on her throat, though she made no real effort to pull it away.

On the contrary, something inside her opened and softened with longing at his dominant touch, and her hands fell away. She adored breath play and erotic choking, and would have melted to the floor if he hadn't kept such a tight, delicious hold on her throat.

"Me?" she managed to gasp.

"You," he agreed, staring down at her with those penetrating, gray-green eyes that stripped her soul bare. "I need to test all these toys before we put them up for sale. You're going to be my volunteer. You're going to get naked and let me use every one of these devious devices on you."

If his hand hadn't been at her throat, she was sure she could have come up with some kind of snappy, witty response to his audacious assumption that she'd go along with the idea, without even asking her permission or discussing her boundaries and limits.

As it was, all she managed was, "Oh, you think so, huh?"

He tightened his grip, and she couldn't stifle a moan of pure, raw lust. "Yes, Ruby. I do."

He let her go. She stumbled back, grateful as he reached out to steady her. "Where were you thinking of conducting these practice sessions?" Her voice came out hoarse and she cleared her throat. "It's not exactly private here."

He lifted his eyebrows, his lips quirking into a sexy smile. "You didn't seem too concerned about privacy yesterday. Why so modest all of a sudden?"

She looked around the large, empty warehouse. "What if some random delivery guy or repairman wanders in?"

"Delivery guy's already been here, and no one else is scheduled to come in, as far as I know. But you're right. Privacy would be a good thing." He reached into his pocket and pulled out a set of keys. "I'll just lock up to be sure. Does that suit you?"

"You're pretty presumptuous, especially for a guy who let me whip his ass." She had tried for sassy, but she was too breathless to pull it off. The thought of submitting to this man again made her all wobbly inside. Unlike the two other times they'd scened, this time they would be all alone as she willingly allowed herself to be restrained and completely at his mercy.

She usually took a little longer to know someone before leaping into an intense scene without anyone else around. But her gut told her she could trust Evan. It wasn't just that he was clearly a skilled Dom who intimately knew his way around a BDSM dungeon. Something in him spoke directly to her core, bypassing language or time. She touched her throat again, recalling his powerful touch, and her own melting reaction.

Evan grinned. "I guess I am." He moved closer, the grin fading to a hint of a smile. Lifting his hand, he stroked her cheek with two fingers, his beautiful eyes locked on hers. "All kidding aside, I felt something with you last night, Ruby. You're an incredibly responsive submissive, and I would be honored if you'd agree to be my partner in testing these devices."

This simple, heartfelt declaration pushed her closer to a yes. She was about to agree, when Evan added, "Check out the packing list of toys. It's on the table in the booth. I'll just go lock up while you look it over."

As he walked away, Ruby stepped into the booth and picked up the piece of thin, yellow carbon paper.

Anal Impaler - 10

Female Bondage Ball - 10

Rack Compactor - 10

Prison Stockade with optional fucking rod - 10

Pussy Spreader - 10

Total Lockdown System - 10

Zeus Electrosex Deep Intruder - 10

Zeus Electrosex Penis Band - 10

Ruby's imagination kicked into immediate overdrive. No question about it, she'd love to try out some of this stuff. Looking at the last item on the list, she grinned to herself.

Evan returned a moment later, two bottles of water and a small stack of towels in his hand. "So, did you make up your mind?"

"I'll do it on one condition."

"Which is…?"

"*I* get to try out the electrosex penis band on *you*."

His face registered a rapid play of emotions, moving from *no way* to *what the hell* in a matter of seconds. Then he shrugged and flashed a grin. "Lady, you've got yourself a deal."

They spent the next hour or so opening one box from each item on the packing list and getting them set up. Ruby came across a padded envelope that contained several tubes of lubricant in various flavors, including wild cherry, luscious watermelon and, naturally, passion fruit.

She kept touching her throat as she worked, Evan's hand having left a phantom tingle of desire there. She was excited at the prospect of an extended scene with him and intrigued with the BDSM toys, some of which were new to her.

"Hmm," Evan said when they were finished assembling the equipment. "We're going to need some impact toys to properly check this stuff out."

Ruby waved toward Taggart's booth. "We have some of the finest gear available right there. I'm sure the Leather Master wouldn't mind if we borrowed some. Let me just text Rylee real quick and see."

"Great idea," Evan agreed.

She grabbed her purse and pulled out her phone, shooting a quick text to Rylee. *"Hey there. Would it be okay if we borrowed a few of Taggart's toys for an equipment demo? We promise to use them gently and clean them thoroughly after use. If that's not cool, no worries. We'll improvise."*

In addition to designing and maintaining websites, Rylee also helped Taggart run his business. While she worked inside their home, Taggart worked in an outbuilding behind the house with his assistants, busily creating all his beautifully crafted implements.

Rylee responded a moment later with a thumbs-up emoticon. *"You don't waste any time, LOL. Tag's right here with me at the moment and he says that's fine. The pieces actually improve as they're broken in."*

Ruby slipped her phone back into her purse. "Taggart says no problem."

"Sweet." Evan walked into the Leather Master's booth and selected the luscious flogger he'd used on her the day before, along with a red long-handled riding crop. "These will do nicely. I'm looking forward to this."

"You love giving them or getting them?" Ruby teased.

Evan laughed and shook his head. "Last night was fun, but don't count on it happening again. My sub days are long over. In fact, that's the first time I've let someone dom me in over a decade."

"Could've fooled me," Ruby said with a grin. "You were into that whipping, boy."

"I was into *you*, Ruby." Evan replied. "And I agree with Tag. A Dom should be willing to undergo anything he expects of his submissive, even if it doesn't float his particular boat. And you know your way around a whip, girl. Do you consider yourself a switch?"

"Not really," she answered honestly. "I mean, it's fun to dom someone as a kind of game, but I'm way too much of a sexual masochist to be a Domme."

He moved closer to her, the sexual tension suddenly ratcheting up between them. "Just a masochist, Ruby?" He placed his hand on her throat again, and she melted in his grip. "I sense there's more here than mere masochism. You need to submit to a Master. You were born to submit."

She swallowed, her throat moving beneath his hard hand. Twisting from his grip, she forced a laugh. "I don't know about that," she said, trying for saucy but not quite succeeding. "I haven't yet found a man who can truly master me."

"*Yet* being the key word," Evan replied, not smiling.

Ruby turned abruptly away, flustered.

~*~

"Let's start with the Total Lockdown System," Evan said. "We'll keep it in the upright position for now." He placed the impact implements on a table next to the lubricant and the water bottles. He couldn't wait to get started.

"Okay," Ruby agreed, eyeing the device with an expression that was part eager, part anxious. Her floor-length sundress was pale blue silk. She pushed the spaghetti straps from her shoulders and let the dress fall from her gorgeous body. Her breasts were bare, the nipples already erect. She was wearing a pair of white, lacy panties.

"Those, too," Evan said, his cock stiffening in his jeans.

She pulled down the panties and set them, along with the dress, on one of the empty display tables. Evan badly wanted to fuck her then and there. He had a condom in his wallet. He could just lift her onto that table and do it, fast and hard.

But she had already walked over to the restraining device. She assumed the position, legs apart to accommodate the ankle cuffs at either end of the spreader bar, arms lifted high over her head to reach the wrist cuffs. She looked at him, her face now a mask of calm expectancy.

Evan stared at her, drinking in her beauty, admiring her poise. He'd scened with too many women to count over the years, and he'd never encountered one who was so self-possessed. It would be a challenge and a pleasure to tear down her reserve and reduce her to a wanton, begging, sexual animal that was his to control—his to claim.

He pulled his T-shirt over his head and tossed it aside. She licked her lips as she looked him over, and he smiled, moving close so he could properly restrain her. He wrapped the Velcro cuffs around her wrists, adjusting the cuff rings so her arms were raised, but not uncomfortably so. Then he crouched to secure her ankles against the spreader bar. Standing again, he attached the collar device behind her head, and brought it around her neck, noting the softening of her features as he tightened it around her throat.

"Your neck is a major erogenous zone, am I right?" he asked, spanning her throat with thumb and forefinger above her collar.

"Yes, Sir," she said, a slight tremor in her voice.

He tightened his grip, cutting off her airway. Her eyes widened, her face reddening. "You like to feel the power of a man's hand on your throat, to know your very life is in his hands," he said softly, his eyes boring into hers.

She grunted, the only sound she could make. She was trembling in her restraints.

He let her go, and she drew in a deep breath, a tremor moving through her entire body. "Fuck," she breathed. "Jesus." Her nipples rose from her round, high breasts, her cheeks flushed, her eyes wild.

Evan reached into his jeans and rubbed his cock, which was hard as a bar of iron. He wanted to feel her hot mouth on his dick. He wanted to ram it down her throat and hold her head in place until he shot his load. Forcing himself under control, he pulled his hand from his pants and turned to the table where he'd set out the other toys they would sample together.

She wasn't in the right position for the anal probe, but the rack compactor looked promising, as did the vaginal e-stim device.

"So many wicked toys, so little time," he said, chuckling. "Before we really get going," he continued, "I know your safeword. You obviously enjoy breath play and can handle a considerable amount of erotic pain." He held up the rack compactor. "Any issues or sensitivity with your breasts I should know about?"

"No, Sir. My nipples are very sensitive, but I can handle compression toys."

"Excellent." He placed the contraption carefully over her breasts, positioning them between the crossbars. He slowly tightened the screws, careful not to make them too tight, as he planned to leave the rack in place for a while.

"That looks so hot," he said, standing back to admire her bunched breasts, the nipples red and engorged. She looked incredibly sexy, arms high overhead, legs forcibly spread, her head held in position by the restraint collar. "I wish I had my nipple clamps with me." He lightly twisted the hard, spongy nubbins until she moaned. He glanced around, wishing he'd brought his gear bag. "I'll just have to crop them instead."

Her eyes were blazing, her tongue visible on her lower lip, her chest rising and falling. She was ready.

So was he.

Chapter 4

Evan picked up the crop and drew it slowly down Ruby's cheek, sending a shudder through her body. "Slow your breathing," he said gently. "Calm yourself. We're only just getting started."

She tried to comply, closing her mouth and drawing air in through her nostrils.

"Better," he murmured. He lifted the folded rectangle of soft leather on the crop to her lips. "Kiss it," he commanded.

As she brushed her lips against it, breathing in the erotic smell of leather, he added, "I'm going to hurt you, Ruby. I'm going to make your suffer."

His words ricocheted through her like a handful of marbles flung against a wall, and she actually moaned aloud. Her clit was swollen and her nipples throbbed.

He started lightly, tapping the crop against her compressed breasts. He smacked her belly and along her inner thighs, slowly increasing the intensity. Moving behind her, he struck her ass with some force, a sudden, rapid flurry of stinging swats that made her jerk in her restraints.

Returning to stand in front of her, he struck her right nipple. An explosion of pain hurtled through her nerve endings, erupting from her mouth as a scream. He struck the second nipple, and she screamed again, unable to help herself.

"Good girl. Breathe through it," he said, now tapping lightly over her purpling breasts. "You're doing really well. You're fucking awesome."

In spite of the pain and discomfort, his words soothed her like a balm, and she relaxed in her restraints.

"I want to push your boundaries. I want to challenge you."

"Oh," she breathed, drawing out the syllable, but she didn't protest. On the contrary, her body and soul thrilled to his dark promise.

He moved behind her, snapping the crop against her bottom in a series of sharp, slapping strokes until she whimpered. He focused on the tender spot where her ass met her thighs, painting searing lines of delicious, stinging pain over her flesh.

She was just about to beg him to stop when he moved again to stand in front of her. His eyes were glittering with lust, his erection clearly visible in his jeans. "You good, baby?" he murmured, his face close to hers.

"Yes," she replied breathlessly. "Yes, Sir."

His leaned closer, kissing her lightly on the lips, pulling away when she opened her mouth, eager for his tongue.

"Time later for sweetness," he said, his smile cruel. He returned his attention to her tortured breasts, snapping the crop against her nipples in a rapid tattoo of stinging swats as she jerked and twisted in her restraints.

"No, no, no, no," she chanted, barely aware she was saying the words.

"What is it, Ruby? Do you need me to stop? Just say your safeword."

She pressed her lips together and shook her head. No fucking way.

He struck her again, and she gasped with pain.

"Say quicksilver and I'll let you down."

A trickle of sweat rolled down her right temple. She was dizzy, her heart pounding, but she felt wildly alive and powerful, as if she'd snorted a line of the best coke on the planet. She blew a strand of hair out of her face. "No," she said, not ready to capitulate.

"You want more?" He lifted his eyebrows with surprise. "You sure?"

"Bring it."

He focused on her breasts, covering every inch of them with stinging fire. Each time he struck her nipple, an agony of raw pain exploded in her brain, but her soul was singing, her spirit soaring. This was what she needed, needed, needed…

Ruby opened her eyes and stared up into Evan's handsome face, completely disoriented. "Wha…?" she managed. "Huh?"

"Welcome back." He was sitting on the floor, cradling her in his arms as he'd done the night before. "You okay?"

"I think so," she said, still not quite sure what had happened. "How did I get from there to here?" She lifted her chin toward the rig where she'd been tethered. "Last thing I remember, I was up there, biting a hole through my lip to keep from saying my safeword."

"You scared the shit out of me. Safewords exist for a reason, you know."

"I didn't want to use it," Ruby said stubbornly. "I wanted to power through it."

Evan shook his head. "Well, one minute you were there, staring me down with this badass expression on your face, and then suddenly your eyes rolled back, your head fell forward and you went completely limp. You've never seen anyone move as fast as I did to get you down. I should have reminded you to breathe. You were hyperventilating."

"Not your fault," she said, managing a smile. "I know better. I can get really stubborn. I don't know what it is. Maybe I was a mule in another life. I can never resist a challenge."

Evan smiled, relief evident on his face. "I can relate. But seriously, are you okay?"

Ruby shifted in an effort to sit up, and Evan helped her, lifting her and setting her down gently beside him. She moved her arms and legs, and touched her tender breasts. "I'm fine, as far as I can tell."

Evan held out a bottle of water, the cap already off. "Here, drink some water."

She took a long swig and set the bottle down.

He got to his feet and held out both his hands. "There's a comfortable couch in the back office. Let's take a quick break before we try the next contraption."

Ruby was both exhilarated and exhausted, as if she'd just won a marathon. A break was probably a good idea. She put her hands in his and allowed him to hoist her upright.

He brought her close and held her, gently swaying. She relaxed into his comforting embrace. Eventually, she pulled away so she could lift her face to his. "Kiss me," she commanded.

He smiled down at her. "You're a bossy little thing, you know that?"

"So I've been told," she said, managing only a weak laugh, still spent from the experience. Circling her arms around his neck, she pulled him down to her.

His lips parted, his tongue entering her mouth. He held her carefully, clearly mindful of her still tender, sore breasts. He cupped her ass with his hands, his cock like steel between them as they kissed.

When they eventually parted, they walked arm in arm back to the office. It consisted of a large room with a workstation in one corner, an arrangement of second-hand living room furniture in the other. Evan sank onto a large, worn leather couch and patted the spot beside him.

But Ruby had a better idea. Evan's obvious erection had been distracting her since their first hello, straining against the faded denim of his jeans like an invitation she was eager to accept.

"I want to thank you properly, Sir, for the amazing session just now."

"Yeah?" Evan replied, a sexy half smile moving over his lips. "And how do you propose to do that?"

"I'd like to worship your cock, Sir," she said sweetly, dropping to her knees in front of him. She placed her hands lightly on his strong thighs. "That is, if that's all right with you."

The half smile broadened into an all-out grin. "That would be just fine and dandy with me." Evan slipped off his shoes and reached for his fly, yanking it open. Getting to his feet, he shucked his jeans and underwear, kicking them away. He stood naked, hands on hips, smiling down at her.

Her mouth watering, Ruby leaned eagerly forward. She curled one hand around the base of his hard shaft and gently cradled his balls with the other. He sighed when she closed her lips over the head.

She took him in deep, loving the weight and heft of him in her mouth and hands. He groaned as she milked his cock with her tongue and throat muscles.

"Jesus," he breathed, twisting his fingers in her hair. "Christ, you are fucking perfect." He held on for a few minutes, but finally gave in to the inevitable. His body stiffened as his jism shot down her throat in a hot stream.

She kept her mouth locked on him as he shuddered his way through a series of aftershocks. His hands fell limply to his sides as he collapsed back onto the couch with a long, satisfied sigh.

Ruby climbed up beside him, as satisfied as a cat that just licked a bowlful of cream. Which reminded her... She snuggled against him and stroked his cheek. "I hate to ruin the mood, but I have to go take care of my hosts' cats. They're due for their walk and lunch."

Evan lifted his head and scrunched his handsome face into a comical scowl. "Did I hear you correctly? Did you just say your hosts' *cats* need a walk?"

Ruby laughed. "I did. I know it sounds kind of nutty, but it's really a pretty sweet gig. I have the run of a huge, gorgeous house and use of their very nice car for the time I'm here, in exchange for spoiling the crap out of their two prized Russian Blues. Part of the long list of requirements includes a lunch of fresh salmon and then taking them for a walk around the very posh neighborhood in their rhinestone-encrusted harnesses."

"Seriously?"

"As a heart attack," Ruby said solemnly. But then she grinned. "They're actually really cool cats. They were wary of me at first, but I think we're starting to bond."

Evan shook his head, smiling. "Hand me my jeans, will you?"

Ruby got to her feet and grabbed Evan's jeans and underwear. She really did have to take care of the darn cats, but she didn't want to leave Evan—not yet. Handing him his things, she said, "Want to come with me?"

"Sure. But I still need to test out the prison stockade. It seems a little complicated. We have to get the kinks out," he added with a wink.

Ruby laughed. "Okay, but what if we take it with us?" She put her hands on her hips. "And don't think I've forgotten your end of the bargain. No way am I going to pass up the chance to use that Zeus electrosex band on your cock."

Before he could respond, she ran from the room, laughing, her heart soaring like a balloon.

~*~

Evan broke down the prison stockade and packed the pieces into a large gear bag he found in the warehouse office. On an impulse, he grabbed another whip from Taggart's booth. He put the whip—a pretty short-handled single tail—into the gear bag along with the flogger and riding crop, making a mental note to properly clean and replace the borrowed items.

He followed Ruby to her place, eager to continue the fun. The house was in a high-end neighborhood, with large, pristine homes fronted by emerald green lawns and huge shade trees. The inside of the home was just as lavish, with lots of polished wood and raw silk upholstery, tasteful oil paintings on the walls.

She led him through to a small, bright room with much shabbier furniture and lots of cat trees in various configurations set up around the room. "Hi, Binky. Hi, Cuddles," Ruby said as she entered the sunny room.

Two elegant cats with silvery coats and light blue eyes turned their attention from the large window, on whose broad sill they had been perched, and jumped gracefully down. They both made a beeline for Ruby, one of them rubbing luxuriously against her leg while the other butted her gently with his head.

Ruby squatted down and stroked the one tangling in her long skirt. "I know. I'm a little late. You guys ready for some awesome fish?"

As if they understood her, both cats meowed in response.

"That's cat for 'shit, yeah,'" Ruby said with a grin.

They followed her from the room, Evan trailing behind, enjoying the sway of Ruby's ass as she walked. In the kitchen, she moved toward a polished granite counter, on which sat a wooden bowl filled with large, shiny red apples.

"These are local," she said, picking one up and tossing it to Evan, who automatically held up his hand to catch it. "They're really good." She brought a second one to her lips, opening her small, pretty mouth to take a bite. "Hmm," she said, closing her eyes in obvious appreciation as she chewed.

Evan took a bite of his apple, suddenly hungry. It was crisp, sweet and tart, and he took another bite, watching as Ruby got a container from the refrigerator and spooned some mashed, pink fish into tiny silver bowls set on either side of a larger water bowl. The cats ate daintily but quickly, and then Ruby retrieved two sparkling harness-leash contraptions from a hook by the back door. "Want to come with us on our walk?" she asked, "or would you rather unload the stuff? We just go around the block."

"I'll go with you," Evan replied, not wanting to leave her side.

They talked easily as they walked, stopping every few feet for the cats to delicately sniff a bush or blade of grass.

"Do those cats sleep with you?" Evan asked, envisioning a hot scene with Ruby interrupted by an unwelcome feline presence. Or worse, one or both leaping onto his back at a crucial moment and giving him a heart attack.

"Actually, it's really weird, but they never come upstairs at all. Their domain includes the kitchen, laundry room and sunroom. They sleep curled up together on one of the sofas or on the large windowsill of the bay window. It's the most adorable thing you ever saw."

Evan, more of a dog person, offered a less than sincere, "How sweet."

As they talked about their travels, the sexual tension buzzed between them like an electric current. Though her "thank you" back at the warehouse had been beyond phenomenal, he was longing to make love to her. But first he would lock her up in that sexy prison stockade and do all sorts of wonderful, terrible things to her.

When they returned to the house, Ruby said, "I don't know about you, but one apple was not enough lunch. You gave me a real workout," she added with a grin.

"We're only just getting started," Evan said. He was more than ready to pick up where they'd left off, but a little sustenance before the next round was probably a good idea.

Ruby went to the refrigerator and pulled out several items as Evan took a seat on one of the barstools. "You pour the Perrier," she instructed, "while I slice some cheese."

She set two wine glasses in front of Evan. As he poured the sparkling water, she prepared a crackers and cheese platter. She selected another apple from the bowl and cut it into segments. "I could make sandwiches, if you like peanut butter and jelly," she offered. "They said I could eat whatever's here, but it's mostly just breakfast foods. We could go out and grab a burger."

"No, this is fine," Evan sat on one of the barstools beside Ruby. He would have happily skipped the food and cut straight to the action.

"That's better," Ruby said after they'd cleaned the plate. "Now, where were we?"

Evan retrieved the gear bag from the car and then Ruby led him up the stairs. They entered the first room on the right, a large bedroom with a queen-size four-poster bed. There was also a bureau, a small writing desk with a chair, and one of those padded benches at the end of the bed.

Evan set the gear bag on the bench, anticipation fizzing like champagne bubbles in his blood. "So much to do, so little time," he said with an evil grin. "I can't wait to check out this prison stockade. I love the idea of you on your hands and knees, completely immobilized while I have my wicked way with you."

Ruby perched on the edge of the bed as Evan pulled out the pieces of the stockade to reassemble. She hugged herself and shivered dramatically. "Oooh," she breathed, her eyes shining. "Yes, please, Sir."

"Good girl. That's what I like to hear. You can start by getting out of all that unnecessary clothing while I put this thing back together."

He couldn't help sneaking glances at her as he worked. He loved how easy and relaxed she was with her body. It made her that much sexier.

He needed to focus to make sure he assembled the stockade correctly so it would be safe to use. The stockade rods could be adjusted for height and the steel collar shaft moved up and down to lock the head at different angles.

He attached the main steel rod between the short perpendicular cuff bars at either end, and adjusted the device for Ruby's height. Next, he attached the upright adjustable steel collar rod near the front cuff bar so he could fully restrain her.

"That thing looks rough," Ruby said, watching him work. "Those metal cuffs and collar could cause abrasions to the skin."

"Oh, I almost forgot. Bring me the gear bag, will you?"

Ruby complied, and Evan rummaged a moment. He pulled out the packet of sheepskin lining that had come with the device. "We can't be damaging the slave merchandise, hmm?" he teased. He tore open the packet and applied the adhesive-backed padding to the insides of the cuffs and collar. "Better?" he said, looking over at her.

"Much," Ruby said with a nod, though she was hugging herself, perhaps a little anxious at what was to come. "Isn't it funny how we worry about stuff like that?"

"It probably does seems weird to the uninitiated," Evan agreed. "People who don't understand that erotic pain is very specific and controlled. There's no comparison between, say, the stinging stroke of a lash lovingly delivered and a clenched fist smashed into a jaw. The lash is erotic. The fist is just violent."

"That's it," Ruby said emphatically. "You get it."

"*We* get it," Evan agreed as he got to his feet. He looked from the stockade to the lovely naked girl, and his cock turned to steel. "I want you to get on your hands and knees. I'm going to cuff your wrists and ankles, and then adjust this collar rod to keep you in place."

"Don't you think you should be naked, too?" Ruby said. "I mean, just in case…" She didn't finish the thought, but she didn't have to. Evan was more than happy to strip alongside her, since he absolutely planned to fuck her.

Ruby crouched on her hands and knees over the stockade's base rod. Her long hair fell in a wavy curtain around her face.

"Do you have something I can pull your hair back with?" Evan asked, glancing around the bedroom.

"There should be something on the bureau," Ruby replied, flipping her hair with a toss of her head.

Evan found a red hair-elastic and returned to her. Leaning down, he gathered her thick, soft hair into a ponytail and slid the elastic over it. "That's better," he said.

"Thanks," Ruby said, twisting back to smile at him. She rested her forearms on the carpet as she placed her wrists in the open cuffs.

Evan squatted beside her and clicked the wrist cuffs into place. Scooting back, he locked her ankles into position. "Comfy?" he inquired, feasting on the sight of the bound, naked girl as he stroked his hard cock.

"As comfy as I can be in this position."

"This will help support you, as well as keep you still." Evan adjusted the knob on the collar shaft until it was the perfect height for her to rest her neck in its lined metal confines. He clicked it closed, a shot of adrenaline kicking through him now that she was once again totally at his mercy.

Even before a scene actually began, he always got a jolt when a sub put herself completely in his power. But with Ruby, the experience was intensified—maybe because she herself was such a strong personality, not a meek or docile bone in that hot body of hers. He wanted to be worthy of her submission, and the feeling was a new one, since usually his thoughts were more focused on his own gratification.

He crouched behind her and leaned forward so his chest was against her back. Letting his weight rest against her, he put his arms around her and cupped her breasts, finding her nipples with his fingers. He rolled them until they were hard.

Ruby moaned.

Keeping her nipples in his grip, he twisted, lightly at first, and then harder.

Ruby drew in a sharp breath, her body tensing beneath his.

"It's good, right?" he murmured into her ear. "You need this pain. You need to suffer."

"Yes," she whispered.

He let go of her nipples and cupped her breasts again as he kissed her ear and her neck. She smelled so good, like lemon and expensive soap. He was glad they'd moved from the openness of the warehouse space to this much more intimate setting.

"You know," he said softly, reaching beneath her to cup her sex, "with the pain comes the pleasure." Still draped over her, he slipped a finger into her cleft, stroking upward over the hard button of her clit. She shivered beneath him as he stroked the soft folds. She moaned as he slid a finger into her silky, wet heat.

"You ready for more?" he asked, pushing a second finger inside her.

"Yes, oh god, yes," she gasped. "Please, Sir, will you fuck me?"

He chuckled softly, withdrawing his hand from her sticky sex. He had her right where he wanted her. "I will, but only if you take a proper whipping first. I want to mark that beautiful ass."

"Yes, Sir," she said breathlessly.

He lifted himself from behind her and went to the bench. Reaching into the gear bag, he pulled out the single tail and snapped it in the air.

Ruby could see him from her position on the carpet. "Where did you get that?" she asked, her eyes wide.

"It's another of the Leather Master's wonderful creations." He snapped it again, a cruel smile lifting his lips. "You already showed me you can deliver a single-tail whipping," he added, "but can you take it?"

Her dark eyes flashed. "Bring it."

He grinned. "I shall." He walked slowly around her, admiring her lovely lines and curves. Her sex peeked from between her forcibly spread legs, the asterisk of her tight asshole begging for attention.

Returning to the gear bag, he removed the plastic grocery bag in which he'd placed some KY and a tube of Arnica. Going over to his jeans, he pulled out his wallet and found the packet of three condoms he always kept there.

Coming around behind Ruby, he bent down and stroked her rounded ass. He smacked her cheeks lightly, readying the skin for the lash. "Ten strokes," he said, recalling the wicked whipping she'd given him in the Byrnes' dungeon. "You will count for me."

"Yes, Sir."

Adjusting his position, he flicked the tip of the single tail against her left cheek.

"One," she said breathlessly, as a small, red welt rose on her smooth flesh.

He flicked the other cheek.

"Two."

Taking a step back, he flicked both cheeks at once.

"Three," she cried. "Ow, that hurts!"

"Doesn't it, though," Evan agreed. He snapped the whip against her sweet bottom in a steady rhythm as she yelped the count, until she finally wailed, "Ten, oh, ouch, ouch!"

Evan dropped the whip and reached for the tube of Arnica. "You did good, Ruby," he said as he rubbed the soothing balm into her reddened skin. "Not exactly the silence I would expect from a trained slave," he added with a chuckle, "but you did okay."

He moved around to crouch in front of her. Taking her face in his hands, he said gently, "Hey, you all right?" He kissed her cheek. Her skin was hot to the touch. "Was it too much?"

Her eyes were fever-bright, her cheeks flushed. "Oh, no, Sir," she breathed. "It was *just* right. Thank you, Sir."

Evan smiled. "Good girl. You ready for your reward?"

She nodded eagerly, making him laugh.

Evan grabbed the condom packet and tore away the wrapper. Crouching behind Ruby, he slid it over his shaft. She looked so hot, cuffed and collared in the stockade, her pussy peeking between her legs. He stroked the soft, swollen folds. She was wet and ready for him.

Unable to hold back another second, he positioned the head of his sheathed cock at her entrance and eased himself inside. He put his hands on her hips and swiveled inside her. She groaned, pushing back against him to take him deeper. Her strong vaginal muscles rippled over his shaft.

"So good, so good," he moaned. He was in heaven, his cock encased in the satiny soft, slick perfection of her cunt as he stroked her from the inside out.

Reaching beneath her body, he found her hooded clit. He circled his finger around it until she was panting. Keeping his hand on her sex, he thrust inside her until she was mewling like a kitten. He willed himself to hold off until she was ready.

"Oh god," she finally cried out. "Oh, god, oh yes, oh please..." She trembled, her vaginal muscles contracting like a glove around his shaft.

"That's it," he panted, his fingers still flying over her sex. "Come for me, Ruby. Now."

She moaned, the sound low and feral, as she shuddered against him. Letting go, he climaxed inside her, the blinding pleasure rendering him nearly unconscious for a moment or two.

When he came to himself, she was still trembling in her bonds, though the shuddering had ceased. Evan eased himself out of her and stripped off the spent condom, which he dropped into the plastic bag.

He got to his feet and moved quickly around her, releasing her ankles and wrists, and finally her neck, from the shackles that held her in place. Before she could fall to the ground, he put his hands beneath her and lifted her into his arms. He carried her to the high bed and set her gently on the pale yellow quilt.

Sitting on the bed beside her, he grabbed one of the bottles of water she'd placed on the nightstand along with a tube of salve.

She lifted her head, her eyes glazed, her color high. He kept hold of the bottle as he tilted it to her lips. She drank and then let her head flop back down on the pillows.

"You okay, Ruby?" A strange tenderness had overtaken him, as if she were the most precious and vulnerable creature in the world, and he held her life in his hands. He didn't quite know what to do with his emotions, which left him feeling rather vulnerable as well—not something he was used to.

Unsure what to do with these new, strange feelings, he pushed them away, focusing instead on aftercare, which he would give to any sub he scened with, even the most casual pickup at a club.

Her wrists, ankles and neck were a little red from the restraints, though the skin wasn't chafed. Taking the tube of Arnica, he smoothed it over the reddened skin, savoring the feel of her soft, supple flesh.

When he was done, he reached beneath her head to gently pull away the hair elastic.

"Oh, yeah," she replied, a smile spreading slowly over her face. "I'm definitely okay. That was fucking *awesome*, Evan. I love that stockade thing. I felt so deliciously helpless. It was really intense. Thank you." She shook her head, fanning her dark, shiny hair over the pillow. Then she sighed contentedly and closed her eyes.

"You're more than welcome, sexy girl." Evan stroked a thick tendril of hair from her face and tucked it behind one perfect ear. He'd managed to recover from the odd sense of vulnerability and was eager for more play. "Ready for the next toy?"

Ruby didn't respond. Her lips had parted, her breathing now deep and even.

Evan shook his head and smiled. "Guess not," he whispered. Stretching out beside her, he took her into his arms and closed his eyes.

Chapter 5

Ruby opened her eyes, momentarily disoriented. She was trapped beneath Evan's arm, which was flung over her chest. His leg was over her thigh. His mouth was open and he was snoring softly, his hair flopped over his eyes.

Easing carefully out from under him, she slipped silently from the bed. Padding to the bathroom, she slid the pocket door closed so as not to disturb him. She used the toilet and washed her face and hands. In the mirror, her eyes were bright, her hair tousled, her cheeks flushed from sleep. She looked happy.

She was happy. Whatever was happening with this handsome man, it was a fun, new adventure. Ruby loved adventure in whatever form it might take. She lived in the moment and, right now, the moment was very, very good.

Returning to the bedroom, she walked back to the bed and lay down beside Evan, leaning up on an elbow as she faced him. He looked younger in sleep, the laugh lines at his eyes and on either side of his mouth less pronounced. His thick, reddish blond lashes brushed his cheeks and his lips were slightly chapped.

On an impulse, she leaned down to lightly touch them with her own. Like an enchanted prince in a fairytale, he opened his eyes at her kiss. He looked sleepily at her a moment, and then he smiled—an open, sunny smile that warmed her heart. He held out his arms and she snuggled into them.

"Hey," he said sleepily. "I thought I wore you out, but I guess it was the other way around."

She chuckled. "I think you wore us both out. That nap was just the ticket." She pulled gently out of his embrace so she could see his face. "Don't think I've forgotten your side of the bargain. You better have packed that Zeus electrosex penis band, boy."

Evan laughed. "So it's boy now, is it? What happened to Sir?"

Ruby shrugged. "A deal is a deal. Your turn to be the guinea pig."

Evan sat up, apparently fully awake now. "I don't know," he said running his hand through his hair. "It's getting kind of late and—"

"Oh, no," she laughed. "You're not getting out of it that easily." She scooted down to the end of the bed and slid onto the bench beside the gear bag. Rummaging inside, she found the plastic-wrapped item she was looking for, along with the e-stim power box that would give it juice. She held the items up for Evan to see.

"Okay, okay," he said with a grin. "Let me pee first, will ya?"

"I guess so," she said in a pretend grudging voice. "But then get that sexy butt of yours back in here. It's my turn to run the scene."

~*~

When Evan returned from the bathroom, Ruby was seated on the bench. She had removed the e-stim toy from its wrappings. It consisted of a fabric strap with a small Velcro cuff on either end. Long wires protruded from each of the cuffs, ready to attach to the power box.

He stood in front of Ruby, his hands on his hips. "If you want to use that thing on me, you'll have to get me hard. I'm not into erotic pain—at least not into receiving it."

Ruby laughed. "You could have fooled me when you took that single tail whipping."

"Uh huh," Evan replied blandly. "But you don't fool me, my sweet little sub girl."

Ruby raised her eyebrows. "I'm definitely a sexual masochist and bondage bunny, but submissive?" She wrinkled her nose. "Not so much."

"We'll see," Evan said lightly, sensing a challenge.

"Let's get this party started." Ruby picked up the tube of gel that had come with the band and squirted some on her fingers. She reached for his cock and he moved closer.

He sighed with satisfaction as she stroked his rapidly hardening cock with the skilled fingers of one hand while cupping his balls and stroking his perineum with the other.

"That didn't take long," she said with a knowing smile. Keeping one hand lightly on his now throbbing shaft, she smoothed the page of instructions that had come with the device against the bench and read aloud, "Get ready for a thrilling experience. The dual bands act like cock rings to keep you hard, while the gentle zing of electricity delivers shivers of pleasure to your cock and balls."

While Evan wasn't especially looking forward to the experience, having Ruby touch and stroke him in the process made it worth it. She squirted more gel onto her fingers and coated his hard cock with it. Kneeling in front of him, she wrapped the Velcro cuffs on either end of the strap around his shaft, one at the base, one just below the head.

As she attached the wires to the power box, she said, "The electricity goes from one cock band to the other. We can position them all sorts of ways to give you different sensations. The directions promise that you're going to love it," she added with a grin.

"We'll see," Evan said noncommittally, though he was mildly curious how it would feel.

"*Puta madre*, right?"

"Uh, yeah," Evan said, a small stab of anxiety poking into his gut.

"Don't worry," she laughed. "I'll be gentle."

The first jolt felt like fizzy champagne bubbling over his shaft. She zapped him again and again, slowly increasing the intensity. As the currents edged from pleasure to pain, the old masochistic hardwiring from his youth must have kicked into play. More likely, it was because a gorgeous, naked woman was kneeling in front of him turning the dial. Whatever the reason, his balls tightened with an impending orgasm.

She wrapped her fingers around the shaft between the cuffs and stroked him while still sending a steady current of buzzing electricity through his cock. Evan gave himself over to the sensations, heightened by his desire for her. Before long, a ribbon of ejaculate shot onto Ruby's lovely breasts.

"You did good," she said approvingly as she detached the wires from the box and then pulled the Velcro cuffs from his deflating shaft. "Though if I were a proper Mistress, I'd make you lick this come off my tits." She scooped a blob of the goo onto her finger and held it up to him.

"In your dreams," Evan replied.

~*~

As they showered together, Ruby marveled at how comfortable she felt with this man she'd only just met. Admittedly, they'd packed plenty of intensity into their brief time together, but it was more than that. On some deep, basic level, she trusted Evan, as if they'd known each other for years instead of merely days. She was used to relying on her gut, and her gut told her Evan Stewart was special. Beyond his drop-dead gorgeous looks and his obvious skill as a Dom, she liked how easygoing he was. She didn't get that sense of neediness or expectation that so many guys brought to a new relationship. He, like her, seemed content to take life as it came.

They dressed, repacked his gear bag and went back downstairs. Ruby was just about to suggest they go out for a pizza or something, when Evan's phone pinged in his pocket.

He pulled it out and glanced at the screen. "Damn. I'm really sorry, but I have to get going. I promised Bob I'd help him unload some equipment."

Ruby at once readjusted her expectations. Maybe it was a good thing to take a little breather. After all, they still had plenty of time to pick up where they'd left off.

"No apology necessary. I had an incredible time."

Evan looked momentarily perplexed. "Maybe I could just tell him something came up and I can't make it. We could grab a bite or something."

"No, that's fine," Ruby assured him. "It's all good. I had a wonderful time, Evan. Thank you." She moved closer and brought her arms around his neck, pulling him down for a kiss.

When they parted, he said, "Let's connect again, soon, okay? You've got my card."

"I do," Ruby agreed. "And we will."

Ruby lingered at the door as he walked to his car. She waved as he drove away.

Back inside, she got the cats their dinner and then hung out with them for a while in the sunroom, still basking in her sense of wellbeing as she stroked their satiny flanks.

She sat up abruptly, startled out of her dream. Binky was on her chest, Cuddles on her head. With a yowl, Cuddles toppled to the sofa, while Binky leaped gracefully to the ground, her tail swishing with displeasure.

"Sorry about that, kittens," Ruby apologized. She got to her feet, her muscles stiff, her mouth dry. "I think a glass of wine and a nice hot bath are in order. What do you two think?"

The cats, who had resettled themselves on the windowsill, pointedly ignored her.

"Suit yourselves," she said with a laugh. "I'll be down later to give you your midnight snack." She went into the kitchen and sliced an apple, which she took upstairs, along with a large glass of red wine.

She drew herself a bath in the huge master bathroom, adding lavender-scented oil to the Jacuzzi. Piling her long hair into a coiled knot on top of her head, she eased herself into the hot, fragrant water. Her body felt properly used and sore in all the right ways. Closing her eyes, she sighed contentedly.

Life was good.

~*~

That evening in the warehouse as Bob and Evan unloaded and arranged the equipment in the dungeon space, Evan couldn't get Ruby out of his head. She was different from most women he hooked up with. Usually—no, always—Evan was the one who pulled away first. While he truly adored playing with submissive partners, he was careful to head off any potential clinginess or neediness at the pass.

He hadn't had to engage in any evasive tactics with Ruby, however, for which he was grateful. She was refreshingly independent. She hadn't even tried to give him her contact information, though now he wished she had. It would have been fun to send her sexy midnight texts to keep her juices flowing until they met again.

Bob and Evan finally finished the equipment setup to both their satisfaction. Bob put his hands on his hips as he surveyed the dungeon space. He had managed to procure several fine pieces of gently used equipment, including two St. Andrew's crosses, two spanking benches, two padded bondage tables and a wicked looking set of wooden stocks. "Looks pretty good, huh? This will save me a bundle."

"Yeah," Evan agreed. "You did good. I'll call the wholesaler first thing in the morning and adjust the order."

His cell phone buzzed in his pocket. He smiled to himself. So much for her assertion she was going straight to bed. "Gotta get this."

He eagerly pulled his phone from his pocket. Turning away from Bob, he clicked on the call. "This is Evan," he said, striving for a nonchalant tone.

"Hi, this is Darlene from Credit Card International," a mechanical voice droned. "Did you know we can help get you out of debt with a rate as low as—"

What the fuck?

Annoyed, Evan clicked off and shoved the phone back into his pocket.

As they walked back together toward the office, Bob said, "So, did you get a chance to check out the new gear we'll be selling at the grand opening?"

An image of Ruby leaped into his brain, naked, trembling, eyes shining, chest heaving, lips parted... His voice came out hoarse when he started to answer. He cleared his throat and tried again. "I sure did. We tried out all the more complex pieces and had no problems. I'm comfortable I'll be able to handle any hands-on product testing during the event."

"That's good to hear. So," Bob added with a leer, "who did you get to volunteer? I bet I can guess."

"Yeah?"

"Yeah. Allie's sexy little friend, Ruby. Am I right?"

"You are," Evan said, unable to stop the smile that spread over his face.

"Man," Bob said with a rueful grin, "what I wouldn't give to be twenty years younger. Ah, well. There are still plenty of submissive fish in the sea interested in an old fart like me." He rubbed his hands together. "How about let's go celebrate with some pizza and beer, my treat? Then I'll take you over to Hardcore. It's ladies night tonight," he added with a comical waggle of his eyebrows.

Ruby was taking up entirely too much space in Evan's head. He pushed her from his mind and said with more enthusiasm than he felt, "Sounds like a plan. Let's do it."

Hardcore was one of the seedier BDSM clubs in Portland. Located in the basement of a gay bar, it provided just the right combination of gritty funk and BDSM action to keep his thoughts from straying where they shouldn't.

After agreeing they'd scope out the place on their own, Bob quickly disappeared with a platinum blonde in a black satin bustier and very high heels.

Evan watched a couple of scenes in progress. A skinny guy in bike shorts lay on a bondage table being worked over with vampire gloves by two girls who looked like twins, both with long black hair and big lips painted bright red. Evan quickly lost interest and moved on to a naked woman bound face forward to a cross. Her voluptuous ass jiggled each time her partner struck her with a wooden paddle, but her loud squeals grated on his nerves, and after a while, he moved away.

Someone put a hand on his arm. He looked down to see an attractive girl with curly reddish blond hair, blue eyes and a splash of freckles over an upturned nose. Her small breasts were bare above a waist cincher, her legs covered only by fishnet stockings held up by garters. She wore clunky platform shoes on her feet. Oddly, she had a small, sparkly crown on her head like something you'd get at a party supply store.

She looked almost too young to be legal, but when she spoke, her voice was deep and confident, though her fake British accent left something to be desired. "Excuse me, Sir," she said, dropping into a rather pretty curtsey, "would you be interested in spilling hot wax on my breasts and then flicking it off with a single tail?"

In spite of himself, Evan's cock nudged in approval at the invitation. If she was old enough to be here, she was old enough to play. If nothing else, it would pass the time well enough while he waited for Bob. "Sure," he agreed. If nothing else, it would pass the time.

The girl led him to a bondage table with a workstand beside it that contained several candles in glass containers, the wicks already lit. Evan doubted the use of such candles was legal in the club, but no one seemed to notice or care.

He helped the girl onto the table. Then he picked up a candle and examined it. "Are these safe for wax play?"

"I use them all the time. I'm the hot wax queen of Hardcore," she replied, touching the plastic and rhinestone crown pinned in her hair. "You're my first prince of pain tonight." She began to undo the tiny hooks that held her waist cincher in place. "Please, your Majesty, cover my breasts in burning wax and then flick it off. I promise a royal reward." She stared pointedly at his crotch.

Evan declined her offer of a reward, but still managed to pass a rather pleasant hour. And he didn't check his cell phone—not once.

CHAPTER 6

The next morning, Ruby drove over to Liam and Allie's place. Allie opened the door, welcoming her inside with a hug. "You get some good rest yesterday?" she asked.

"Uh, not exactly," Ruby said with a laugh.

"That sounds intriguing," Allie said as she led Ruby back to the kitchen. "Rylee did mention you and Evan might be hooking up."

When Ruby didn't deny it, Allie added with a grin, "You do realize I'll require full details."

"Can I get a cup of coffee first?"

"Sure. How about some breakfast?"

"No, thanks. The cats and I already ate and did our morning exercises together." She looked around the large, modern kitchen. "Where's Liam?"

"Liam's not here, unfortunately. He's a grant writer for non-profits. Usually he works from home, but he went out to meet a client."

"That's cool you can both work from home," Ruby said. "No commute, no fixed schedule."

"Yeah, it is pretty great." They sat down together at the kitchen table, coffee mugs in hand. Allie set out some homemade chocolate cookies. "I remembered these were your favorite back in college."

"Yum," Ruby said, picking up one of the cookies, which was still warm from the oven. "Cookies definitely don't count as breakfast."

"Absolutely not," Allie agreed, also taking a cookie from the plate.

Ruby moaned appreciatively as she took the first bite, her eyes fluttering shut with bliss.

"These are Liam's favorite, too," Allie replied around a mouth full of cookie. "I lived alone for so long that I had pretty much given up baking. I've enjoyed rediscovering it now that I have an appreciative partner with a sweet tooth."

"You've made quite a life for yourself, Mrs. Byrne," Ruby said. "A husband, a house, a successful career doing what you love. What's next? Babies?"

Allie grinned and shrugged. "We've been married two years now, so, yeah." She patted her flat stomach. "It's definitely something we've been talking about."

"You have to do more than talk about it to get pregnant," Ruby teased. "Seriously, though, you guys will make gorgeous babies." She put her hand over her old friend's. "You look so happy, Allie. There's this joyous, serene glow about you that I've never seen before."

Allie sighed happily. "Liam is the love of my life. And the best part is he's not only my husband, he's my Master. He owns me in the best possible way."

Ruby nodded, trying to imagine what it would be like to settle down with just one guy in just one house in just one city forever and ever and ever... She couldn't suppress the shudder of horror that slithered along her spine at the thought of voluntarily placing such shackles on her life.

Allie shook her head and laughed. "You should see your face, Ruby. You'd think I was describing life in prison with no chance of parole."

"Oh, no. I'm sorry," Ruby said quickly, embarrassed she'd been so easy to read. "I think it's fantastic. Truly, I do. But you know me. If I stay in one place for too long, I get antsy."

"Sure, I know that," Allie replied. "And I get it. But that doesn't mean you can't fall in love, right? Speaking of which, I now demand full details on your hookup with Evan Stewart."

Ruby grinned, her heart skipping a delightful beat as she thought about Evan for the hundredth time that morning. She adopted a posh British accent. "A lady doesn't kiss and tell."

Allie guffawed. "Since when? Tell me everything this instant. That's an order."

Ruby snorted a laugh. "Okay, okay. After I helped Rylee with Taggart's stuff, we went to breakfast. When we came back to the warehouse, he was there. Turns out he needed a volunteer to try out all this extreme restraint equipment Bob had bought for resale."

"A likely story," Allie interjected with a snort of her own. "But a good one."

Ruby spent the next twenty minutes detailing the intense, delicious hours she'd spent with Evan, getting hot all over again at the sexy memories. Allie hung on her every word, squealing with excitement as Ruby described the various scenes. It was as if they were back in their college dorm room all those years ago.

"So what's next?" Allie asked, when she'd wrung every possible detail from Ruby's memory. "When are you going to see him again?"

Ruby shrugged. "We didn't really make any plans."

"You totally *have* to see this guy again," Allie said emphatically.

"What if he's Master Right?"

"I'm not looking for Master Right," Ruby replied with a laugh, though an odd pang of longing shot through her, if just for an instant.

"Okay, okay," Allie capitulated. "But still, you gotta see him again, right? Don't you want to?"

"I do want to," Ruby admitted, her smile lingering. "There was something between us—something I haven't experienced for a long time. If I *were* looking for someone, he might be the one…" She trailed off, her mind veering suddenly toward the secret fantasy she only let out occasionally, and then usually only when she was alone in her bed at night, her hand between her legs, her defenses lowered by the impending orgasm she was spinning with her fingers.

"Hey," Allie said softly, startling her. "Where did you go, Ruby? Your face went all dreamy and still."

"Oh," Ruby said, snapping her head up. "I was—nothing." She shook back her hair and pushed away from the table. "We'd better get up to your workshop or we'll never get started on those canes."

~*~

Evan looked at his phone for the umpteenth time that morning. He was tempted to throw the stupid thing against the wall. In spite of staying out later than he'd meant to, he'd woken early, grabbing his phone in case he'd missed her call or text the night before, but the screen was blank.

He took a long run in the neighborhood to clear his head, purposely leaving his phone behind. When he got back, however, it stared up at him like a silent reproach.

What the hell's the matter with you, Stewart? If I didn't know better, I'd say you were falling…

He shook away the ridiculous thought before it was fully articulated.

He managed to busy himself for a few hours. When he couldn't think of another thing that needed doing, he picked up the phone once more, cradling it in his palm as he silently willed Ruby to call or text him.

Why hadn't he gotten her damn number yesterday? What the fuck was wrong with him? He never should have left her in the first place. He should have insisted on taking her out to dinner and then brought her back to her place so they could have made love for the rest of the night, Bob and BDSM Connections be damned.

He scrolled through his phone and found Taggart's contact information. Since he'd already met and hung out with Taggart a couple of times on the BDSM convention circuit, Evan felt comfortable reaching out to him. Before he could overthink it, he thumbed a quick text. *"Hey there, Tag. Any chance you have Ruby Beckett's contact info? Or maybe Rylee's got it?"*

It took a minute or two, but Taggart finally responded. *"Sorry, buddy. I don't have that, and Rylee's not around at the moment. But I do have Allie's number. She'll know how to get in touch with Ruby. Glad you're reaching out to her. You two make a great couple."* He added Allie's phone number, along with a winking smile emoticon.

Evan snorted. Were they all matchmakers in Portland? Still grinning, he copied the number into his contacts, along with her name. Then he clicked on the message tab and typed, *"Hey there, Allie. Evan Stewart here. I need to get in touch with Ruby Beckett. Any chance you have her cell number handy?"*

Almost immediately, the wavy ellipsis appeared, indicating she was responding.

"She's actually here with me in my workshop. I'll let her know you're trying to connect."

"Great. Thanks."

His phone dinged a moment later.

"Hi, Evan. This is Ruby. What's up, handsome?"

In spite of himself, Evan's heart lurched, making him grin at himself. "Jesus, Stewart," he said aloud. "You've got it bad." He shrugged. What was the big deal? Why hold anything back? He'd be gone in two weeks, and Ruby would just be another fond—albeit very fond—memory.

"Thinking about you, gorgeous," he texted. *"We were just getting started. Care to pick up where we left off?"*

There was a longer pause this time. Then she replied, *"That sounds fun. Dinner tonight?"*

No, damn it. I want to see you *now.*

"Sounds good. I'll pick you up at 7:00?"

"It's a date."

Somehow, Evan made it through the rest of the day. When Ruby opened her front door, she moved immediately into his arms, pulling his head down for a long, hot kiss that made him forget all about dinner. He was ready to scoop her up and carry her back into the house, but she pulled away.

"There," she said, blowing out a breath. "I just wanted to make sure the spark was still there."

Evan grinned. "Is it?"

"You have to ask?" she teased with an adorable toss of her head. She looked especially sexy tonight, wearing a short dress that molded to her curvy figure and showed her shapely legs.

"Let's skip dinner and move right to dessert," he growled, lunging for her and pulling her close again.

They kissed for a long moment, and again it was Ruby who broke the contact and pulled away. "We've got all night. I'm hungry. Knowing you, I'm thinking I'll need fortifying," she added with a devilish grin.

Evan laughed. "That you will, little girl. I have all kinds of devious plans in mind for you."

"That's what I like to hear," she replied with a laugh.

They went to a seafood place Taggart had recommended. The large restaurant was crowded but somehow they snagged a small table in a secluded alcove. They ordered a bottle of white wine to share with their meal. After the waitress had opened the bottle and poured them each a glass, Evan lifted his toward Ruby. He tried to come up with something clever to say, but then spoke from his heart. "To us."

She clinked her glass against his with a smile.

While he would have happily skipped the meal and gotten right down to the fun stuff, he enjoyed getting to know her a little better outside a dungeon or bedroom. Ruby was well traveled and interesting. She shared funny stories about mishaps and misunderstandings that had resulted from cultural differences. She seemed genuinely interested in what he had to say and asked questions about his business and the BDSM scene in general that showed her understanding and passion for the lifestyle.

Eager to learn everything he could about her, or even just hear her smooth, sexy voice, Evan said, "So, tell me about your childhood. Do you have brothers and sisters?"

"Boy, do I," she replied with a rueful grin. "I've got four sisters and two brothers. I'm the youngest. I never had a room of my own, or any clothes that hadn't been worn by at least four other kids. My dad ran a hardware store and my mother was a stay-at-home mom. We only had one bathroom until I was eight."

"Wow," Evan said. "No wonder you travel the world alone. You need your space after all that. I bet all of you couldn't wait to get out of there."

"Nope. Every single one of my siblings still lives within twenty miles of our parents in upstate Massachusetts. They're all married with kids. I'm the aberration, the one they talk worriedly about in hushed tones until I enter the room. Then they all look up with false, bright smiles and pretend they were talking about the weather or something." She laughed, no trace of bitterness in her tone. "My mom's given up asking me when I'm going to settle down and have children. She just prays for me at church on Sundays."

Evan laughed. "Sounds rough. My parents were both dentists who worked all the time. I just have one brother. He's two years older than me, unhappily married, with two kids."

"That's too bad. The unhappily part, I mean," Ruby replied with a frown. "I don't know if my siblings are truly happy or not. I doubt it's something they would even take into account. In my family, you date one person starting in high school, eventually get married and have kids and go to church and that's that. Divorce is not an option, and feelings aren't something we discuss."

"How in the world did that family produce *you*, Ruby? You're like the polar opposite of all that."

"Even when I was little, they used to joke that I was switched by accident in the hospital nursery, and Mom was too tired to notice. I don't even look like the rest of them. I used to fantasize that it was true, and my *real* parents, who were adventurers who lived on a boat and traveled from port to port all over the world, would come back to get me and take me with them."

She shrugged, her smile a little sad. "They never showed up, though, so I just took off on my own." She took a sip of her wine. "What about you? Where are you from originally? Do your parents know what you do for a living?"

Evan shook his head. "Not precisely. They know I set up events and conventions that require me to travel a lot, but I'm vague about the details. Easier that way. And we're from California—the San Francisco Bay area."

"You still live there when you're not traveling for work?"

"I have a small house there that I inherited from an uncle when I turned twenty-one. It's the only thing I kept from my divorce. I do short-term rentals for most of the year, keeping it vacant for when I need a place to land. The rents make me more money than my actual job," he added with a laugh.

"Your divorce," Ruby repeated, homing in, as he'd known she would, on that particular detail. Normally, he didn't mention his failed marriage to girls he hooked up with. Why had he told Ruby?

Because you can trust her, a voice whispered in his head.

He and his ex had both been twenty, juniors in college and very much in love. At least, Evan had been. Marriage hadn't been on the table, at least not in the near term, until Marissa had discovered she was pregnant, despite using a diaphragm. Evan, a hopeless romantic at the time, agreed with both sets of parents that marriage made sense. Marissa had been less sure, but she'd caved under the pressure.

Ignoring her hesitation, Evan had been stupidly, deliriously happy on their wedding day, chalking up her lesser enthusiasm to new-bride jitters. But when she'd miscarried only three months into their marriage, everything had changed.

Despite Evan's best efforts to comfort his grieving wife, she steadily withdrew from him. The cracks in his heart grew longer and deeper as the months passed, and yet he doggedly tried to force the marriage to succeed. Though she stuck it out for a full year, Marissa finally admitted she'd never loved him the way he'd loved her, and she wanted a new start.

He had been devastated. It had taken a long time to get over losing her, but it had been fifteen years, and plenty of scar tissue now covered those old cracks. No point in raking all that muck up. He wouldn't bore Ruby with the sordid details of his sad but probably all too common tale.

Forcing a light tone, he offered only, "Yeah. It was years ago. We were still in college. She got pregnant, we got married, she miscarried, we divorced. End of story. Stupid shit." He looked away, hoping the heat that suddenly scorched his face wasn't showing as a blush.

"That's not stupid shit," Ruby said gently, putting her hand over his. "That's a lot for two kids to handle."

Evan shrugged. "Yeah, it was rough. But probably for the best. Anyway, it's ancient history." He forced a smile. "So, what about you? Ever been married? In a long-term relationship?"

"Never married," Ruby replied. "As to a long-term thing, I guess it depends on your definition. I've lived with various guys over the years, some of them vanilla, most of them into the scene. I was pretty serious about one guy, but we called it quits after about two years. He wanted to settle down in one place, while I still wanted to travel. And, probably more at the crux of things, I wanted more intensity in our BDSM relationship than he felt comfortable giving me. We parted as friends, though."

Evan leaned forward, intrigued. "Tell me about that—about you wanting more intensity. Are you talking about erotic pain, or something more encompassing, like a 24/7 thing?"

"Oh," Ruby said, suddenly flushing. "I don't know. I guess some of both. Sometimes you want to find out if your secret, dark fantasies could be brought to life, you know?" She looked away, emitting a small, nervous laugh. "Just ignore me. That wine went right to my head."

"What dark fantasies, exactly?" Evan leaned over the small table and placed his hand on her bare arm. He was both excited and intrigued by her sudden discomfiture. "Don't be shy. Tell me. You've piqued my curiosity."

The waitress chose that precise moment to appear with the bill. Instead of discreetly melting away once she'd left it, she stood there, staring down at them, her expression both impatient and apologetic at once. Evan realized then they'd been there quite a while, their food having been cleared some time ago. She probably needed to turn over the table. Having been a waiter himself back in the day, Evan could sympathize.

He was determined to pursue the intriguing conversation they were having, but decided to let it go, for now. He pulled out his wallet, refusing Ruby's offer to split the check. As they got to their feet, he said casually, "Shall I take you back to your place? Pinky and Noodles probably need their pedicures."

Ruby laughed. "They should be all right a while longer. I was thinking we could take a walk along the lake we passed on the way here. It's such a beautiful evening."

"Your wish is my command, my lady," Evan said with a mock bow.

They drove in companionable silence the few minutes to the lake, and Evan parked in the lot beside it. As they walked along the path in the cool evening air, stars glimmered in the velvety black sky and only a few clouds scudded across the nearly full moon. Evan reached for Ruby's hand, which was cool and soft in his. His cock hardened just from touching her, and he led her to a bench and pulled her gently down beside him.

Taking her into his arms, he kissed her for a long time, exploring her mouth with his tongue as he pulled her close. He loved the feel of her breasts against his chest, separated only by the fabric of their clothing.

When they finally parted, she stared up at him with shining eyes, her lips gleaming from their kiss. He could feel her desire, which matched his own. "I want you, Ruby. I want to make love to you again."

"Yes," she whispered. "Take me home."

Once inside the front door, Evan dropped the gear bag he'd packed in hopes she'd ask him back to her place after dinner. He wrapped his arms around Ruby and hoisted her into the air.

She clung to him, wrapping her legs around his waist. Her skirt rode up high on her legs, and Evan gripped her ass as he kissed her. His cock was throbbing. He fell back against a wall, Ruby still in his arms. Keeping her aloft with one hand, he reached for his jeans fly and yanked down the zipper, along with enough of his underwear so that his cock sprang free.

"Yes," Ruby breathed, reaching between her legs to pull her panties aside. "Do it, Evan. Fuck me. Fuck me hard. Fuck me now."

Wild with lust, he shifted, managing to position his cock at her entrance. Just as he was about to plunge into her, he came to his senses. "Fuck," he swore softly.

"What?" Ruby gasped, her legs and arms still wrapped around him. "What is it?

"A condom. I've got one in my wallet—"

"No," she interrupted. "Don't. It's okay. I'm on the pill. I'm clean."

"Me, too. You sure?"

"I'm sure." She shifted in his arms, angling herself as one hand sought his cock. "Fuck me. I want you."

"I want *you*." He eased into her wet heat, groaning with pleasure as it enveloped him.

They rutted like animals, panting and grunting. Evan held her ass as he thrust into her. She gyrated against him, her fingers digging into his shoulders. "Oh, yes, yes, yes, just like that. Like that, like that," Ruby cried, her voice rising. Her cunt muscles spasmed around his shaft, sending him over the edge. He came in a series of convulsive thrusts, his face buried in her hair.

He slid down the wall, Ruby still in his arms. They sat like that, Ruby on his lap, until their breathing returned somewhat to normal.

Something soft and feathery brushed against Evan's arm, startling him.

"Hey, Binky," Ruby said, smiling at the cat, who meowed loudly in response. "Snack time." She untwined herself from Evan and got to her feet, pulling her dress back down. "And I found some great gelato in the freezer. Want some?"

Evan sipped some sparkling water as he watched Ruby eating sea salt caramel gelato. Just watching her eat a bowl of ice cream was sexy as hell. The quickie in the front hall had taken the edge off, but the night was young, and he was ready for more.

Happily, she seemed to have the same idea, because when she'd finished her dessert and tended to the cats, she fixed him with a sexy gaze and said, "Shall we go upstairs and explore what you packed in that gear bag of yours?"

"You read my mind," Evan replied.

~*~

"This looks like something my grandmother would hang her stockings on to dry," Ruby said, pulling out a large metal ring about nine inches in diameter. It had six clothespins attached to thin, stretchy black bands that were tied equidistant from one another around the ring.

Evan's smile was at once cruel and sensual. "That's one of the toys Bob ordered. It's called a pussy spreader, and I can't wait to try it out on you."

Ruby made a face. "Ouch. I'm afraid to ask what the clothespins are for."

"They're exactly what you think they're for." They were sitting on the bed, the gear bag open between them. Evan reached for the toy. "You need to get naked and lie on your back, knees bent, feet flat, legs spread wide. Then I'll press the ring between your thighs, right over your cunt and use the clothespin to open you wide. I brought the electrosex e-stim toy along as well. Once I have you spread wide, I'll shock that pretty little pussy of yours from the inside out."

He reached into the bag and took out what looked like a hair-curling wand, except it was shaped like a penis. It was made of black rubber with metal plates attached on either side, a handle with a cord beneath it. Presumably, he'd brought the power box she'd used on his cock as well.

Ruby was both intrigued and nervous at the thought of submitting to these strange erotic torture devices, neither of which she'd experienced before. She hugged herself, hesitating. "Hmm," she said aloud. "I'm not sure about that."

Evan lifted his hand to her throat, spreading it so his forefinger and thumb framed her jaw. As he increased the pressure, a frisson of delicious erotic fear tingled through her nerve endings, making her nipples hard. She swallowed in his grip, a pulse beating at her throat. She melted inside, any words of protest vanishing from her vocabulary.

He squeezed a little harder. "You'll do this for me, Ruby, because it pleases me." He kept his hand on her throat as he stared into her eyes, but his expression softened. "And because you know you can trust me."

Yes. She did know that. Somehow, she'd known it since the first moment she'd seen him. Still caught in his grip, she managed a small nod, her heart pounding.

He released her, his eyes smoldering. "Take off your clothes and lie on the bed like I told you, on your back, knees spread."

"Yes, Sir," she whispered.

Evan placed the ring between her legs, holding the cold metal against the backs of her thighs, the clothespins dangling inside it. Crouching in front of her, he pulled her left labia taut and closed one of the pins onto it.

"Ah," Ruby cried as it pinched tight against tender flesh.

Evan moved quickly, attaching all the pins, three on either side, until her cunt was spread wide, the ring held in place against the backs of her thighs by the tension of the pins on their elastic bands. Each time she shifted or struggled the tension only heightened, the clothespins tugging harder against her taut flesh. Better to remain still, if she could.

He stared down at her, an erection visible in his jeans. "You look so hot like that." He picked up the e-stim wand. "I'm going to shock that pretty little pussy."

"Yes, Sir," she whispered, her exposed clit throbbing. Her labia had grown numb in the grip of the clothespins. She bit her lip as she watched Evan lubricate the dildo, her heart was beating wildly against her breastbone.

He positioned the tip at her spread cunt and pushed it carefully inside her. It was hard and thick, and her muscles contracted and spasmed involuntarily against it as it invaded her.

"You doing okay?" he queried. "You took the whole thing."

"It feels really full, really intense," Ruby replied breathlessly.

"It's about to get a whole lot more intense." Evan picked up the power box. "I'll start slowly. We'll see what you can handle." He twisted a small knob on the box, sending a jolt of electric current through Ruby's body.

She squealed, more from surprise than pain. In fact, it had tickled.

"Okay?" Evan asked, searching her face.

She nodded.

"More?"

"Yes, please, Sir." She was curious now to find out how much she could handle. The second jolt was a little stronger than the first, and her muscles shivered in protest, though her clit continued to throb, made hypersensitive by the tension added from the taut clothespins.

"More?"

"Yes, please, Sir."

Evan gripped the handle of the dildo that was lodged inside her. He shifted it somehow, increasing the friction against her G-spot. Ruby had always envisioned her clit as three dimensional, with the outer part visible, but the underside deep inside her. Whatever Evan was doing with the dildo sent radiating waves of pleasure through her clit from the inside out, and she moaned her appreciation.

Another jolt of electricity shot through her, intensifying the pleasure with a buzz of erotic pain. "Oh," she cried out. Another jolt, and then another, until the current was moving through her in a steady, pulsing beat, penetrating deep muscle tissue and triggering hidden nerve bundles as it sent shudders of raw pleasure all through her.

"Oh, oh, oh, oh," she chanted, as he increased the intensity a little more, and then more still. She trembled as a powerful orgasm rose from deep inside her. She wailed as wave after wave of dark pleasure crashed over her senses.

When she opened her eyes, Evan was peering at her from between her legs. He'd pulled the electrified dildo from her body, though her cunt was still spread wide by the pinching clothespins. "I'm guessing you liked it?" he said with an impish grin.

"Fuck, yeah," she breathed.

He frowned. "Now comes the hard part. We have to get this thing off you." He touched the rim of the metal ring pressed against the backs of her thighs. "It's better if we do it now, while the endorphins are still coursing through your blood."

Ruby tensed, aware the releasing of the pins would hurt as much as, if not more than, when he'd attached them. "Okay." She closed her eyes.

One by one, he released the pins, moving quickly. Ruby sucked in her breath. It hurt, but not as much as having clamps removed from sensitized nipples, which had a lot more nerve endings than labia.

Bringing his mouth to her sex, he licked the tortured folds. His tongue was like wet satin, his hands on her inner thighs only adding to her pleasure. He kissed and licked her pussy until another orgasm rose on the heels of the last one.

"Ask me," she heard Evan say over the pounding of her heart and the pant of her ragged breath. "Ask me for permission, sub girl."

"Please," she begged, too far gone even to think of protesting.

"Please, Sir, can I come?"

"Yes."

He lowered his head and focused on her clit, giving her a shuddering, powerful climax that left her senseless.

After a while, she opened her eyes to a rustling sound. Evan was stripping off his shirt and jeans, revealing his hard, muscular body. His cock jutted toward her like a divining rod. Sitting next to her on the bed, he growled, "I want to fuck that gorgeous ass of yours."

Still reeling pleasurably from her orgasm, Ruby nodded. She had always enjoyed anal sex, not so much the act itself, but the submissive aspect of it. She rolled onto her stomach and rested her head on her arms.

Evan crouched behind her. Reaching for her hips, he pulled her up to her knees. His fingers, gooey with lubricant, smeared over her sphincter. The hand was withdrawn, replaced a moment later by the spongy head of his cock.

"Relax," he crooned, leaning up over her as he pushed carefully past the tight ring of muscle at the entrance. There was a moment of pain, and then her muscles relaxed and opened to him, drawing him in as she pushed gently back.

He reached beneath her body with one hand, cupping her cunt as he moved inside her. The skilled dance of his fingers against her sex was perfectly juxtaposed with his thick, hard shaft as it moved and thrust inside her. He came before she did, emitting a sudden, sharp cry as he slammed against her. They both fell forward onto the mattress, she pinned beneath him, his hand still between her legs.

But instead of pulling away, as she'd expected, he continued to stroke and tease her, his cock still buried in her ass. He didn't stop until he wrested yet another strong, wild orgasm from her exhausted body.

They lay as they'd fallen for a long while after that. Ruby tried to summon the energy to speak, to move, to get up, to think. But the powerful urge to sleep tugged at her senses, dragging her down until at last she gave in to its sweet, dark peace.

CHAPTER 7

When Ruby opened her eyes the next morning, the bed beside her was empty. She lifted herself on her elbows. "Evan?" she called. There was no reply. She got out of bed and went into the bathroom, which was empty. Maybe he was downstairs already, making coffee. She smiled at the thought as she used the toilet and brushed her teeth.

Back in the bedroom, she noticed that his gear bag was gone. "Hmm," she said, for the first time considering that he'd flown the coop without so much as a goodbye. She looked around for a note, then remembered what century she was in and went in search of her phone.

At first she couldn't think where she'd left her purse, but a little digging revealed it under the small heap of clothing she'd thrown off the night before. Pulling out her phone, she woke up the screen and checked her messages. There it was.

"Hey, sexy girl. You were sleeping like an angel. Didn't want to disturb you. Text or call when you've recovered." He added an emoticon of a grinning devil.

"Hey, sexy guy," she texted back. *"I'm recovered, are you? Gotta do some stuff today. Let's connect later."*

Still smiling, she pulled on a nightshirt and went downstairs to take care of the kitties and make coffee.

Grabbing her phone, she texted, *"Hey, Allie. I've got time today if you need more help with the walking canes. Let's hang out."* She added a heart and a smiley face.

Allie's reply came quickly. *"Great! Wood order expected today. Hurry over. I have buttermilk pancake batter with fresh blueberries that has your name on it."*

Ruby's stomach rumbled in anticipation. *"Yum. See you in thirty."*

The cats were happily ensconced in the sunroom. Ruby sent a quick text and a short video of Cuddles and Binky to her hosts, letting them know everything was going great and the cats were eating well. Then she returned upstairs to straighten up and make the bed. She pulled on an old red T-shirt and a pair of faded jeans, good work clothes for whittling and staining wood. She smiled at herself in the bathroom mirror as she pulled her hair back with a pretty red leather barrette shaped like a Celtic knot that she'd picked up in Ireland.

She felt good from her head to her toes, and Evan was the reason why. She loved that he was as highly sexed, adventurous and energetic as she was. Not many guys who weren't avowed subs would feel comfortable enough in his own skin to let a woman whip his ass or use an e-stim toy on his cock. She liked that he was still in touch with that part of himself. Even better, he was a real Dom, and that, at least in her experience, was a rare find. Most guys who enjoyed BDSM play could put on a good show during a scene, but as soon as they came, the party was over. Evan, she sensed, was someone who could sustain a D/s relationship for the long term.

Not that Ruby was thinking long term, but if she were...

Her stomach reminded her blueberry pancakes were waiting. Grabbing her purse, she headed back downstairs. She planned to spend most of the day at Allie's working on the canes. It would be a real pain to leave in the middle of a project. Maybe just this once the cats' schedule could be altered without extensive psychological damage.

She pulled out the container of the specially prepared cat food her hosts had provided and put some into the cats' matching china food bowls. When they got hungry again, their noses would lead them back to the kitchen. She would give them an extra long walk when she came back. Guilt averted, she headed out to the car.

Liam pulled open the front door before she'd even had a chance to ring the bell. He held out his arms for a hug. "Good morning, Ruby. Come on in. It's great to see you again."

She stepped into his arms and stood on tiptoe to kiss his cheek. "You, too."

"Allie's in the kitchen. Come on back and have some breakfast."

Ruby walked beside Liam through the living room. He used his cane expertly, so that his limp was barely noticeable. Allie had told her about the devastating car accident, and all the dark stuff he'd put himself through as a result. Thankfully, he seemed at peace with it now.

"Hi, sweetie," Allie said as they entered the kitchen. She was standing at the stove, a spatula in her hand. They embraced and Allie pointed to a bowl of batter filled with plump berries. "Our friends Bonnie and Matt Wilson stopped by this morning and dropped off these great locally grown blueberries. I've got some bacon too."

"Sounds delicious," Ruby said. "Can I do something?"

"Everything's still on the table. Just have a seat. Pancakes coming right up."

Liam, who had moved to a counter, opened a cabinet and took out a mug. "What do you like in your coffee, Ruby?"

Ruby laughed. "You guys are spoiling me. I could get used to this." Turning to Liam, she added, "Just a little cream, thanks."

Liam brought her mug to the table, a second mug in his other hand. "If you lovely ladies will excuse me, I need to get my butt in gear and get to work." He kissed Allie on the top of her head and left the kitchen.

Allie brought over a plate stacked with hot pancakes, several pieces of crisp bacon beside them. "Let me just get another cup and I'll join you."

Ruby added some butter and syrup to the steaming pancakes. She took a bite and nearly swooned with pleasure. "I swear, Allie, you're a fantastic cook."

Allie grinned as she slid into a chair across from Ruby with her coffee mug. "I like to bake and make breakfast—that's about it. But thanks."

The doorbell rang. Allie jumped up. "That's probably the wood supplier. I got some black cherry and walnut, just like you suggested. I'm excited to get started."

"Great. Me, too."

As Allie left to get the door, Ruby took several more bites of the delicious breakfast. She sipped her coffee, which was strong and hot.

Allie returned a few minutes later and sat back down. "Yep. That was the wood guy. I had him take it right up to the workshop, so we can get started right after breakfast." She took a drink from her mug. "But first I need an update on the Beckett/Stewart romance since yesterday."

Ruby laughed. "I don't know if it can be called an official romance, but it's been pretty intense, I have to say."

"Details, details, details," Allie said, leaning forward eagerly.

Ruby filled her in, Allie asking questions and interjecting commentary along the way. "You two sure can pack a lot into the space of a few days," she said with an approving laugh. "That's what's so great about a true D/s connection. The intensity is immediate and sustainable. You've got a built-in spark and love just keeps the flames fanned."

"Whoa," Ruby said with a grin. "Who's talking about love? I just met the guy."

"Don't discount it, Ruby," Allie said seriously. "Love at first sight isn't just the stuff of romance novels. It happened to me, and now he's my Master." She fingered the tiny gold heart on the red leather collar around her throat. "I was watching you during the whipping demo the other day, and then again at dinner and down in the dungeon. There was something happening between the two of you from the second you set eyes on each other that went beyond casual play. Something special."

Ruby couldn't deny it, but nor was she quite ready to confirm it. Instead, she pushed back from the table with a contented sigh. "That was absolutely delicious, Allie. If you keep feeding me like this, I'm going to need a new wardrobe." She got to her feet and picked up her plate to take it to the sink. "Now that I'm properly fortified, let's get to work."

As they always did when Ruby was engaged in a creative process, the hours flew by. The smooth wood and the woodworking tools felt good in her hands, like old friends she'd been away from too long. Allie and she worked in companionable silence, losing themselves in their craftsmanship.

At one point, Liam brought them sandwiches and lemonade. He sat with them as they took a break to eat. "You're just like Allie," he said to Ruby, flashing an indulgent smile at his wife. "You both get lost in your art and forget to eat."

"Guilty as charged," Ruby agreed, suddenly hungry at the sight of the food. They cleared a space on one of the tables to eat their lunch. When they were done, they returned to their tasks, quickly becoming absorbed.

"Something's dinging."

Ruby, engaged in her task, took a moment to process Allie's voice as words. "What?"

"I said, something's dinging on your butt," Allie said with a grin. "Someone's texting you."

"Oh!" Ruby put down the staining rag, wiped her hands and reached into the back pocket where she'd stashed her phone.

It was a text from Evan. Her heart quickened as she clicked on the message.

"Been thinking about you. Can't wait to try out a few more toys."

"It's from Evan," she said, looking up at Allie.

"I knew that from the goofy grin on your face. What'd he say?"

She showed Allie the screen.

"Oh, that sounds promising," Allie said with a sly grin. "Tell him to come here. We need a break, anyway. It's already past two. We've been at it for hours."

"I'm at Allie's place. She says why don't you come by?"

"And what do you say, Ruby? Do you miss the feel of my hand on your throat?"

A shiver of desire moved through Ruby's body at the image his words conjured, her hand moving unconsciously to her throat.

"What?" Allie said, holding out her hand to see the screen. "What did he say?"

Ruby showed her.

"OMG, Ruby. He's so hot. Tell him yes!"

"Are you sure you don't want me to set *you* up with him, Allie?" she teased.

Allie laughed. "Hey, a girl can look, right? He's very easy on the eyes. Seriously, tell him to come over. You guys could use the dungeon." She began to put her tools away. "You could go down and wait for him. Wouldn't that be so hot? You down there, naked and on your knees, head bowed, waiting to serve him."

Ruby laughed again. "What're you, my BDSM social director?"

Allie shrugged. "It's a tough job, but somebody's got to do it. Anyway, doesn't it sound super hot?"

Ruby couldn't deny that it did. A good night's sleep and a half day away from Evan, and she was more than ready to pick up where they'd left off. "Yeah," she agreed. "It does at that."

She thumbed back a reply. *"Yes, Sir. Yes, please."*

Evan rang the doorbell at the Byrne house and took a step back. He felt more like eighteen than thirty-six, puppy-dog eager to see Ruby again. But when the door opened, Allie, not Ruby, greeted him.

"Hi, Evan. Welcome." She gave him a quick hug and stepped back. "Come on in."

Evan entered, looking around. Ruby was nowhere in sight. "Uh, Ruby's car is out front but...?"

Allie grinned. "Yes, I'm doing fine, thanks."

Evan flashed an embarrassed smile. "I'm sorry, Allie. It's really good to see you again. I had a great time the other night."

"You're forgiven. I was just teasing. Ruby's here. She's waiting for you."

Evan raised his eyebrows.

"Downstairs," Allie added, her pretty blue eyes twinkling. "In the dungeon."

"In the dungeon," he repeated, slow to process the import of her words. "She's down there now? Waiting for me?"

"That's right. Hopefully naked and on her knees."

Evan's stomach flip-flopped, his pulse quickening. He was dying to race down immediately, but now mindful of being rude. "Should I...?" he queried, uncertain.

"Go," Allie urged with a laugh. "The dungeon is all yours. No one will disturb you."

Evan smiled. "Thanks, Allie. You're a good friend—to both of us."

He walked down the stairs, his cock already stiffening in anticipation. At the bottom, he drew in a breath at the lovely vision before him. Ruby was naked and on her knees, her hands clasped behind her head, her breasts thrust proudly forward.

"Jesus," he breathed aloud. "Perfect."

In two strides, he was in front of her. Bending down, he lifted her upright and caught her in his arms, his mouth seeking hers.

Having satisfied that initial overwhelming need to touch her, Evan gently disengaged from her embrace and put his hands on her shoulders. He stared down into her eyes. Though he didn't need a dungeon to continue where they'd left off, he was excited by the opportunities this new situation presented. He had been thrilled to see Ruby again, but hadn't thought much beyond that, content to see where things stood between them after the intensity of the day before.

To find her waiting for him, naked and on her knees in this awesome dungeon, went beyond anything he'd dared hope. She was like a gift from the BDSM gods, and he couldn't wait to claim her even more fully.

"Are you ready to go further today, Ruby? I want to take you past your comfort zone. Does that suit you?"

Ruby licked her lower lip, the gesture achingly sensual. "Yes, Sir," she said in a low, throaty voice that stroked all his senses.

"How comfortable are you with rope bondage? We haven't really explored that yet."

"I love it, Sir," she replied eagerly. "I love the feeling of the rope against my skin. I love the erotic helplessness, and also the security and comfort of being tightly bound."

"That's a good thing, because bondage is something of a specialty of mine. I studied with an excellent Shibari Master back in California."

Ruby flashed him a radiant smile that made his heart squeeze almost painfully in his chest.

He let her go as he looked around the large, well-equipped space. "I left my gear bag in the car, but we should be able to find whatever we need here." He went to the wall where whips and rope were neatly arrayed on hooks. He chose several hanks of red-dyed jute, perfect for intense bondage.

Returning to Ruby, he said, "Lift your hair out of the way and put your hands behind your head."

She executed some kind of girl maneuver with her hair, tying it into a loose knot on top of her head, and then laced her fingers behind her neck.

Evan unwound the strong, soft rope, keeping a piece in his hand and setting the rest on the ground nearby. The sight of the lovely, naked girl standing in that submissive pose was making his jeans uncomfortably tight.

He unbuttoned his shirt and set it aside. Then he pulled off his boots and removed his jeans, leaving on only his black silk boxers. Ruby was watching him with hungry eyes that pleased him.

While Evan enjoyed both the power rush and the aesthetic appeal of binding a woman, he especially loved how it made *her* feel. He adored creating that sense of erotic helplessness sexual masochists craved, and Ruby's comments only reinforced his desire.

He started with a basic chest harness, using a lark's head knot to join two of the shorter pieces of rope. He wrapped her breasts carefully, using a figure eight around their contours to hold them tight. As he worked, her breathing deepened, her chest rising and falling, her cheeks flushing. He could sense her arousal, which increased with each knot and tug of rope, as well as that sweet, powerful ascent into submissive headspace that he was honored to help bring about.

When he was satisfied, he said, "You may lower your arms."

She brought her arms down to her sides, her luminous eyes fixed on his face.

"Place your hands in a relaxed position in front of you, palms touching." He used a simple double column tie to bind her wrists.

Her entire face was now lit with a submissive glow, her eyes bright. Her breasts, lifted and compressed by the ropes, sported dark red, distended nipples that fairly begged for clamps. Unable to resist, he bent and sucked each perfect nipple until she moaned. He left them shiny and hard, the areolas puckered.

She was more than ready to be led deeper into submissive headspace, and he couldn't wait to take her there. She had reacted very strongly to the water play they'd witnessed on Saturday, and he was eager to explore her personal boundaries in that regard.

Taking her bound wrists in his hand, he led her back toward the water play area, bringing her to a stop in front of the submersion tub.

Ruby stared at it with wide eyes, her teeth worrying her lower lip. He took her head in his hands and searched her beautiful, expressive face. "I watched you the other night when the girls were bound to the water wall. I sensed both your fear and excitement. Have you ever been held down under water?"

"No, Sir," she whispered, her lovely, dark eyes widening.

"Would you like to experience that at my hands?" As he asked the question, he placed his hand at her sex and slipped a finger between her labia. She was soaking wet.

She drew in a sharp breath. "I'm not sure. I mean, it would be sexy, but scary too."

Evan nodded. "A good combination for a masochist, no? Think of the rush."

"Yes," she said, the word sibilant in her mouth.

"Do you trust me, Ruby?"

She nodded.

"Good. Are you ready for a new adventure? I promise to keep you safe. I will take you to the edge, but I won't push you over. I've done this before and I know what I'm doing."

Again she nodded.

Satisfied, Evan leaned over and turned on the hot water faucet. The tub filled rapidly, and he adjusted the temperature to that of a warm bath. When it was two-thirds full, he turned off the water and helped Ruby climb in, supporting her shoulders as she settled herself in the water.

Then he pulled down his boxers and kicked them away. He stepped into the large tub behind her and eased himself down into the warm water, extending his legs on either side of her. She leaned back against him with a contented sigh.

Reaching around her trussed body, he cupped her exposed breasts in his hands. "You're bound in rope," he murmured into her ear as he rolled her nipples between his fingers. "You are completely at my mercy. When you're ready, I'm going to gently press your shoulders to submerge you completely under the water. I will keep you under until I decide to let you up. Your safe signal will be lifting either of your legs out of the water. But don't worry, I won't let it get to that point. You can actually hold your breath a lot longer than you think you can, as I'll soon show you. When I take my hands from your shoulders, that's your cue to come up for air. It's an exercise in trust and control—a true act of submission."

Ruby tensed against him, though she made no protest.

Releasing her nipples, he massaged her shoulders, gently easing the tension from her muscles until she relaxed. He dipped his head to nuzzle her neck and murmured. "Are you ready, Ruby? Are you ready to submit to me?"

"Yes, Sir," she said in a slightly tremulous voice.

A dark thrill of heady power surged through him as he positioned his hands on her shoulders. He had entered what he thought of as Dom-space, a particularly lucid, serene state of mind in which he felt uniquely connected to his sub.

For Evan, being a Dom wasn't just about the rush that came from having the power and the control over a scene and another human being. It was most essential to have control over oneself. Your partner trusted you to create a safe and intimate space for them to fully experience their darkest desires.

As Evan eased now into that headspace, he experienced a combination of arousal, tranquility and incredible focus. It was exhilarating to lead a sub through their fear and desire to a higher plane, secure in the knowledge that he controlled both their pleasure and pain.

"On the count of three," he said. "One... Two... Three."

Evan pushed, slowly but firmly, causing her to slide forward and down until she was fully submerged. The top of her head touched his chest, her face just a few inches below the water, eyes squeezed tightly shut.

Sensibly, their hosts had hung a large clock on the wall by the tub, and Evan carefully tracked the second hand's sweep. He was keenly aware of Ruby's reactions, intimately connected to her every gesture and response. Unlike the intense impact play sessions, which fit neatly into Ruby's existing masochistic groove, this water play had lifted her out of her comfort zone, and Evan was determined to make the experience one she would never forget.

The D/s bond between them was so strong at that moment that Evan felt as if he and Ruby inhabited the same space. He could feel her heartbeat and the pressure in her head as she held her breath.

He waited until precisely the right moment and then removed his hands from her shoulders.

Ruby bolted upright, gasping for breath.

Evan shifted so he could see her face. He reached for a hand towel from the stack on the side of the tub and gently wiped the water from her eyes. "You okay?"

"I think so," she gasped. "Being bound like this, unable to move at all, it was pretty intense. How long was I under? A minute? I thought my lungs were going to explode."

Evan chuckled. "You were under for ten seconds. A healthy person can hold their breath for about two minutes."

"Are you sure? It definitely felt like longer."

Evan pointed to the clock. "I timed it. It felt longer because you're tensing up. Relax." He pulled her gently back against him. "While I'm counting down this time, take a deep breath, nice and slow. The rope harness is loose enough that it shouldn't be an issue. Then give in to the process. Submit."

"Yes, Sir," she said, no longer tremulous but still a little breathless.

"Breathe deep," he reminded her. "I'm going to count to three and then down you go. One… Two… Three."

She drew in a deep breath.

He pushed gently on her shoulders until she again slid beneath the water. He tracked ten seconds on the clock. She was doing better, and he let another ten seconds go by. She started to tense. He kept his hands on her shoulders until thirty seconds had elapsed.

Again she sprang up, gasping for air. "How long?" she cried. "How long was that?"

"Thirty seconds," Evan said. "You did good."

She frowned. "Just thirty? I can do longer. Let's do it again."

Evan laughed. "Eager now, huh? Or is it just the challenge?"

"I guess that's part of it. I feel both powerful and vulnerable, all at the same time, if that makes any sense."

"It makes perfect sense. It's part of the submissive mindset—it takes real courage to submit, to allow yourself to be so completely vulnerable and reliant on another person, and that's a pretty powerful feeling."

"Yes," she cried excitedly. "That's it exactly."

He placed his hands again on her shoulders. This time he held her down for nearly a minute. She began to panic at around the fifty-five second mark, her body tensing. Before she had a chance to fail, he released her and pulled her upright.

He wrapped his arms around her as she gasped for air. "Shh," he crooned. "You did good, Ruby, nearly a full minute under. That's enough for our first time. I'm proud of you."

He wiped her face with the towel and then pulled her gently back against him. Reaching around her body, he released the knot at her wrists and unwound the rope from her arms, tossing it out of the tub.

"Just relax in the water for a minute while I dry off," he said, getting to his feet. He stepped out and toweled himself quickly before wrapping the towel around his waist. Leaning down, he held out his hands, and Ruby took them. He helped her to stand, keeping his hand on her arm as she climbed out of the tub.

Her bunched breasts were dark pink, the nipples crimson. Evan stroked the hard globes, running his hands over them. He bent to kiss each rock-hard nipple. Then he released the knots that held the chest harness in place and let the wet ropes slide to the ground. Grabbing one of the terrycloth robes that hung on a nearby hook, he draped it over her shoulders and helped her to slip her arms into the sleeves.

Feeling both tender and lustful, he lifted her into his arms. She snuggled against him as he carried her to the recovery couch. Sitting with her on his lap so she was facing him, he dipped his head for a kiss.

She responded ardently, pulling him closer, her tongue dancing in his mouth, her bare breasts pressing against his chest as her robe fell open. "That was so hot," she gasped between kisses, before seeking his mouth once more. "It was thrilling. I've always been afraid of that kind of play, but you made it both safe and sexy. Thank you for that, Evan. Thank you." Her smile could have lit up a small town.

Evan grinned back, delighted and aroused in equal measure. His cock and balls were aching, and he still felt the rush of domination from the water play. Without thinking about it, he brought his hand to her throat, finding the sweet spot on either side of her jaw with thumb and forefinger.

Ruby stilled at once, her eyes widening as he tapped into this particular erogenous zone. He tightened his grip and said softly, "What's your darkest fantasy, Ruby? The secret one you've never told another soul?" He kept his hand firmly on her throat.

"What?" she gasped, a deep blush blooming on her cheeks as she looked away. "What are you talking about?"

"You know what I'm talking about," he said, certain by her reaction he had struck a key nerve. "Don't try to make it pretty, or soften it because you think I'll judge you. I want to know the truth. I want that secret, Ruby. The darkest, dirtiest, scariest fantasy you keep hidden and only take out at night, when you're alone in your bed, your hand between your legs."

He loosened his grip on her throat, but only a little.

"Jesus," she whispered. "Who are you?"

"Who do you want me to be, Ruby?" he murmured, his eyes locked on hers. "Tell me."

"A Master," she finally managed.

"Go on," he said softly, trying to keep his excitement tamped down. "Tell me everything. Don't hold back. Tell me your secret. I'll keep it safe." He kept his hand on her throat, but now it was only a touch, a reminder that, for this moment at least, he owned her. "Tell me," he urged gently.

"It's just a fantasy," she said, laughing nervously. "Sometimes, I fantasize about a guy who keeps me locked up, naked and on my knees. I'm his possession, his toy, his sex object. He decides when I sleep, when I pee, when I eat, when I service him, how I service him. He whips me daily and trains me to be his perfect, obedient submissive sex slave. He punishes me harshly when I misstep and owns me completely."

Her words bypassed Evan's brain, lodging directly in his core. Without meaning to, he tightened his grip on her throat.

A shudder moved through her body and she jerked in his grasp.

He let his hand fall away, and she rolled from his lap to the couch beside him. She pulled the robe closed around her body and rocked forward. Her hair had come loose, and it fell in a damp curtain, obscuring her face.

"Like I said, it's just a fantasy." She glanced nervously at him.

"It's an incredibly hot, sexy fantasy. One I would love to help bring to life, Ruby."

Her mouth fell open, her eyes widening. "What? You mean...you and me? Do a Master/slave thing in real life?"

"That's exactly what I mean. Not forever, obviously. But just for a few days. As an experiment."

She shook her head, her hands twisting in her lap. "I don't think I could do that. Not in real life."

"You're afraid," he offered, placing his hand lightly on her thigh. "But what an adventure it could be. Think of it," he enthused, swept away in the possibilities. "You would give yourself completely over to another person. I would control your every move, your every action. I would take you deeper than you've ever gone in your submissive exploration. I'd keep you safe. I think you know that, Ruby."

A spark of excitement kindled in her expression, bright as a candle. "Gosh. I don't know." She shook back her wild hair and laughed. "I mean, come on. I'm an independent woman who takes what she wants and then moves on. A masochist, yes. A submissive slave? Not so much."

"Hey, don't think I don't get that. This isn't a lifetime commitment, far from it. It would be an experiment, something we could explore together. I don't think of myself as a Master, either. But I have to say, the idea of claiming a woman, of taking full control of every aspect of her life and training her to serve me with complete obedience and submission sounds pretty fucking wild. It's a super hot fantasy, Ruby. Incredibly sexy."

He turned to her, taking her face into his hands as he stared down into her eyes. "It takes a very special person to submit to that degree. Someone who's strong enough to undergo intense sexual and submissive training without losing their essence. A woman like that has to be secure in herself, courageous enough to take the leap, and willing to engage in that ultimate exchange of power. I've never found a woman like that. Until now."

He leaned forward and kissed her lightly on the mouth. "I would be deeply honored to be that man for you. I know you like a challenge. What do you say? Are you in?"

CHAPTER 8

Ruby stared at Evan, her mind reeling. What would it be like to be kept naked and chained 24/7, constantly used and deliciously abused by a Master who was fully in control?

But was Evan the man for the job? While she'd had an incredible connection with this awesome guy so far, did she know or trust him enough to give herself over so completely? Did she want to?

"Ruby?"

"Hmm?"

"I'm waiting for your answer. Do you have the courage to submit? The desire to see your dreams brought to life?"

Yes, yes, yes, yes, yes, a tiny voice whispered emphatically inside her.

But this was crazy. Even if she'd known him for years, there was no way she could sustain that kind of intensity for more than an hour or two, nor was she sure she really wanted to.

Liar.

She blew out a breath as she marshaled her thoughts. "It sounds really hot and sexy in theory, but I'm not sure it's something I could actually do in real life."

"You know," Evan said slowly, "One of the many things I love about BDSM is that it can take you to places you never thought you'd go. It's like drugs, only way safer and a thousand times more intense. I love the idea of going further, delving deeper, than just a short-lived scene. I've never taken full control, 24/7, of another person, but I think it could be a really powerful experience, not just for you as a sub, but for me as a Dom."

He took her hand. "I guess the question you have to ask yourself is, are you willing to surrender your body, heart and soul to another person? That person would literally hold your life in his hands. If you were willing to trust me with that kind of total power exchange, I promise I would cherish and honor that gift, Ruby—the gift of your submission. If we do try this thing, we would agree in advance on limits and boundaries, and your safeword would still be sacrosanct."

Ruby pulled the robe tighter around herself. Her mouth had gone dry and her heart tap-danced in her chest. She closed her eyes and drew in a deep breath in an effort to calm herself down.

"I don't know," she finally replied. "I want it, or at least, I think I do, but it also scares me."

"A little fear can be a good thing," Evan said, his voice husky. He brought his hand again to her throat, and though she knew he was doing this to arouse her, that didn't stop it from working. Heat washed over her face, starting at her throat and moving upward to the roots of her hair.

"I-I..." she stammered.

All at once, Evan withdrew his hand and rose from the couch. He looked so hot standing with only a towel around his waist, with his sexy tattoos and rippling muscles. She wanted to eat him up.

He rubbed his face and ran a hand through his hair. "Hey, I'm sorry," he said ruefully. "I'm rushing you. I'm pushing buttons to get the answers I want and that's not cool." He held out his hand, and she took it, allowing him to pull her upright.

"We don't have to decide this now," he continued. "Maybe we need a break. I should probably get going."

"No," she said abruptly, his sudden withdrawal allowing her to acknowledge what was in her heart.

"No?" he said, lifting his eyebrows.

"I mean yes," she blurted, flustered but determined. "Yes, I think—no, I *know* I want to try it."

"You want to try what, exactly? Help me be sure I understand what you're saying, Ruby."

"I want to try being your 24/7 submissive sex slave," she said, barely believing the words were coming out of her mouth. A rush of exhilaration shot through her body. She wanted to leap into the air and dance around the room, though she forced herself to remain still. "I don't know for how long, or if I can even do this, but I want to try, Evan. I want you to bring my darkest fantasy to life."

"Yes," he breathed softly, his eyes glittering. "That's what I want, too." He placed his hands on her shoulders, applying pressure so that she sank down to her knees before him.

He placed a hand on her head, like a priest offering a benediction. His voice was soft but authoritative as he said, "From this moment until we decide otherwise, you belong completely and unequivocally to me. I own your body, your will, your obedience and your submission. You will abdicate complete control of every aspect of your life to me. You will not eat, sleep, pee, dress, orgasm or touch yourself sexually without my express permission. I will bind you, whip you, spank you, choke you and use your body as it pleases me. I will push every erotic boundary you possess. The word 'no' will not exist in your vocabulary. You will be my slave in every sense of the word. Do you understand?"

Ruby had forgotten how to breathe. He'd reached down into that dark, secret core of her fantasies and pulled out its heart, which he now held, bloody and pulsing, in his hand.

"Yes, Sir," she finally managed, her voice tremulous, her heart beating wildly against her ribs.

Evan held out his hands and pulled her upright. As he wrapped her in a firm embrace, she tried to get control of her whirling thoughts. Was she really going to do this? Was she out of her mind? Maybe that was a good thing—to get out of your own head for a while. He had offered her the chance to seize another wild adventure in a life lived on the edge. One more leap into the unknown, one more thrill to be explored to the fullest.

As if sensing her turmoil, Evan let her go and looked down into her eyes, his expression gentle. "Trust me, Ruby," he said softly. "Trust us."

"Yes," she breathed. "Yes, Sir."

Together, they cleaned the tub and water play area and hung the Shibari rope to dry. Then they dressed and went upstairs. They found Allie and Liam in the kitchen, sharing a glass of red wine. "Hey kids," Allie said with a knowing grin. "Decided to come up for air?"

Liam eyed Ruby, apparently noting her still-wet hair. "Enjoyed a little water play, hmm?"

"We did, indeed," Evan replied. "We hung the Shibari ropes to dry on the towel rack. I hope that's okay."

Liam raised his eyebrows, but said only, "Sure, that's perfect."

"Thanks very much for the use of the dungeon," Evan added.

"Yes, thanks to you both," Ruby said. Her gaze strayed to the kitchen wall clock. "Oh, man. The cats. I have to get home. They're probably freaking out, being neglected for so long. They missed their afternoon walk."

"Cats?" Liam said, clearly perplexed.

"Very special cats," Allie explained.

"Royal cats," Evan added with a laugh. "Listen, I hate to run out like this, but I have to handle something for BDSM Connections and then"—he fixed Ruby with a meaningful stare—"I have an appointment with a certain sexy sub girl."

"Well, listen, don't be a stranger, Evan," Liam said.

Allie stood and moved toward Ruby, giving her a hug. "Thanks for the help. We got a good start today." Leaning closer, she whispered, "I want a full report when you get home. Call me."

"I will." Ruby smiled.

The couple walked them to the front door, with everyone again exchanging hugs, or, in the case of the guys, handshakes.

At their cars, Evan said, "I just need to stop by the warehouse and take care of a few things for Bob. Then I'll swing by the bed-and-breakfast and pack some things. I'll grab a bite along the way. So, I'll see you in about two, two and a half hours. Does that work for you?"

"Sure." The dark spell Evan had woven over her had loosened its hold, though prickles of anticipation still bubbled in her gut. She stood on tiptoe and kissed him. "See you soon."

Back at the house, she parked and went out the garage door, pushing the code into the keypad beside it to close it. She walked to the front door and reached into the mailbox beside it for the daily delivery.

As she entered the house, two beautiful, glaring cats greeted her, their tails waving high with indignation.

"Okay, okay," she said with a laugh as she set the day's mail on top of the growing pile on the side table beside the front door. "I'm sorry I wasn't here to take you on your walk." She bent down to stroke them. "Let's get a snack and then off we go, I promise."

She took her phone with her on the walk, eager to reconnect with Allie and tell her the astonishing news. "There you are," Allie said when the call connected. "What happened down in the dungeon? Did you use the water wall? Isn't it awesome? There was definitely something hot simmering between the two of you. Liam and I both felt it."

Ruby shared the intense water immersion experience, and they compared notes on the subject for a while.

"What?" Allie finally said, somehow reading Ruby's mind. "There's something you're not telling me. What is it? Is everything okay?"

"I honestly have no idea," Ruby blurted. "Or, no, that's not exactly true. Evan's heading back over in a while. We've agreed to, that is, I've agreed to... Well, it's really crazy, but..."

"What? What is it, sweetie?

"Okay. I'll just tell you, and then you can tell me I'm insane." She confided in Allie about the 24/7 Master/slave arrangement they'd made, not quite believing as she said it aloud that she'd agreed to it.

But when she was done, far from admonishing her for signing up for something crazy, Allie squealed with delight. "Oh, Ruby, that's so hot! You're going to *love* it. I'm Liam's full time slave girl, even if it doesn't look like it from the outside. I mean," she rushed on, "he doesn't tell me when to pee or eat or that kind of stuff, but I most definitely belong to him. He calls the shots in everything to do with our love life, and I absolutely adore it."

"I know you do," Ruby said, stopping with the cats so they could inspect a dead toad at their leisure. "But I'm not like you. I'm a free—"

"A free spirit. Yes, I know," Allie said with a laugh. "But you're also nothing if not adventurous. This has got to be the adventure of a lifetime. There's something incredibly freeing about giving yourself over completely to someone else, Ruby. You'll see—it's like nothing you've ever experienced. And anyway," she added, "it's not like you're signing some seven-year servitude contract or something. You guys agreed to try it for a day or two, right? You can do anything for a day or two, surely?"

"You're right, of course. Thanks for talking me down off the ledge," Ruby said. "When I get past the noise in my head, I'm actually super turned-on by the idea. It's my darkest fantasy, and he wants to bring it to life."

"I love it," Allie said. "Just remember, I'm going to need a full accounting, so take notes."

"Uh huh," Ruby said with a laugh. "I'll just post a video on YouTube, why don't I?"

"Even better," Allie teased back.

When Ruby got back to the house, she led the cats to the back door since they always liked to stop at the laundry room litter box after a walk. They were apparently too ladylike to relieve themselves out in public, and she couldn't blame them.

The cats taken care of, Ruby handled a few emails and turned on the TV in the living room. She was antsy and couldn't pay attention to what she was watching. Instead, she put on some music to do a little yoga, which always calmed her down. After about forty minutes of stretching and exercising, she had worked up a sweat.

It was already nearly seven—where the hell was he? She was too wound up for a proper meal. She grabbed an apple from the dwindling bowl in the kitchen and took it with her, eating as she climbed the stairs.

She decided to shower and fix her hair, which had dried into a tangled mess after the water play. As she washed and groomed, her mind drifted to Evan—to all the things they'd done so far, and all the things they were going to do...

As she dried off after the shower, her clit throbbed, begging to be stroked. She pressed her thighs together in an effort to relieve the ache, but that just made it worse. The Master/slave dynamic wouldn't really start until Evan showed up, right? A quickie orgasm would at least take the edge off.

Returning to the bedroom, she lay on the bed. Closing her eyes, she slipped a hand between her legs. She sighed with pleasure as Evan rose in her mind's eye, a long, curling whip in his hands...

~*~

His obligations satisfied for BDSM Connections, Evan returned to the bed-and-breakfast to pack a few things. He let the hostess know he might not be back for a few days, but to keep his room for him.

This was definitely not his usual MO—to basically move in with someone he'd known for only a few days. But it wasn't like that, he reassured himself. They were conducting an experiment, and it wouldn't work if they didn't commit to it 24/7.

Though he'd never harbored any particular Master/slave fantasies himself, her strong, visceral reactions as they'd talked about its potential had excited him deep in his dominant core.

He only hoped he could make it work for her. While her complete erotic servitude was definitely a hot concept, he didn't really have the first idea of how to be a so-called Master.

Sitting down on his bed, he opened his laptop and went to a few how-to websites that detailed proper Master/slave protocol and offered concrete advice for the domination of a BDSM slave. There were a ton of sites and plenty of information, some of it credible, some of it insane. He read for a while, absorbing what made sense to him and discarding the rest.

Yes, this was definitely going to be fun. Ruby's fantasy included all the key aspects of a true Master/slave total power exchange, and Evan was excited to bring it to life for her. He was determined to stick to his guns. He wouldn't let her get away with any misbehavior. She expected and needed to be controlled, directed and properly punished as part of her training. He wasn't sure if he could actually pull this thing off, but he was hell-bent on trying.

Overnight and gear bag packed, he stopped at a supermarket on the way to Ruby's place, since she didn't seem to have all that much food in the house. He filled the cart with whatever struck his fancy, also buying a prepackaged sandwich and a can of soda for dinner, since he'd told her he'd grab a bite along the way, and it was already past seven.

Done with the shopping, he headed to her house, eating his sandwich as he drove. He thought about texting to let her know he was coming. No. It would be more fun to surprise her.

When he arrived, he pulled in the driveway and cut the engine and the lights. Grabbing his bags from the trunk, he headed up the front walk to the door. He was about to ring the bell, but on impulse tried the doorknob. To his delight, it wasn't locked.

He entered the house, locking the door behind him. All was quiet. He dropped his duffel and gear bag at the bottom of the stairs and carried the grocery bags into the kitchen.

No Ruby.

He put away the things that needed refrigeration. Back in the front hall, he grabbed his bags and walked quietly up the stairs, in case she was napping.

He was ready to become Ruby's Master, at least for a little while.

~*~

"What do you think you're doing, slave?"

Startled, Ruby's eyes flew open, and she squealed in frightened confusion. She slammed her legs closed, instinctively grabbing the quilt to cover herself. "Oh my god! What the—? Evan! You scared me to death. How did you get in?"

"The door was unlocked," he said as he dropped his bags to the ground, his expression grim. He strode toward the bed and yanked her upright, the quilt falling away as he pulled her to her feet. "What the hell were you doing just now?"

Ruby's face flamed with humiliation and chagrin. Who the hell did he think he was, just barging in like this? She tried to pull her arm away, but he held her fast.

"Answer the question, slave girl." His voice was softer now, but there was steel beneath it.

She looked down, her face hot. "Well, I-I, that is, I was just..." she trailed off, unable to finish the sentence. Though she knew it was a game, it sure as hell didn't feel like one. She was both deeply embarrassed and, if she were honest, thrilled to her core.

Evan placed his hand under her chin, forcing her to look at him. "You're already going to be punished for that infraction. Don't compound it by failing to answer a direct question."

Jesus, was he for real? Ruby wasn't entirely sure what she'd expected, but it had included easing a little more slowly into this thing. But he was already in full Master mode and clearly determined to make her toe the line.

He was a head taller and fifty pounds heavier than she, all of it muscle. Though she instinctively trusted him, how well did she really know the guy? A frisson of genuine fear ricocheted through her. What if he took this thing too far? At the same time, every fiber of her being was alive with a wild, pinging energy as she embarked on this new adventure.

"What was the question, Sir?" she asked, her heart fluttering wildly in her chest.

"I asked what you were doing."

Ruby looked away. He was really going to make her answer what was obviously a rhetorical question. She forced herself to look up at him, lifting her chin to give herself courage. "I was touching myself."

Evan nodded. "Yet, we agreed only a few hours ago that your body belonged to me, and you were not to touch it sexually without express permission. Isn't that right?"

Ruby blew out a breath. "Yeah. But I thought—"

"I'm not interested in what you thought right now. A simple yes or no is all that's required."

"Yes," she admitted.

"And what happens to slave girls who break the rules?"

"They get punished," she muttered, biting back the urge to protest, to explain, to cajole.

Because he was right—if they were going to do this thing, she needed to give it her all, or else it would be nothing more than a game.

"I'm sorry, Sir," she said sincerely. "It won't happen again."

"No," he agreed, letting her go. "It won't. Get on your knees and stay quiet while I unpack some things."

Ruby lowered herself to the ground, her heart hammering. Evan lifted his gear bag onto the bench at the end of the bed and unzipped it. Ruby watched with widening eyes as he laid out several items, including a ball gag, some leather cuffs and a slave collar, two hanks of thin rope and what looked like two large metal wall hooks.

Finally, he sat on the edge of the bed. He looked down at her. "Before I punish you, I want to be sure you understand the parameters of our arrangement. We've already established that I own you, and I will use your body as it pleases me. While you are serving as my slave, you'll wear what I choose from your wardrobe, when you wear anything at all. You'll submit without protest or hesitation to my every command. You will address me as Sir, or Master, as you see fit. For my part, I promise to dominate and use you as befits a slave, and I promise not to harm you or endanger you in any way. Do we agree so far?"

"Yes, Sir," she said, startled when her voice came out shaky. Jesus, he was good at this.

"Good. Now, I need to understand your hard limits—anything that is an absolute game stopper for you, or any health issues that we need to take into account."

"No health issues, Sir. I guess my hard limits would be no scat play or golden showers, and no bestiality."

Evan nodded. "Any trigger with face slapping, anything like that?"

Ruby, who adored the intensity of face slapping and could almost fly from that stimulation alone, shook her head. "Face slapping is a turn-on for me, Sir."

"What about blood play? Knives? Needles?"

"Those are soft limits, Sir. I can handle it as long as I trust my partner."

"And do you trust me, Ruby?" Evan's husky voice softened, his eyes searching hers.

"Yes, Sir," she whispered.

"Good." He stood from the bed and pointed to the wall. "Get on your hands and knees and crawl over to the wall. You will stand with your back against it while I prepare your punishment."

Crawl? That seemed so...degrading. But was it? Or was it simply another way to indicate her complete submission to this man—this Master?

She lowered herself to the ground and placed her palms flat on the floor. She glanced up at Evan through the veil of her hair and was electrified by the intense, smoldering expression in his eyes. *I'm in charge*, his look seemed to say. *You're mine to do with as it pleases me.*

To her surprise, far from being demeaned by her position on her hands and knees, she felt incredibly vibrant and sensual. She moved slowly, her hips and breasts swaying provocatively as she crawled to the wall.

Evan followed her. He reached over her to remove the large oil painting that hung there. He set it against the desk on the opposite wall as she got to her feet. He walked to the bench and picked something up. "Now, it's time for your punishment."

Ruby's stomach swooped like an elevator suddenly dropping as Evan approached her with the metal hooks in his hand. They were the kind of hook that had an adhesive backing and could be removed without marking the wall, only they were larger than any she'd seen before.

Following her gaze, Evan said, "These are industrial removable hooks. They each support about twenty pounds, so be mindful you don't put too much stress on them. They should work nicely for our purposes, however. Lift your right arm overhead so I can get the hook placement right."

Ruby did as instructed. She watched as Evan pulled the adhesive from one of the hooks and pressed the hook firmly against the wall near her right wrist. "Okay, you can lower your arm," he said. He held the hook in place for half a minute or so while it adhered.

To her surprise, he placed the second hook on the wall several feet from the first. She was dying to ask why, but held her tongue.

He returned to the bench and grabbed the cuffs and collar. He crouched in front of her and wrapped a cuff around her right ankle, buckling it into place. Ruby sighed happily as he secured the other ankle cuff and then moved to her wrists. She loved the feel of leather against her skin. Finally, he placed the collar around her neck, his hands moving beneath her heavy hair as he buckled it into place.

Taking a step back, he eyed her with obvious appreciation and then said, "Are you familiar with a-symmetric bondage?"

"Um, I'm not sure, Sir."

"Most bondage is symmetric," Evan explained. "Like when you're bound to a St. Andrew's cross, for example. Your arms and feet are equidistant apart when you're cuffed into place."

"Yum," Ruby said, the image sending her to a lovely place. Too bad they were doing this slave experiment thing in a vanilla household, but at least Evan had brought a well-stocked gear bag.

"Yum, indeed," Evan agreed with a smile, his eyes crinkling at the corners. "You would look especially lovely like that, Ruby. But in addition to its being hot and sexy, if you're like most subs, that kind of bondage can be very relaxing, in a paradoxical way. It allows you to surrender to whatever you're feeling, while safe in your bonds."

He went to the bench, this time returning with the hanks of rope. "Lift your left arm to the hook," he instructed. He unraveled a hank and pulled one end of the rope through a ring on her wrist cuff, knotting it into place. He looped the other end of the rope over the hook above her head. Pulling the rope down behind her, he looped it again, this time though one of the rings at the back of her collar.

As he worked, he said, "A-symmetric bondage is harder to handle. There's no natural balance to it. Your mind processes the experience differently, even a mind hardwired to enjoy bondage."

The rope dangled behind her back.

"Put your free hand behind your back," he instructed.

Ruby obeyed, the position slightly uncomfortable with her other arm extended taut against the wall.

Evan looped the rope through the O-ring on her right wrist cuff, pulling at it until her bent arm was forced upward, tying it off at an O-ring on her collar. He took a step back, his smile suddenly cruel.

"Now, for the fun part." Crouching in front of her again, he looped the end of the second hank of rope through an O-ring on her right ankle cuff, tying it tight. Getting to his feet, he pulled the rope, forcing her to lift her leg until it was straight out along the wall beside her, perpendicular to her body. He tied the other end of the rope onto the second hook.

Ruby jumped in place a few times on her left leg as she struggled to find her equilibrium in this awkward position.

"See what I mean?" Evan said. "A-symmetric bondage can be uncomfortable. It's definitely harder to endure than symmetric bondage. That's what makes it so good for punishment."

He moved closer, placing his hand on her mons. He cupped it, rubbing his palm sexily against her clit. While the bondage was unusual, and she did indeed feel off-balance, it was also exciting, especially with his hand moving with such perfect friction against her. The heady combination of erotic discomfort and the rising pleasure of an impending orgasm made her moan aloud.

Abruptly, Evan pulled his hand away.

"Oh, don't stop," Ruby blurted, on fire with lust.

"Oh, dear," Evan said. "Did you forget the rules again? No worries. I have the perfect remedy." He moved to the bench and grabbed the ball gag, returning to her with it held at the ready. "Open wide," he ordered.

With a sigh, Ruby opened her mouth.

Evan pressed the squishy rubber ball between her teeth, wedging it securely before buckling it around her head.

Ruby immediately began to drool. She hated ball gags, much preferring the sensuality of a satin sash. Her cunt continued to throb, and she was already finding it difficult to maintain her position without pulling over-hard on the temporary wall hooks. She hopped on her grounded foot, trying to get better purchase.

What would he do to her? Whip her with a single tail? Clamp her nipples? Fuck her standing up? She waited in anxious, excited anticipation.

But Evan did none of those things. Instead, he returned to the bed. He pulled off his shirt and then reached into his jeans pocket to pull out his phone. He lay down on the bed and began to play with his phone. Without looking up at her, he said, "There. I set the timer. You'll stay against the wall like that for fifteen minutes. I'll be right here with you."

Wait. What?

He looked down at his phone, his thumbs flying, apparently absorbed in whatever he was doing. Shit, the bastard was completely ignoring her. Ruby hated to be ignored, especially when she was bound and primed for play.

As the minutes ticked slowly by, Ruby focused at first on the physical sensations. She'd managed to balance herself in such a way against the wall that she no longer needed to hop about on her foot. Bound as she was, she definitely wasn't going to fall, even if she'd wanted to.

The rope was tight, but not uncomfortably so. She was quite limber from years of yoga, and having her leg extended along the wall wasn't difficult, though it did feel strange. The arm tied behind her back was mildly uncomfortable, but nothing she couldn't handle, for a little while at least.

Fifteen minutes seemed like an awfully long time to be left in this contorted position. Was it safe?

You can trust him, she told herself. He had proved every step of the way that he knew what he was doing when it came to BDSM play. If only she hadn't fucked things up right out of the gate...

If only she could wipe the damn drool off her chin.

She was keenly aware of her bare, spread pussy. Her clit still pulsed from his touch, engorged and sensitive to the slight draft of air that wafted over her naked, bound body. Her nipples ached for the feel of his tongue and lips, or the twist of his fingers. Maybe he could fuck her standing up, though it would be a little awkward with her leg raised as it was. But it would feel so good to have him slide his big, hard cock into her...

Ruby opened her eyes, the fantasy slipping away as she shifted in an effort to get more comfortable.

Why was he *ignoring* her?

Then she got it.

That was the point.

That was the real punishment.

Chapter 9

As the minutes ticked by with agonizing slowness, Evan found it surprisingly hard to leave Ruby tied up in that awkward position. As he stole glances at her, his cock hardened in his jeans. What would it be like to fuck her in that position?

Stop it, he ordered himself. *She's being punished right now. This is not about you.*

He glanced at his cell. Nine minutes to go. Had he made the time too long? Was the rope too tight? Could he get her out quickly enough in the event of an emergency?

Had he gone overboard, punishing her right off the bat?

Then her words came back to him. *He whips me daily and trains me to be his perfect, obedient submissive sex slave. He punishes me harshly when I misstep and owns me completely.*

She wanted this. She needed it. If he was going to make this real for her, he had to stand firm and enforce the rules they had agreed on. He was determined to give her the experience she craved.

All at once, he glanced sharply at her. Her eyes were closed, her head tilted back against the wall. She didn't appear to be in distress, but damn it, he'd forgotten to give her a safe signal.

Of course, there was the universal sign of distress common in BDSM dungeons of closing and opening one's hand. With all her dungeon experience, she would know that, surely. But what if she didn't?

He didn't want to disrupt the punishment, but he would rather err on the side of caution. He rose from the bed and moved quickly to the bathroom. He grabbed a washcloth from the cabinet and returned to the bedroom, approaching the awkwardly bound girl.

"That's enough with the ball gag," he informed her as he reached behind her head to unbuckle it. He pulled it free and then gently wiped away the drool from her chin and breasts.

"Phew," Ruby said, working her jaw. "Thank you, Sir. I hate that thing."

"You're welcome. How you doing? Circulation okay?"

She hopped a little on her free foot and made a comical face. "This isn't exactly a comfortable position, Sir."

"It's not supposed to be," he reminded her, not quite managing to suppress his smile. "You're being punished."

"Yes, Sir," she whispered.

He waited a beat, half expecting her to beg him to let her down, but she said nothing further. If she had begged him, what would he have done? He honestly wasn't sure. All he knew was this Master/slave gig was going to be harder than he'd anticipated.

This is what she wants, he reminded himself.

He returned to the bed with renewed determination. Picking up his phone, he pretended to ignore her.

Finally, the timer dinged. Evan leaped from the bed and hurried over to her. He released her raised leg first, and then quickly undid the ropes that bound her arms.

As she swayed toward him, he scooped her into his arms. He carried her to the bed and lay her gently down. Stripping off his jeans and boxers, he climbed onto the bed beside her.

"You okay?" he asked softly as he massaged the life back into her cold limbs.

"Yes, Sir," she whispered. She didn't seem angry or in the least upset by what he'd done. On the contrary, her eyes were shining as she stared up at him.

Something painful bloomed in his chest, as if the thick layers of scar tissue were being torn away. He pushed away the feeling, not ready to examine it.

"Punishment is over," he said. "You start with a clean slate."

"Works for me," she said, adding only belatedly, her face twisted into a wry smile, "Master."

Would a proper Master have punished her for that sass? Maybe so, but he didn't care. Her sass was part of her charm.

He brought his mouth to hers and kissed her, gently at first, and then with increasing passion. He draped his body over hers. Her thighs fell open in invitation as he nestled his erect cock between them.

She was deliciously wet and ready for him. Apparently the punishment hadn't been too traumatizing. He stopped thinking as her strong vaginal muscles clamped around his shaft. He put his hands under her ass, lifting her slightly as he thrust even deeper.

"Yes," she cried breathlessly. "Just like that. Yes, yes, yes. Don't stop."

She hadn't said "Sir" but Evan didn't give a fuck. He swiveled inside her, excited by her breathy cries and trembling body.

She has to ask to come, a voice in his head suddenly reminded him. "Ask permission," he grunted, trying to hold back his own orgasm.

"Please," she cried breathlessly. "Please, Sir, may I come?"

"Yes," he hissed, slamming into her as an avalanche of orgasmic pleasure rocked through his body. She trembled and moaned beneath him, her cunt spasming around his cock.

Her heart tapped against his as they lay tangled together in a post-orgasmic heap. After a while, he mustered the strength to lift himself from her and roll away. He turned his head to see how she was doing.

She lay on her back, arms and legs spread out, a dreamy expression on her face. As if feeling his eyes on her, she turned her head, a smile ghosting the edges of her mouth. "Hi," she said softly, the smile revealing itself more fully. "Can I do something more to serve you, Sir?"

"Hmm," he said, pretending to consider. "You can go down to the kitchen and make me a chocolate milkshake."

She actually started to lift herself into an upright position. "I could check if the Martins—"

"Hey, I'm just kidding," he interrupted with a laugh. He reached for her, pulling her into his arms. "You can serve me by curling into me and laying your head on my chest. I want to fall asleep with you in my arms."

"Now you've got me thinking about milkshakes," she replied, but then she yawned and curled like a cat around his body.

~*~

Ruby was roused by something nudging at her lips. She opened her eyes, surprised to find the pale light of a new dawn filling the room. Her last memory was of placing her head on Evan's firm chest and closing her eyes.

She was on her back on the high bed, but positioned sideways across the mattress, her head right at the edge. The cuffs were no longer on her wrists or ankles, and the collar wasn't around her neck. It was hard to believe she'd slept through all that, but she had no memory of his removing them.

He stood at her head, his erect cock in his hand. Fully awake and aroused by what he was doing, she parted her lips. As he slid his shaft into her mouth, he pulled her by the shoulders so that her head now hung off the mattress.

She gagged on the thick, hard shaft as it lodged deep in her throat. A small, jagged edge of panic rose in her gut when she became aware she couldn't breathe.

"Relax," Evan said. "You will serve your Master by worshipping my cock." He pulled back to allow her to draw in some air and then pressed again into her throat.

Ruby's body kicked into full arousal mode, her nipples stiffening, her sex moistening. Without thinking what she was doing, she put her hand between her legs to massage her throbbing clit.

Leaning over her, Evan slapped away her hand, startling her. "Don't touch my property without permission, slave," he said, his voice hard.

A thrill of raw desire, edged with just a hint of fear, hurtled through her body and soul.

"Pull up your knees and put your feet flat on the mattress," he directed in the same hard, sexy voice. He continued to slide his cock in and out of her mouth, choking her each time she tensed her throat muscles. "Spread your legs wide and lift up your pelvis so I have access to your cunt."

Ruby eagerly did as she was told, more than ready to feel the stroke of his sexy fingers on her sex as he fucked her mouth.

A sudden, sharp sting exploded over her vulva. She slammed her legs together in shock, her gasp of pain muffled against his shaft. It took her a second to realize Evan had slapped her pussy with the flat of his hard palm.

"Open your legs this instant," he commanded. "I didn't tell you to close them. Reassume your position, slave."

Her heart jumping like a jackrabbit, Ruby did as he said, her labia still stinging. He slapped her again, just as hard as before, while keeping his cock lodged in her throat.

Tears sprang to Ruby's eyes, but somehow she found the wherewithal not to close her legs or twist away.

"That cunt is mine," Evan said sternly. He slapped her again as his cock moved in and out of her open mouth. "If you touch it again without permission, your punishment will be much more severe than a mere slap."

He pumped in and out of her mouth, slamming into her throat with choking thrusts. Ruby struggled to open herself to the onslaught. A sweet, dark sense of surrender spread inside her like ink blooming in water. As she gave in, her mind stilled and her body relaxed.

Evan continued to pummel her mouth, his hands now on either side of her head, holding her in place. After several minutes, he groaned, his body stiffening. Then he spurted, the jism sliding hotly down her throat. He stayed that way a moment or two before finally pulling back, his cock falling away from her open mouth.

"Ah," he breathed, smiling down at her. He sat beside her on the bed and pulled her head up and into his lap. "That was awesome, sexy girl." He ran his thumb softly down her cheek. "Now it's time to get up. We have a busy day."

He led her into the bathroom, and they brushed their teeth in the dual sinks.

Ruby walked toward the toilet, but before she could sit down, Evan said, "Slave girls need permission to pee, remember?"

Oops. She'd forgotten sharing that detail of her fantasy with him. "Please, Sir," she said as submissively as she could, "May I use the toilet?"

"No."

She startled. "What?"

"No, you may not use the toilet. You may stand in the tub and pee in front of me."

She pursed her lips, about to remind him of her limit of no golden showers, but this didn't really fit that definition. Her bladder protested again, and she climbed into the tub and faced him. She couldn't decide whether she was aroused or irritated.

Evan stood watching her intently, his hands on his hips.

She spread her legs and willed her bladder to release. Her usual lack of self-consciousness deserted her. She really had to go, but for some reason she couldn't, not with him staring at her. How did guys do it all the time in front of each other in public bathrooms? She closed her eyes, willing herself to relax.

"Open your eyes," Evan snapped. "Keep them on my face while you pee."

A wave of heat washed over her cheeks. She hadn't blushed this much since she was a teenager. She forced herself to obey, fixing him with a defiant stare. Finally, her bladder cooperated, and a stream of urine splashed down between her legs.

When she was done, Evan reached over and turned on the hot and cold water. He climbed into the tub and pulled the shower curtain closed. Reaching around her, he moved the lever from bath to shower.

As the warm water cascaded over them, Evan pulled Ruby into his arms and kissed her mouth. She wrapped her arms around his neck as he cupped her ass. After a while, they parted, and Evan pressed lightly on Ruby's left shoulder. "Kneel and wash my body, slave." He handed her the bar of soap.

"Yes, Master," she said, unable to suppress a grin. Rubbing her hands all over that hard, sexy body would be a pleasure. She soaped up his strong legs and then cradled his balls as she washed his cock. Despite his recent orgasm, it stiffened and lengthened at her touch. Pleased, she continued to stroke and tease it until he pushed her hands away. "Focus on your task, slut," he said with a laugh.

She got to her feet and soaped the rest of his body as he washed his own hair. When she was done, he took the soap from her and said, "Now, it's your turn. I'm going to wash and groom you."

"Groom me?" she asked, lifting her eyebrows.

"That's right. I'm going to shave those sweet pubic curls away, not because they displease me, but because a slave girl should provide full access to her Master. I want to be able to see your cunt better."

Ruby frowned. She had never cared for the current trend. Hers was a woman's body, and she was proud of it. She shook her head. "No, I don't think—"

Evan cut her off by placing two fingers over her lips.

"You don't need to think, slave. You just need to do as you're told. We have a verbal contract, remember? You promised to obey my every dictate during this experiment. It pleases me to shave your cunt. Are you refusing to comply with your Master's wishes?"

Ruby's protest died in her mouth as she stared up at him. The easygoing rogue was nowhere in evidence. A stern Master had somehow taken his place. His expression was serious, his gray-green eyes boring into her soul as he waited for her response.

Of course, she could refuse and that would be that. But he was right. They were either all in, or they weren't. Evan had offered her the chance to finally realize the darkest, most secret sexual fantasy of her life, and she owed it to him—to herself—to give it her best shot. And it was only hair, after all. It would grow back. "I'm sorry, Sir. You're right. I'll do better."

"Good girl." Evan reached for the soap. His sure hands sent shivers of pleasure over her skin as he lathered her body and then washed her hair.

She would have liked to pull him down into the tub so she could straddle that hard, gorgeous cock and ride herself to orgasm. Aware that wouldn't be behavior becoming of a slave girl, she instead stood docilely as he rinsed her hair beneath the spray.

When he was done, he turned off the water, opened the curtain and climbed out of the tub. He handed Ruby a towel and then reached for another, which he wrapped around his waist.

As Ruby towel-dried her hair and body, Evan took another towel and laid it on the counter between the two sinks. He turned on the hot water in one of the sinks and dropped a fresh washcloth into it.

Turning back to her, he said, "Come sit up here for your grooming."

Swallowing her trepidation, Ruby wrapped her hair in the towel and stepped out of the tub into the steamy room. Evan helped her up onto the counter.

Reaching into his shaving kit, he took out a small pair of barber shears. He stood in front of her and pulled some of her pubic hair taut with his left hand. He snipped the curls and tossed them into the small trashcan under the sinks. Ruby tried not to twitch as he worked. Finally, he rinsed the shears and set them aside.

Returning to his shaving bag, he extracted a disposable razor and removed its plastic covering. He set it in the sink and again reached in the bag, this time taking out a small can of shaving cream. He squirted some onto his fingers and smeared it over her shorn mons.

"Scoot to the edge of the counter and keep your legs spread wide."

"Yes, Sir," she whispered, both fascinated and nervous at what he was doing.

He took the razor from the hot water and drew the blades carefully over her flesh, leaving baby-pink skin behind. He rinsed the blade and stroked again, scraping away the hair until she was smooth.

"Now for the tricky part," he said, crouching in front of her. "Stay very still so I don't nick you."

Ruby swallowed hard. He'd been very gentle up to this point, but this was intricate work, and if it had to be done, she'd rather do it herself. "Please, Sir," she began, "can I—"

"No, you cannot," he interrupted, cutting her off. "I know what I'm doing. Submit to the process."

This is what I wanted, she reminded herself.

"Yes, Sir," she said aloud.

His touch was delicate, the razor gliding smoothly over her folds. When he was done, he gave her a hand mirror for her to see the change. She stared down at her shaven pussy. She didn't look at all like a little girl, as she'd feared. Her labia were swollen, the folds dark pink, a hint of moisture at her entrance. They looked like orchid petals. "Wow," she breathed. "That's kind of cool."

Evan grinned. "It's kind of beautiful, is what it is." He took a small bottle of baby oil from his shaving kit and squirted some onto his hand. He massaged the oil over her mons and labia, his fingers moving sensually over her hard, aching clit. As he stroked her, she moaned, the pleasure rapidly mounting inside her. "Oh, god," she breathed. "It feels so good, Evan. So, so, so good..."

He rubbed faster, making her pant with pleasure.

"Please, Sir," she gasped, delighted with herself for remembering the rules, even in the face of the powerful orgasm about to engulf her. "May I come?"

All at once, he pulled his hand away. "No, slave. You may not."

~*~

Evan watched the play of emotions moving over her face, from confusion to outrage to acceptance, if grudging, within the space of a few seconds. She pressed her lips together in a thin line and looked down. Obviously, she didn't have the mindset of a true slave, but he had to give her points for trying.

He was impressed and pleased she'd let him shave her, and while he would have enjoyed making her come, his online crash course in slave training had taught him that it didn't do to let a slave come too often during training. They had to earn their orgasms. They didn't just get them for free.

"I'll let you come when it pleases *me*, not you," Evan said, though he kept his voice gentle. "Do you understand?"

"Yes, Sir."

In the bedroom, he pulled on a pair of jeans, watching as Ruby removed the towel from her head and let it fall to the ground. She ran her fingers through her damp hair and tucked it behind her ears. She was breathtakingly beautiful, and he had to resist the sudden urge to throw her on the bed and make love to her again. But, no. She would have to earn that privilege, too.

He watched the sexy sway of her voluptuous ass as she returned to the bathroom to hang her towel. She came back into the bedroom a moment later and went to the closet, reaching in for her robe.

"Hang that back up," Evan said. "You'll remain naked while you're in this house, except for your cuffs and collar."

She replaced the robe on its hook and turned to him, her arms wrapped protectively around her body.

It was interesting that this woman who had been so comfortable in her nudity was suddenly acting like a shy girl. Could it be because before it was *her* decision, and now that decision had been taken from her?

"Don't cover your body," Evan instructed. "Don't forget. It belongs to me."

As she dropped her arms to her sides, he added, "Stand at attention, feet shoulder-width apart. Lift your hair from your neck and keep it out of the way."

"Yes, Sir," she said quietly, assuming the position.

Evan gathered the cuffs and collar from the nightstand. He went to the gear bag and pulled out a foot-long hobble chain with clips on either end. He stuffed the chain into his back pocket.

So far, things were going well. Maybe he really could pull off this Master thing. How far should he take it? How far would she let him?

He stood in front of her and placed the collar around her throat, reaching back to buckle it into place.

She started to lower her arms, but he stopped her with a shake of his head.

"Keep your arms up." He clipped a cuff around each wrist. "I want you to lock your fingers behind your neck and stay that way until I tell you."

As he crouched in front of her, he could smell the light, intoxicating scent of her arousal. Her sweet, newly shaven pussy peeked at him between her thighs, and his cock twitched in response. He looked up at her face. Her lips were softly parted, her eyes shining. She seemed to be entering the proper headspace, and the realization excited him.

He wrapped the second set of cuffs around her ankles. Getting to his feet, he said, "You can put your arms at your sides." He held out his hand. "Let's go downstairs. I took the liberty of buying some groceries. You can take care of the cats and make breakfast."

"You bought food? Apples, cheese and crackers not enough for you, Sir?" she asked in a teasing voice.

"Afraid not," he replied with a smile. Maybe a real Master wouldn't allow his slave girl to banter as she did, but he didn't care. This was their fantasy—nobody else's.

When they got down the stairs, Skittles and Pinky, or whatever the hell their names were, appeared almost at once. They purred loudly as they rubbed against Ruby's bare legs. She bent to stroke them, making cooing sounds.

Evan fingered the hobble chain in his back pocket. He'd wait until after breakfast.

There was a coffeemaker on the counter and Evan found the beans in the cupboard above it and set about making coffee while Ruby took care of the cats. When she was done, she walked to the refrigerator and pulled open the double doors. Examining the contents, she said, "Bacon, eggs, milk, orange juice, cold cuts, potato salad, strawberries, oh, and a chocolate cake! You must have been hungry when you went grocery shopping."

"I got bread, too, and a pint of chocolate gelato."

"Nice," she said, pulling out the orange juice, eggs and bacon, along with butter and cream. The aroma of freshly brewed coffee filled the air. Turning to him, she asked, "How do you like your eggs, Sir?"

"Scrambled is good, thanks," Evan replied as he got out mugs for the coffee. "And how do you like your coffee?"

"A little cream please. That is, if Masters are allowed to get coffee for their slave girls," she quipped.

"Masters are allowed to do whatever they want," Evan replied with a laugh.

As Ruby busied herself at the stove, looking sexy as hell in nothing but collar and cuffs, Evan prepared their coffee, poured glasses of orange juice and found napkins and silverware.

The kitchen table was set into a nook, a padded bench against the wall, two chairs opposite it. Evan slid onto the bench, sipping his coffee as he watched Ruby cook.

He picked up a cushion from the back of the bench and placed it on the floor beside the table.

Ruby came to the table with two plates of scrambled eggs and bacon. "Breakfast is served," she said, placing the plates on the table. She pulled out one of the chairs across from Evan.

"Whoa," he said. "What're you doing?"

She looked confused. "Huh?"

"You're not thinking of sitting on that chair, are you, slave girl?"

Her mouth fell open, understanding dawning.

Evan pointed to the cushion he'd placed on the floor. "You will kneel on that and put your hands behind your back. I'll feed you."

"Feed me? Oh, but I can feed myself...Sir."

"Of course you *can*, but you won't," Evan replied firmly. "Now, do as you're told."

Ruby moved toward the cushion and sank down onto it, color rising in her cheeks. She knelt up and put her hands behind her back.

Evan pulled her plate over beside his. Picking up a fork, he speared a generous bite of eggs and held it out to her.

Ruby parted her lips. He placed the fork in her mouth and pulled it back, watching her chew. As she licked her lips, he tackled his food. The eggs were perfectly cooked. He took a bite of bacon and then a sip of orange juice.

He fed her more eggs and held out a piece of bacon for her. As she chewed, he picked up her napkin and dabbed at her chin, a curious tenderness moving through him. He held her coffee mug to her lips and tilted it gently, allowing her to sip the hot liquid.

She kept her gaze on his face as he fed her, her dark eyes wide. Her rosy red nipples were like ripe cherries he wanted to bite. His cock hardened, forcing him to adjust it as it tented his jeans.

Evan had intended the feeding exercise to be more about control than something erotic, but he couldn't deny the sexual tension that was rising between them as he fed her. It was as if the balance of power was finally shifting definitively, both in fact and in her mind. She was giving herself over to him with each submissive parting of her lips.

When both plates and juice glasses were empty, he dabbed at her chin and gave her the last of her coffee. "You may place your hands in your lap," he said.

She brought her arms from behind her back and clasped them together on her thighs.

"Is that the first time you've ever been fed in a sexual context?" he asked, curious.

"Yes, Sir. I've never gotten into that whole food as part of sex thing. The Hershey's syrup and whipped cream stuff, you know?" She wrinkled her nose. "No, thank you."

Evan laughed in spite of himself. "But this was different, wasn't it? You were actually submitting to me by your surrender of control. How did that make you feel?"

She pondered a moment. "Yeah, you're right. It was different than what I'd imagined. I had no idea the experience could be so powerful."

"Agreed," Evan said, thrilled with her response. "It was hard for you at first, but you surrendered to the process—to me."

"Yes, Sir," she said, her eyes shining. "Thank you, Sir."

Evan smiled and leaned down to stroke her soft cheek. "You're more than welcome." He rose from the table and reached into his back pocket for the hobble chain.

"Stand up, slave. You're going to wear this hobble chain while you clean up. Then meet me upstairs. I'll be waiting."

Chapter 10

Ruby moved carefully in her hobbled state as she carried the things to the sink. She washed their dishes and placed them in the drying rack. After wiping her hands, she cupped her shaven mons, still not quite believing she'd let him do that.

In spite of her trepidation, it had been a deeply erotic experience. She'd nearly lost her mind when he stroked her with the baby oil. The pleasure was intense, and even his refusal to let her come had been a turn-on.

It was exciting to give up control in ways she hadn't previously considered expressly erotic. She'd never found the idea of food play of any kind to be sexually exciting, and yet Evan had made it so. Even clearing and washing the dishes had taken on a different feel, not only because of the cuffs and chains hampering her movements, but because her Master had instructed her to do it.

Yes, it was only a game. Of course it was. But it was a very hot and sexy game, in some ways even hotter than her secret fantasies, because someone else was now involved. This wasn't just happening in her mind. It was real.

Kitchen reasonably straight, she headed out to the stairway. The chain made climbing the stairs difficult, but using the bannister and putting both feet on each step, the way a small child would, she managed her way without tripping.

She hesitated at the bedroom door. Evan was sitting at the desk, his back to her. He was still in jeans, his broad, muscular back bare. He had brought his laptop and was busy tapping away on its keyboard.

He had apparently managed to fit the pieces of the Total Lockdown System into his gear bag, because there it was, reassembled, though without the collar cuff or the spreader bar. Ruby's pulse quickened at the sight of the restraint device, her clit perking to attention.

"Hey there," she said to get Evan's attention, belatedly adding, "Sir."

He turned his head and flashed a smile. "All done? I'll just be a second. You may kneel up at attention by the rig, palms resting on your thighs, knees spread, until I'm finished."

Ruby lowered herself to her knees, careful not to trip herself on the hobble chain in the process. He'd unpacked more of the gear bag, the items set neatly along the bench at the end of the bed, which he'd made, if a little haphazardly.

What especially caught her eye was the bondage ball, which she recognized from the warehouse on Sunday morning, still in its original shrink-wrap. Less than a foot from stem to stern, it consisted of a steel ball the size of a golf ball at the end of a small rod that had been soldered onto the center of a curved, perpendicular bar with metal figure-eight shaped loops on either end. She couldn't quite envision how it worked, but figured she was about to find out.

Placing her hands palms-down on her thighs, she closed her eyes. She had learned some meditation techniques in her travels, and she brought them to bear as she focused on relaxing her body and stilling her mind.

"There. I've taken care of the things requiring my immediate attention and managed to clear the rest of the schedule, so I'm all yours for the rest of the day."

Ruby opened her eyes at the sound of Evan's voice.

He rose from the chair and walked toward her. "Or rather," he added, raking her naked body with hooded eyes, "you're all mine."

Coming to a stop in front of her, he placed his hand on her head. "This morning I'm in the mood for some predicament bondage. In the process, I'll be assessing your endurance and ability to handle erotic pain."

Like most sexual masochists, Ruby had a love/hate relationship with predicament bondage.

"I'm going to cuff you into the Total Lockdown System, and this time, we'll add the bondage ball to keep you on your toes." Evan grinned evilly. "We're going to have some serious fun."

He held out a hand, and she took it, allowing him to hoist her upright. "Do you need to use the bathroom before we get started?"

"Yes, Sir."

Evan crouched in front of her, removing the chain between her ankles, though he left the cuffs in place. He did remove her wrist cuffs, and then said, "I'll get things ready while you use the bathroom."

Ruby was glad he didn't make her pee in the tub, and even gladder that he didn't want to watch her. While she got the control aspect of the exercise, and had articulated it as part of her fantasy, in real life it just wasn't that sexy.

When she was done using the bathroom, she returned to the bedroom, butterflies dancing in her stomach.

Evan held the bondage ball in his hands, now unwrapped. "This goes between your legs, front to back. It's designed so the ball is inserted inside you. Then ropes are attached to these rings. When I secure the ropes in front and in back of you to the top of the apparatus, it'll hold the ball in place. I'm going to force you up on your toes with the rope. If you come down flat, you'll feel the pressure increase and the ball will pull up hard inside you. Hence the predicament."

Ruby stared at the diabolical device, her heart skittering in her chest. "That sounds pretty intense."

"That it does," Evan agreed, his erection visible in his jeans. "Think you can handle it?"

Ruby blew out a breath. "In theory," she said nervously.

His eyes glittered. "We'll find out. Before we get started, remind me of your safeword."

"Quicksilver," Ruby said, her stomach doing a flip-flop.

"Quicksilver," he repeated, nodding. "Take your position on the rig."

Ruby stood with her back to the main pole and lifted her arms to settle her wrists into the attached cuffs. Evan set down the bondage ball and moved to her. He closed the cuffs, his body close to hers as he worked. As always happened when she was bound, a shiver of raw desire worked its way through her, igniting all her nerve endings. On an impulse, she leaned forward and kissed Evan's smooth chest as he worked. He didn't seem to mind.

Stepping back, he picked up the bondage ball from the bench, along with a tube of lubricant. He covered the steel ball generously with the lube and then stood alongside Ruby to position the device between her legs. Slowly and carefully, he eased the ball into her body.

She sucked in a breath as it penetrated.

"You okay?" Evan asked, tugging lightly to make sure the ball was in place.

"Yeah," she said a little breathlessly.

He retrieved the coils of black rope that had come with the toy and used a slipknot on the rings in front and back. He raised the ropes above Ruby's body, adjusting them until he'd forced her onto her toes. Then he tied the two ends around the ring at the top of the restraint rod.

He came again to stand in front of her, cupping her breasts in his hands as he dipped his head to kiss her mouth. She kissed him back hungrily, deeply excited by her restraints and by the hard ball inside her lodged snugly against her g-spot.

Letting her go, he stepped back and took something from his bag. He held up a short-handled black leather whip with only two narrow throws. They were split like a snake's forked tongue. Evan smiled cruelly as he snapped it in the air. "I call this the Dragon Kiss. It's one of my favorites. It delivers a sharper sting than your standard impact toy, and it leaves lovely welts. I'm going to whip your entire body with it. Your job will be to stay on your toes, unless you want a rather nasty reminder of how that bondage ball works." He moved closer and brushed the deceptively soft leather throws over her breasts. "Are you ready to suffer for me, slave girl?"

Ruby's mouth had gone dry, her heart beating a rapid tempo against her sternum. But at the same time, her clit throbbed and her nipples ached. Her skin tingled in anticipation of the wicked-looking lash. "Yes, Sir," she breathed.

He moved behind her. The whip whistled in the split second before impact. The sting was sharp and immediate, and Ruby gasped at the sudden pain. He flicked it again and again, focusing on her ass, until she began to adjust to the steady barrage of stinging strokes.

Then, in a lightning strike of pain, the whip struck her left shoulder.

Unprepared, Ruby yelped, her feet landing hard on the carpet. The sudden downward movement created nearly unbearable pressure in her cunt.

She flexed instantly back on her toes, which resulted in immediate relief, though the snapping whip behind her delivered another stinging kiss.

"That bondage ball hurts, huh?" Evan asked, moving to her front.

"It was more pressure than pain," she gasped. "But that fucking whip stings like a bastard." As Evan frowned, she realized her words had been something less than slave-respectful. "Uh, Sir," she added.

Evan lifted his eyebrows, but made no comment. Stepping back, he snapped the forked whip against her left breast.

Ruby hissed her pain as she stared down at the dual red lines the whip left in its wake.

He struck her right breast. Tears sprang to her eyes. "It hurts, it hurts, it hurts," she cried, hopping from foot to foot, still on her toes.

Taking a step back, he snapped the whip against her thighs, each stroke a line of fire on her skin. Sweat prickled under her arms and on her upper lip. It was too much. Too much.

"I can't," she cried, nearly overwhelmed. "I can't stay on my toes."

"You're resisting me," Evan said calmly, letting the whistling whip land on her left breast. "You need to surrender, to let go. You're white-knuckling your way through this."

He was right, but she was too stressed and exhausted from the effort of staying on her toes to obey. She pressed her lips together to keep from cursing or yelling her safeword. A single tear rolled down her cheek.

Evan dropped the whip and reached for her cheek, wiping away the tear with his thumb. "Enough. You've had enough." He reached up over her head and released the ropes that held the bondage ball in place.

With a sigh of relief, Ruby lowered her feet. Evan gently pulled the bondage ball from her body and set it on the bench. Then he released her restraints and led her to the bed.

Pulling back the quilt and sheet, he helped her lie down on her stomach. Sitting beside her, he smoothed soothing balm over the welts on her ass and shoulders. He rolled her gently to her back and stroked her cheek, tucking a tendril of hair behind her ear. "You okay? You took a lot."

She nodded. "You're right, though. I was resisting. I was afraid and I couldn't work through the fear."

He squeezed more Arnica on his fingers and gently smoothed it over the welts on her breasts. "This is where communication is so important, Ruby. We're still pretty new together, and I don't know all your unspoken cues. I can read your body up to a certain point, but I can't read your mind. You have a safeword for a reason. I get it if you don't want to use it and bring things to a halt, but there are ways to slow things down. You can just tell me it's too much. Say you're having a hard time and need to slow things down. Promise you'll let me in going forward—that you'll let me know when you need more or when you need less. I have to trust that you'll let me know your limits or I'll never be able to take you where I sense you want to go."

Ruby lifted her head and met his gaze. "You're right. I promise to do better."

~*~

Evan stripped off his jeans and boxers and lay down beside Ruby. He'd never known anyone like her. She was such a delicious combination of sexual masochist and sassy, kickass woman. Being around her made him feel vital and alive, and more turned on than he could remember being in his life. But how did this new "slave girl Ruby" fit into things? Was he supposed to quash those sassy impulses—to admonish her for behavior unbecoming to a slave?

He put his arm around her and pulled her close, trying to still the turmoil in his mind.

She snuggled against him. "Um…" She drew out the word, but didn't continue the sentence.

Evan looked down at her face. "What? What is it?"

She smiled nervously and ducked her head, not meeting his eyes. "It's just that I haven't had an orgasm since last night, you know? I mean, you started out your morning with one, and then you teased the crap out of me when you were grooming me, but I haven't… I mean, I took a pretty good whipping, Sir. Do you think maybe I've earned an orgasm?"

Evan burst out laughing. "You are a piece of work, Ruby Beckett. A proper slave doesn't ask for orgasms. She doesn't inform her Master that she's earned an orgasm. You wait until your *Master* decides."

Ruby's face twisted into an adorable pout. "I know, but—"

"But nothing," Evan said, pulling his arm from beneath her and lifting himself upright on his elbows. "But you are reminding me that it's time to begin our orgasm control work." He rolled from the bed and got to his feet. "We'll make it interesting," he continued as he retrieved her wrist cuffs from the bench, along with four short hanks of rope. "I'm going to tie you down and alternate between sexual stimulation and erotic torture. Your job is to handle the pain with grace and to hold off your orgasm until I give you specific permission to come."

"Yes, Sir," she whispered, her eyes wide.

He returned to the bed. "Lie flat on your back," he instructed. He clipped the leather cuffs onto her wrists. The ankle cuffs were still in place. Taking a pillow, he said, "Lift your hips so I can slide this under you. I want easy access to that beautiful cunt."

She did as instructed, and he pushed the pillow under her ass, forcing her to tilt her hips, giving him an excellent view of her shaven sex. He attached rope to the O-ring in each of the four cuffs, and secured the other ends around the bedposts, pulling her arms and legs taut.

Excitement and power buzzed along Evan's nerve endings, along with the heightened awareness of his sub's feelings and reactions that always kicked in when a scene was right. He loved her willingness, her trust, her vulnerability, and the rush of power taking erotic control always engendered in him.

Ruby lifted her head as much as she was able in her spread eagle position, watching as he selected his toys from the gear bag. He chose a curved, purple g-spot stimulator and a pair of clover nipple clamps and set them on the bed beside Ruby.

He reached for the clamps. "You have sensitive nipples. How do you do with clover clamps?"

"I hate them, Sir. Oh, and I love them, Sir," she added with a laugh.

"The masochist's dilemma," he agreed with a smile.

He reached for her left nipple, rolling it between his thumb and forefinger. It engorged quickly. He pulled it taut, while pushing open one of the clamps with his free hand. Carefully, he placed the round metal pads on either side of the base of her nipple and then released the clamp.

"Ah," she cried softly, squeezing her eyes closed and wrinkling her nose as she struggled to adjust to the pain.

He did the same with the second nipple. His cock hardened at the sight of her compressed nipples, the black chain between the clamps resting against her lovely olive skin.

To distract her as she adjusted to the tension of the clamps, he put his hand between her legs. He rubbed her sex, finding the hard marble of her clit amidst the folds.

The moment she sighed with pleasure, he removed his hand. Slowly and surely, touch by touch, moment by moment, he planned to ratchet up the sexual pleasure and the erotic pain until there was no longer a distinction between the two.

Picking up the g-spot stimulator, he slipped it out of its sterilized wrapper. Positioning it between her legs, he nudged it against her slick entrance and pushed the fat bulb slowly inside her. In her position, with hips raised, the dildo should stay in place. He twisted the base, and the dildo vibrated to life.

"Ooh," she moaned as it teased her from the inside out. Moving closer, he rubbed his fingers in a circle around her clit. She sighed and arched her hips toward his hand, her fingers curling around the ropes above her cuffs.

When her eyes fluttered closed, he lifted his other hand and slapped her cheek, the sound reverberating over her breathy sighs. She gasped, her eyes flying open.

He slapped the other cheek.

Her mouth fell open, her chest heaving.

He continued to stroke her sex as the g-spot dildo vibrated inside her tight tunnel.

She moaned.

"Focus," he said, slapping her again. He had slipped effortlessly into Dom-space. It was as if he could feel the sting on his own face each time his palm struck her. His breath quickened along with hers as the entwining pleasure and pain edged toward sensory overload.

It was up to him to keep her grounded so she could get through the tumultuous intensity to the vast, serene and deeply fulfilling submissive acceptance he knew she craved.

"You're nearly there, my love," he breathed, watching her intently.

Her pupils were dilated, her breath a pant. He slapped her over and over, whipping her head from side to side. All the while, he stroked her clit, which was hard and slippery beneath his fingers.

"Breathe," he reminded her. "Take in the pleasure and the pain. Let it lift you."

She drew in a long, shuddering breath and let it slowly out. His lungs emptied along with hers, their hearts beating in tandem. He stared into her dark eyes, sensing her longing as if it were his own.

She whispered something.

"What?" he asked, leaning closer to hear her.

"Again," she breathed. "Again, Sir."

"Yes," he agreed, understanding her need. Cupping his palm, he slapped her again—once, twice, three times in succession.

She groaned, her cheeks red, her breath ragged, but her eyes remained fixed on his, fever-bright.

He rubbed her sweet cunt, his fingers flying as the vibrator thrummed inside her.

"Oh, oh, oh, oh," she chanted, and he felt the rise of her impending orgasm.

"Don't you dare," he snapped, aware of his promise to be her

Master. He slapped her to bring her back from the brink. "Not until I say so."

She groaned, attempting to shift her hips away from his touch.

"Stay still," he commanded, his cock throbbing in sympathy, his balls tight with need. "Take what I'm giving you." His fingers flew over her sticky sex. He slapped her again, making the chain between the clamps fly.

"Oh, oh, oh, oh!" she wailed, her hips lifting from the pillow.

"Now," he commanded, slapping her yet again as he rubbed her wet pussy. "Come for me now, slave girl."

She thrashed as the dildo vibrated relentlessly inside her. "Oh, god, oh god," she cried, her body convulsing in a long orgasmic shudder.

When she stilled, he gently eased the dildo from her body and turned it off. He reached for the slipknots that held her spread eagle and plucked them loose. Leaning over her, he stroked back the wild tangle of her hair from her face.

Tenderness threatened to consume him, the feeling nearly overwhelming him. He wanted to climb over her and sink his cock into her sweet heat. He longed to lose himself completely in her loveliness, but he remained mindful of his duty as her Master, and forced himself to maintain control.

"Ruby," he said softly.

She opened her eyes slowly, her gaze unfocused, her expression bleary with post-orgasmic bliss.

He placed his fingers on either side of the clamps, which still held her nipples captive in their grip. He shook his head and said with mock sorrow, "You know what they say, my love. With the pleasure must come the pain."

Then he squeezed, releasing the clamps.

He covered her yelps with kisses and then lowered his head to suckle and lick each tortured nipple until her whimpers turned to moans of lust. Giving in at last to his own desperate need, he draped himself over her warm, yielding body, his cock hard against her thigh.

She shifted, her legs falling open. "Oh, fuck me, fuck me, fuck me," she begged sweetly, her hands cupping his neck as she arched her hips upward to receive him.

With a groan of pent-up longing and desire, Evan complied.

~*~

Ruby made spaghetti and meatballs for dinner. Evan had once again hobbled her, telling her the chain and the cuffs on her wrists and ankles would remind her of her status as his slave. While it was sexy as a fantasy, she found the hobble chain annoying while she moved around the kitchen, stirring sauce, boiling water for the pasta and cutting vegetables for the salad.

Evan was more into the Master/slave thing than she'd expected, and while the scenes had been extremely intense and satisfying, they'd also left her with a strange feeling of unease she didn't entirely understand.

As she mixed olive oil, vinegar and spices together for the salad dressing, she thought about what was bothering her. The primary issue was how different Evan was as "Master Evan" versus just Evan, the sexy, fun guy she'd gotten to know over the past week. And while it was thrilling to always call him Sir and surrender to whatever delicious, diabolical torture he came up with, at the same time it was frustrating to give up so much control.

It was tedious to ask for permission to do anything, and while the feeding thing was kind of sexy in a way, it was also frustrating. She'd had to exert all her self-will during their meals not to grab the fork out of his hand. Plus, it changed the tenor of their meals, which, before the experiment, had been a time when they'd talked easily about their lives and travel adventures. Now, he just fed her and himself, his focus on his task almost grim.

That was it—that was the crux of the matter. This Master/slave thing was too freaking *formal*. It went against her grain, and she suspected, against Evan's as well.

She glanced over at Evan, who sat like a king at the kitchen table, not lifting a finger to help her get dinner ready. He had brought the bottle of red wine and the glasses to the table—his total contribution to the preparations. Normal Ruby wouldn't have put up with such nonsense, but slave Ruby understood he was still engaged in the fantasy. Apparently Masters sat around playing on their iPads while their slave girls did all the work.

The timer dinged for the pasta, and she carried the hot, heavy pot to the sink, moving carefully in the stupid hobble chain. She poured out the boiling water slowly, careful not to let any of the scalding liquid hit her bare skin.

That was another thing. Being naked was all very well, but being constantly naked... It took away some of the allure. Sometimes a little clothing was sexier than nothing at all.

She brought all the food to the table, moving slowly back and forth in her chains. Evan was watching her now, his beautiful gray-green eyes fixed on her, his lips slightly parted. He was gorgeous—she had to give him that. And while he was clearly aware of his own charms, he wasn't a dick about it.

Food on the table, she pulled back the chair across from him and started to slide onto it out of habit. He immediately stiffened and frowned. "Slaves don't sit on the furniture," he intoned.

Ruby couldn't bite back her sigh of annoyance. "Come on, Evan, can't we—"

"Slave Ruby," he barked, pointing imperiously at the cushion on the floor. "You know the rules. Obey them or be punished."

That depends if the punishment's sexy enough, she wanted to quip, but didn't quite dare. Instead, she moved to the cushion and lowered herself carefully to her knees, the process made awkward by the hobble chain.

Evan prepared their plates. "This smells delicious," he said as he ladled sauce over the pasta. He twirled some noodles around his fork, breaking off a piece of meatball with the tines, and then lifted the large bite to Ruby's mouth.

She was hungry, and she leaned forward eagerly, her lips parted.

As he lowered the fork, the whole mess fell from the fork and onto her chest, the hot sauce burning her skin. "Ouch," she cried, jerking back reflexively.

"Shit," Evan said at the same time. "I'm sorry." He grabbed a napkin and began dabbing ineffectually at her, which caused the noodles to slide down between her breasts and onto her thighs. Evan reached out again, his elbow catching a glass of wine in the process and sending it hurtling to the floor. While the glass didn't break, the wine went everywhere, splashing over Ruby and alarming the cats, both of whom had been hovering nearby in case of dropped treats.

Evan leaped up, pushing the table away from the bench, and causing the second glass to topple over, spilling its contents into the bowl of spaghetti. "Goddamn it," he cursed, grabbing the empty goblet as it rolled toward the edge of the table, and catching it just in time.

As the cats streaked away with yowls of alarm, Ruby and Evan stared at one another, the corners of their mouths quirking upward. In a moment, they both burst out laughing.

"I'm so sorry, Ruby," Evan said between guffaws as he helped her to her feet. "I ruined the meal."

"Hey, no big deal," she managed, between chortles of glee that verged on hysteria, she was laughing so hard. "I was thinking when I made it that the sauce could use a little more red wine."

They held onto each other as they continued to laugh. Eventually they got a hold of themselves, though they continued to grin at each other.

Ruby wiped away the tears of laughter and shook back her hair. "I better clean up this mess." She took a step forward, intent on getting the mop from the pantry closet, and forgot she still wore the hobble chain. She stumbled forward with a yelp.

She would have fallen onto her face if Evan hadn't been there to catch her in his arms. "I hate that damn chain," she blurted without thinking. "Can you take the fucking thing off, for crying out loud?"

Evan's smile fell away. "Is that how a slave speaks to her Master?"

"Maybe not," Ruby said, exasperated. "But it's how I'm speaking to you."

He took a step back, holding her by the shoulders as he stared down at her face, his expression grave. Then the quirk that had lifted his lips a moment before was back, and he grinned, shaking his head. "Yes, ma'am," he said, dropping to a crouch in front of her with a chuckle. "Right away, ma'am."

~*~

"It's not working, is it?" Ruby said as they cleaned up the mess and piled the dishes in the sink. "This whole Master/slave thing. I mean, it's been super sexy but it's not..." she trailed off, looking anxious, as if what she was saying was going to upset him.

"It's not who we are," Evan supplied, relieved she'd been the first to say it, as he hadn't wanted to let her down. "It's definitely hot, dominating you like that as part of our bedroom play, but this 24/7 thing, the rules and protocol"—he made a face—"it's so much *work*." He winced as soon as the words were out of his mouth. They made it sound like he hadn't enjoyed the fantasy, and he *had*—to a point.

"Wait, I didn't mean it to sound like that," he rushed on. "You're the sexiest slave girl ever, and I loved being the one to bring your fantasy to life, but I—"

She stopped him midsentence by flinging her arms around his neck and pulling him down for an impassioned kiss. When they parted for breath, she said, "It's okay, Evan. Really. We're on the same page with this. You were a fabulous Master—really sexy and dominant and just like I fantasized. And like you said, it's really hot in short bursts. But this 24/7 thing"—she wrinkled her nose in that adorable way she had—"it's just not who we are."

"No," Evan agreed. "You're way too much of a smartass to be a proper slave."

"Hey, who're you calling a smartass?" she retorted with a grin, giving him a shove with both hands on his chest.

He caught her wrists, holding them tight. "*You*, my sexy, smartass gypsy girl," he said with a laugh, pulling her close. "Now, let's go out to dinner. I'm starving."

Chapter 11

"Mmm?" Ruby murmured, not wanting to let go of her dream. The annoying sound persisted, however, yanking her from sleep. Sun was streaming into the bedroom window, and the bed beside her was empty.

She realized the buzzing sound was her cell phone. She vaguely remembered that Evan had tried to rouse her sometime around the crack of dawn, but all she could recall was his leaning over her, already dressed, to kiss her on the nose and say goodbye.

She fumbled for the phone on the nightstand and pulled it to her, already smiling at the thought of him.

After a nice dinner, they'd returned to the house and tumbled into bed. She was surprised at herself. Usually after such an intense interaction as they'd shared over the past twenty-four hours, she would have needed a break, but hanging out with Evan seemed as natural as breathing. It was as if they'd always known one another.

Maybe Evan would be her next relationship? He'd been clear he was only in town for a short while. Maybe she'd tag along to wherever he was headed next—if he didn't mind.

They'd made love several times over the course of last night, and all of it vanilla—nary a rope or flogger in sight. It was actually a refreshing change after the intensity of the Master/slave experiment.

There was only so much bondage, domination, sadism and masochism a girl could handle.

Ruby stared down at her phone, but instead of seeing Evan's name, *Janice Martin* appeared on the screen. Were the daily texts and videos not enough for the cat-crazed couple? Did they now want to FaceTime with the cats?

"Hello?" she said, hoping she didn't sound like she'd just woken up, since it was definitely past the cats' breakfast time.

"Thank *god*," Janice cried, alarming Ruby. "I *finally* got you. What's happened? Where have you been?"

"What?" Ruby hoisted herself upright on the pillows. "What do you mean?"

"I've been calling since last night. I've been frantic with worry."

It was then Ruby saw the three missed calls and four missed texts. Shit.

"I must have missed your calls. I'm so sorry I worried you. Everything's fine here. Binky and Cuddles are doing great."

"Thank heavens," Janice said dramatically. "But the damage is done. We're coming home."

"I'm sorry, what? I'm not following you."

"I said, we're coming home. I *told* Frank two weeks was just too long, but he wouldn't listen. When I didn't hear back from you, naturally I assumed the worst. I'm glad to know you were just being irresponsible, rather than lying dead somewhere while my poor cats were left alone, starving and hysterical. Nevertheless, I simply cannot be without Binky and Cuddles another day. We've booked a flight for first thing in the morning. That was the soonest we could get out."

Ruby blew out a breath, fully awake now. She'd been around people like Frank and Janice before. Having never had children of their own, their pets were their surrogate babies. She could hear in the resolute tone of Janice's voice that no amount of reassurance was going change her mind.

Rather than responding to the comment about being irresponsible, she said calmly, "All right. What time will you be arriving? I'll pick you up at the airport."

Janice gave her the flight information, and Ruby promised to be there. Setting down the phone with a sigh, she climbed out of bed and padded to the bathroom. She used the toilet, brushed her teeth and took a quick shower.

She didn't like to think she'd upset the Martins, but she recognized Janice Martin was a little unhinged. It was quite possible, even if Ruby hadn't missed the calls, that Janice would have found some other reason to cut their trip short.

Normally such a sudden change in plans wouldn't have fazed her, but now there was a guy in the picture. He was still around for another week, and she wanted to be, too. Toweling off and combing out her wet hair, she pulled on a T-shirt and jeans and went downstairs to see to the precious felines.

Janice would have been pleased to know they were not at all hysterical or starving. They both seemed perfectly content. Binky, the toes of her front right paw splayed, was giving herself a meticulous tongue pedicure while Cuddles busily swiped at the fake mouse that hung from a string off the cat tree.

As Ruby entered the sunroom, Binky leaped gracefully from the bay windowsill and approached to rub against her ankles, while Cuddles lifted her delicate face toward Ruby and gave a plaintive meow.

They followed her into the kitchen, where she opened a can of the gourmet cat food specially imported from Denmark and spooned it into their china bowls. She had brought her phone with her, and as her coffee was brewing, she texted Allie. *"I know I owe you an update on the M/s experiment. Oh, and I just got evicted. Crazed cat parents are on their way home."*

As she waited for Allie's reply, she texted Evan. *"I have a vague memory of your leaving sometime before dawn, but I can't for the life of me remember what you said."*

Evan responded almost immediately. *"Putting out a few last minute fires for Bob. Some issues with permits and other crap. Stay naked and needy for me. I'll expect you on your knees when I return."*

Ruby laughed, shaking her head. *"Dream on,"* she texted, including a winking smiley face. She hit return and then added, *"I'll probably head over to Allie's today. Good luck with the fires."* She would tell him later about the eviction, once she figured things out.

She poured a mug of coffee and added some cream. Just as she was taking her first sip, her phone rang. She glanced at the screen and took the call. "Hey, Allie."

"Finally," Allie almost shouted into the phone. "I've been dying to know how the whole Master/slave thing is going, but I didn't want to ruin the mood by texting. So, tell me everything right this second. Oh," she added as an apparent afterthought, "and what's this about you being evicted? What's going on over there?"

"Everything's fine," Ruby said. "I'll answer your questions in reverse order." She took another sip of her coffee. "The Martins, well, specifically Janice Martin, are having cat withdrawal symptoms. They've actually cut their trip short because I missed some of their phone calls, and Janice freaked out and assumed the cats and I were lying dead in a pool of blood or something."

"But that's crazy."

"Yep. Apparently crazy is her typical MO, at least when it comes to the cats. I talked to her this morning. While she was relieved to know her babies are fine, the damage, to quote her, is done. I have been deemed unworthy. They're heading back from Canada in the morning. I'll be picking them up at the airport."

"They're still going to pay you the full amount, right? I mean, you did nothing wrong."

"I don't know," Ruby replied with a shrug. "I didn't ask. It doesn't matter. I mainly took the gig so I could see you. And I feel bad about that, Allie, because I've been spending all my time with Evan."

"Not all your time, and anyway, I totally understand. When loves comes knocking, we have to open the door."

"Love, huh," Ruby retorted. Allie had always been such a romantic.

"That's right. And I'm actually glad that crazy cat lady is coming back. Now you can come stay with us, right? Or wait, are you going to stay with Evan at his hotel?"

"He doesn't know I've been evicted," Ruby replied. "He had to leave early this morning for work."

"And he left you naked and in chains, right? Does he know you're using the phone, slave girl?" Allie asked in a teasing voice.

Ruby laughed. "No slave girls here at the moment. The experiment was intense. It was super exciting to have a real Master bringing my fantasy to life. I learned a lot about myself as a submissive and a masochist, but I also learned that there's a big gap between fantasy and reality. We both agreed that kind of lifestyle isn't for us, at least not 24/7."

"I get that. Liam and I started out super intense, because that's what I needed at the time. I still think of myself as his sub girl, and I wear his collar, but I wouldn't call myself a slave. That's a tough relationship to sustain for the long term, for sure. But tell me, was it fun while it lasted? Was it hot? Details, girl. I need details."

"Okay, okay," Ruby replied with a laugh. "I promise a full report. How about I come over now? I'm sure you can use more help."

"I absolutely could," Allie replied. "I've been working on a commissioned bracelet that I promised would be ready by tomorrow, and it's taking longer than I expected. It's put me behind on the cane making, so getting your help would be ideal right now. Oh, and I've got warm cranberry muffins here with your name on them."

"Be right there," Ruby said, her stomach rumbling.

~*~

Evan looked at his phone far too often over the course of the morning, but there was nothing from Ruby. He almost texted her at least a dozen times, but managed to restrain himself. Since they'd agreed to give up Ruby's slave fantasy, the dynamic between them had changed. Though she still seemed responsive and eager, he wasn't entirely sure where he stood. If he still hadn't heard from her by the end of the day, he'd shoot a casual, *"What's up?"* in her direction.

Though he had agreed it wasn't really who they were, he'd enjoyed the control aspect of the Master/slave thing. He wasn't used to asking for what he wanted when it came to most women—he was used to taking it. But then, Ruby wasn't like most women. She wasn't like anyone he'd ever met before.

This thing with Ruby—it was just infatuation, right? And yet, he hadn't felt this way since... Well, not since Marissa. Normally, he would have been perfectly content with a bit of hot, spicy, whirlwind sex with a dash of sweet romance thrown in. He would have been already itching at this point to take a break—to put some distance between himself and his latest conquest. It was simpler that way, since his lifestyle didn't accommodate anything long-term.

Yet, with Ruby, he didn't want less. He wanted more.

Stop it, he chided himself, alarmed at the direction of his thoughts. *After the grand opening, I'll be moving on. That's how it always goes. That's how it's got to be.*

But did it?

Maybe he'd stay a while longer, just to make sure Bob had everything up and running. After all, there was no rush. He had no commitments in the near future. Maybe Ruby would stay too.

Meanwhile, enough time had passed, and it wouldn't hurt to check in with Ruby about their plans for the evening. Maybe he'd take her to Hardcore and put her through her paces there. Yes, that sounded good. He smiled, his cock hardening in anticipation.

Grabbing his phone, he typed out a quick text. *"Hey, sexy. How about a date tonight at Hardcore? There's a whipping post there I'd love to chain you to."*

To his delight, the wavy dots started up almost instantly. Maybe she'd been waiting by her phone for *him*.

"Sounds fun, but I'll need to take a rain check. I promised to go to a movie with Allie and Rylee tonight."

Evan frowned. They only had a few days left together, and she was choosing her girlfriends over him? He pushed down his childish reaction. After all, it wasn't like they were joined at the hip.

"Okay, that's cool," he made himself text back. *"See you later tonight at your place?"*

"Just finishing up in the workshop. Need to update you on some stuff. I'll call you in a few, okay?"

That sounded kind of mysterious, even ominous, but Evan refused to speculate. He had no intention of playing the needy guy. That was not who he was. He sent back a thumbs-up emoji.

She finally called a half hour later. Though he had his phone in his hand, Evan let it ring three times before taking the call. "Hey," he said, grinning in spite of himself.

"Hey," Ruby replied. "All your fires out?"

"More or less. So what's all this about updates?"

"The Martins are coming back early. They'll be here tomorrow morning at eleven. I'm going to pick them up at the airport."

"The cat people? Why're they doing that? Is something wrong?"

"It's pretty crazy. They're cutting their trip short because I didn't answer the phone last night or early this morning, apparently, and they freaked out. I think Janice was looking for an excuse to get back to her cats. The trip to Canada was his idea, not hers."

"So," Evan said slowly, trying to get a handle on this unexpected change, "tonight's our last night at the cat resort?"

Ruby chuckled. "Yeah, I guess it is. Listen, the movie starts at seven. We're going to grab a bite first. I should be back by ten or so. You're welcome to come and stay over, if you want to. You can just go in through the garage." She gave him the code.

"Okay. Then we'll have to figure something out. I'm staying at this B&B right now. It's just a room inside someone's big, old house. How about I get a suite over at the Residence Inn near the convention center? We could stay there."

"I have another idea, if you're interested. Allie and Liam have invited us to stay with them. They have a guest bedroom. It actually would work out great, because Allie and I are kind of under the gun to get these canes finished before the grand opening. If I'm staying there, we'll be more likely to get everything done."

Evan didn't reply instantly as he grappled with the whole idea. By agreeing to the arrangement, he was tacitly admitting to the world that they were a couple.

On the other hand, what was so bad about that? He definitely wanted to continue seeing Ruby. And he liked the Byrnes, not to mention their kickass dungeon, which would certainly come in handy. If things didn't work out, he could always find somewhere else to stay.

Who was he kidding?

These were all old arguments—defenses he had built around himself to keep casual relationships from getting overly complicated. The truth was he would do anything to be as close as possible to Ruby for as long as possible. And here she was, offering him the perfect setup.

"Sounds like a great idea," he enthused. "I'll take care of Dinky and Doodles and see you after the movie."

~*~

Evan left for work early the next morning. Ruby changed the sheets and put them, along with the towels they'd used, in the washer. She remade the bed with fresh sheets and tidied the house, making sure everything was pristine before the Martins returned. Once the towels and bedding were dry, she folded and put them away. She fed the cats and then cleaned their litter box one last time. Satisfied everything was in order, Ruby headed out to retrieve the Martins from the airport.

Frank drove home. Janice, beside him in the front, twisted back toward Ruby in the backseat, peppering her with questions about the cats' daily habits and behavior, things Ruby had already told the woman via texts and emails. Forcing herself to be patient, she answered the questions as pleasantly as she could. Fortunately, they didn't live far from the airport, and Frank had a heavy foot.

Back at their place, once Janice had made sure her precious babies were intact and happy, she allowed Frank to pay Ruby half of what they'd initially agreed upon, since, Janice said with a sniff, "You've only completed half the job."

Ruby didn't bother pointing out the obvious—that Janice was the one who had cut their trip short because of her own neurotic obsession. Money was never a driving factor for Ruby. She took the cash with thanks and tucked it away in her purse. Frank offered to give Ruby a ride to Allie's place, which she accepted.

As they drove, Frank, who had said almost nothing when in the company of his wife, said apologetically, "I'm sorry about all this craziness. You didn't do anything wrong."

"I'm sorry I missed the phone calls. I hate to think she worried on my account."

"Nah," Frank said with a shake of his head. "She would have found some other excuse to cut the trip short. I guess the real miracle was that she agreed to go away in the first place." He glanced at Allie, his expression suddenly beseeching. "She really is a good woman, but it's been tough for her. You see, Janice and I were never able to have kids, and that's all she ever wanted. We tried for years, and we talked about adopting, but it never really worked out. I think she went a little nuts as a result. As I'm sure you've observed, the cats are kind of her baby substitutes. You've seen her at her worst, but she's a great gal. Truly she is." He smiled suddenly, his eyes soft with love. "This trip was a big step forward for her. Now that she sees it's possible, maybe I'll convince her to do another trip in a few months."

"Maybe you can do something that involves the cats," Allie suggested with a grin. "Get a camper or something."

"Maybe," Frank agreed with a laugh.

As they pulled into Allie's driveway, Frank reached into his pocket and pulled out his wallet. He removed several bills and held them out to Ruby. "Please, take the rest of what we agreed to. It's not your fault we're a little neurotic."

"Oh, that's okay," Ruby said with a shake of her head.

"Please," Frank pressed, setting the money on top of her purse. "I insist. It'll make me feel better for putting you through this."

With a smile and a shrug, Ruby slipped the rest of the money into her bag. "Thanks, Frank. And thanks for the ride. Good luck with your future travel plans."

"Let me show you the guest bedroom so you can put your things in there," Allie said as they walked together up the stairs. "The master bedroom is downstairs," she added with a wink. "So you and Evan don't have to worry about making noise."

Ruby laughed. "You mean, so you and Liam don't have to worry," she teased back. "That's kind of unusual in these older houses, isn't it? Having bedrooms on different floors?"

"Yeah," Allie agreed. "Liam actually had what was the maid's room and the old butler's quarters off the kitchen expanded into one room back when he had his car accident. He couldn't manage the stairs for quite a while after, so he had those rooms converted into an en suite bedroom."

"He gets around great now, though, huh?" Ruby said admiringly. "It's so cool that he uses the cane you made him."

"Yeah, he gets around fine. He's made huge strides since we've been together, especially in his mental outlook. That accident and the shit that went down really did a number on him, but he's truly come to a place of peace with it all. I'm so proud of him."

"He's lucky to have you, Allie," Ruby said sincerely, smiling warmly at her dear friend.

"I feel like the lucky one," Allie replied, her expression glowing. At the top of the stairs, she rubbed her bottom and flashed an impish grin. "Want to see the gorgeous welts he gave me last night?"

"Sure," Ruby said with a laugh.

Turning, Allie lifted her short dress and tugged down her silky bikini panties. Her small bottom was marked with two dark red welts, delivered in parallel lines across both cheeks. There were myriad fading welts beneath in pale pinks and purples. A non-initiate to the scene would have been horrified, but Ruby understood Allie regarded her constant marking as a source of pride and courage.

"Oh," Ruby said softly. She reached out and drew her finger lightly over one of the ridged welts. "That's beautiful, Allie."

The guest bedroom was at the end of the hallway on the second floor, past Allie's workshop and Liam's study. The room wasn't large, but it accommodated a queen bed with an upholstered headboard, a bureau set across from it. It had its own bathroom, a definite plus.

"This will be perfect," Ruby said, setting down her travel bags. "Evan should be coming by later today when he's done at work. He said something about bringing a couple pizzas, if that works for you guys."

"As long one of them has mushrooms, green olives, onions, artichoke hearts, red peppers, extra sauce and extra cheese, that'll be perfect," Allie agreed with a grin. "Tastebud makes the best pizza around, but House of Pie works in a pinch."

"You should text him directly," Ruby said with a grin. "I'll never remember all that."

"Okay. I will." As they left the bedroom, Allie said, "Ready to get to work?"

"You bet."

They settled in quickly, each working at a separate table. Ruby worked on the cane construction, while Allie did the handles and added the silver filigree and gemstones accents.

At Allie's insistence, Ruby gave her a blow-by-blow description of the Master/slave experiment. That topic eventually exhausted, they talked casually of this and that. Eventually they quieted, each lost in her work.

Out of nowhere, Allie surprised Ruby by saying, "I have a confession to make. Something I never told anyone, not till Liam."

"Oh, yeah?" Ruby said, turning her head expectantly toward her old friend. "What's that?"

"I used to fake orgasms when I was with guys. Not sometimes. All the time."

Ruby's mouth fell open. "No way," she breathed, shocked. Allie had always seemed to be so sexually at ease and confident.

"Yeah, I know, right?" Allie said, shaking her head. "I could never climax with a guy. I used to worry I was broken or something, and I worked myself up so much over it that it became a self-fulfilling prophecy. It got to the point where I was so stressed out that I just decided to fake it without even trying. I got really good at it, so good I could make my own heart pound. I would pant, tremble, sweat, the whole deal. I even half convinced myself I was coming, but it was all just an act."

"So what changed?"

Allie smiled, her whole face lighting up. "I met Sir Liam."

"So it was that easy? You met Master Right, and wham, you're cured?"

Allie shook her head. "No. I lied to him, too, at first. But he figured it out. Not exactly what I was lying about, but that I was holding back. When I finally confessed, he wasn't at all judgmental. He made it safe for me."

"How did he do that?" Ruby asked, intrigued.

"At first he forbade me to orgasm. He took it off the plate, and that took all the pressure off, you know? Then he showed me, slowly and with love and patience, how to trust my own body. He taught me to let go."

Ruby smiled. "That's so romantic, Allie. I'm glad you've found the love of your life."

"Yeah, I am pretty lucky." Allie was quiet a moment, and then she asked, "What about you? Do you think Evan might be *the one*?"

Ruby shrugged. "Normally I'd say no way, since neither of us has plans to stick around, but we definitely have something special between us. Something unique. I love being with him. I love that he delved into my secret fantasies and wanted to bring one to life for me. And I love even more that he got it when I said it wasn't working for me. It's like we're really in tune with each other, and we kind of fit, if you know what I mean."

"I do," Allie replied. "There's a definite connection. But I think it's more than that. I think he's in love with you."

Ruby smiled but shook her head. "Nah. I don't think Evan's the falling in love type. He downplayed it, but he was badly burned in the romance department when he was pretty young. I think that's kept him from getting too close to anyone."

"What a load of crap," Allie retorted. "He might tell you that. He might even tell himself that, but I see what I see. Liam agrees with me."

When Ruby said nothing in reply, Allie continued, "What about you? Can you see yourself settling down with just one guy?"

Ruby paused to consider it. "I honestly don't know. I've had some long-term relationships, if you consider a year long-term. When it's good and it's working, it's wonderful. And when that's no longer the case"—Ruby shrugged philosophically—"then I know it's time to move on."

"What if it's still wonderful with Evan after next week? Have you guys talked about where you go from here, once they do the grand opening, and he moves on to his next gig?"

"We really haven't talked about it." Ruby was quiet a while as she pondered what it would be like to no longer have Evan in her life. The thought actually made her sad, which surprised her, since she usually had no trouble letting someone go. She had always believed that if things were supposed to work out, they would. She wasn't one to try to influence the outcome, especially if the other person had made it clear they weren't in it for the long term.

But it did feel different with Evan. Was Allie right? Was it possible Ruby was falling in love? Was that a good thing or a bad thing? Aloud, she said, "We haven't talked about the future." Then she laughed. "We still have a whole week. Anything can happen."

CHAPTER 12

Evan moaned with pleasure as he came awake. It took him a moment to understand what was happening, and why he felt so incredibly good. Lifting his head, he saw Ruby crouched between his legs, her dark head bobbing over his groin. Her mouth was warm and wet around his cock. She cradled his balls in her hands as she licked and sucked his pulsing shaft.

He wanted to make it last, but it was a lost cause. With a groan, he let himself go, shooting his hot seed down her throat. She didn't pull away until he was completely spent. Only then did she let his cock slide from her lips. Lifting her head, she smiled at him, her eyes dancing. "Morning, cutie pie."

"Man," he said with a satisfied sigh, "what an awesome way to wake up."

"You have that goofy, milk-drunk smile on your face," Ruby said, scooting up to snuggle against him.

"Milk drunk?" Evan repeated, confused.

"Like a baby drunk on mother's milk," she explained.

Evan laughed. "I never heard that one before." He put his arm around her and pulled her closer. "I might have to reinstate the Master thing so I can order you to do that every morning."

"No orders required," she replied with a grin.

Evan drifted pleasantly for a while. He actually had the day off for the first time since he'd arrived in Portland. Ruby had wanted to explore the city, and this seemed like the perfect opportunity.

Then his cell phone began to ding. "Let it go to voicemail," he said, when Ruby lifted her head inquiringly.

She put her head back on his chest, and he stroked her thick, silky hair. The room they were staying in was nice, the bed very comfortable. Everything should have been perfect, but Evan couldn't deny the unpleasant niggle of discomfort at the back of his mind since he'd checked out of the B&B and moved in here as Ruby's "other half."

While most of him was very happy to be part of a couple with this wonderful woman, the old Evan—the careful Evan who always kept an escape hatch open and his suitcase packed—was a little nervous about how quickly things were moving between them. The knowledge that they'd both be moving on at the end of the week should have provided the comfort he needed, but he found that troubling, too. It was as if there were several different Evans in his head, each one fighting to be on top. One Evan wanted to spend every spare second with Ruby, while another Evan was looking around anxiously for an exit. A third Evan was actually asking what the future held, something he normally rigorously avoided even thinking about. The easiest thing to do was put it all out of his mind. Things had a way of working out, if he just let them be.

The phone rang again.

"Maybe you'd better see who it is," Ruby said sleepily.

Fully conscious now, Evan reached for his cell and saw it was Bob Benson. "Hey, Bob. What's up?"

"Glad I got you. Listen, I agreed to let this Femdom group use the space today, even though we're not officially open yet. I was going handle it, but something's come up and I'm not going to be able to make it. Could you cover for me? The event starts at four, but the organizers will probably show up around three thirty to get things ready. They're going to conduct a branding ceremony first off, and then they've rented the dungeon space for a few hours of play afterward. I'll be there to close the place up before they leave. I just need you to stick around during the actual branding. The last thing we need is for these guys to burn the place down before we open." He guffawed.

Evan suppressed a groan, jealous of his time with Ruby. But he prided himself on being a full service, 24/7 event coordinator and so he said without a trace of impatience, "Sure, no problem. I can handle it."

They talked for another minute or two and said their goodbyes.

Ruby lifted her head as Evan set the phone back on the nightstand. "Who was that?"

"Bob Benson. Looks like I have to go in to work for a few hours later this afternoon. A group is coming in to conduct a branding ceremony, and he wants me to oversee them since he can't make it till later."

"I've always been curious about ritual branding. Can I come with you?"

Evan grinned, delighted she wanted to join him. "Sure."

Sunshine was pouring through the windows. He threw the covers back and swung his legs over the side of the bed. "Want to go out for some breakfast?"

Ruby got to her feet, lifting her arms into an elaborate stretch, her chin raised, her eyes closed, utterly relaxed in her nudity. She looked so lovely that he considered scratching the breakfast idea and hurling her back into the bed.

As he took a step toward her, she opened her eyes and looked pointedly at his crotch. He followed her gaze, seeing that his cock, so recently sated, was hardening again. "Shame to waste it," he said with a comically leering grin. "Breakfast can wait, right?"

"You greedy boy," she teased. "There's more to life than sex, you know."

"There is?" he asked, trying but failing to keep a straight face.

She tossed her hair with a laugh and headed into the bathroom. Still grinning, Evan followed.

"It's a gorgeous day," Ruby said as they were washing up. "We have time before you have to be at the warehouse. How about let's do some hiking. Allie was telling me about all these cool trails right in the middle of the city. We can pick up breakfast on the way and eat it at the top of a mountain."

"Sure," he said with a smile, letting go of any lingering thought of taking her back to bed. "That sounds fun."

They decided to go to Mount Tabor Park. It wasn't too far from the BDSM Convention Event Center, and there were several relatively easy hiking trails they could do within a few hours.

Evan was glad Allie and Liam were still sleeping, so they could slip out without a fuss. Ruby found a thermos in the kitchen and left a note to let their hosts know where they were going. They stopped at a bakery, where Ruby selected various muffins and pastries. She had Evan stop next at a convenience store, where they filled the thermos with coffee, and also bought a couple bottles of water, plus two cups of coffee to drink right away.

"You're good at this organizing stuff," Evan noted with admiration as Ruby neatly packed the items away in the small pack she'd brought along for the purpose.

At the park, the lot was relatively empty. They walked hand in hand toward the hiking trail entrance without seeing another soul.

"This is so cool," Ruby said as they stood in front of a sign reading about the park's various trails. "Underneath all these pine trees, this mountain is actually a three-million-year-old volcanic butte."

They chose the blue trail, the most challenging of the three that led to the top. In spite of himself, Evan was impressed with the rugged, natural beauty surrounding them. You could completely forget you were in the middle of a city. It felt good to stretch his limbs as they moved slowly upward along the dirt paths.

Though Ruby was petite, she was strong and fast. While Evan could keep up with her, she was clearly the more experienced hiker. "Hey," she said, turning back to regard him as they climbed single-file up a narrow path. "I told you my darkest, most secret sexual fantasy. What about you? What's yours?"

Evan shrugged. "I don't really have one. I mean, nothing as complicated as your Master/slave thing. I'm not nearly as imaginative as you are."

"Okay. So what's your fantasy when you masturbate? You know, the scene that flashes into your mind that gives you that push you need to finish?"

An image leaped instantly into Evan's mind. He pushed it away, not used to sharing such private moments. He started to shrug again, but stopped himself. Ruby had bared her soul to him. She'd trusted him with her deepest secrets. He owed it to her to be as honest with her as she'd been with him.

"There was this photo I ripped from some porn magazine I'd managed to buy back when I was fifteen or so. It was of a beautiful girl in this flowing, gauzy, see-through dress. She was barefoot, her hair wild around her face. You could see her nipples and the small patch of her pubic hair underneath her dress. She was locked in a full-sized upright cage, her hands on the bars, a beseeching expression on her face. The picture always gave me an instant erection."

"Do you still have the photo? I'd love to see it."

Evan gave a small laugh. "It finally fell apart from too much handling but I've never forgotten the image. It had a powerful impact on me and was one of the factors that propelled me into the scene."

"And yet, you said when you were first exploring, you were a sub?"

"I was never really a sub," Evan replied with a snort. "It was more that I wanted to get into Mistress Marta's panties. She was this gorgeous older Spanish woman I met at the first BDSM club I ever ventured into. In order to do that, I had to agree to be her slave boy. It was fun while it lasted, but it was just a game, nothing more. I knew right away my interest lay in domination, but I'm not sorry for the experience. I learned firsthand what it feels like to be bound, whipped, spanked and controlled by another. That's important for a Dom to know."

"Agreed," Ruby said. "You're a pretty cool guy, you know that?"

A rush of warmth moved through Evan's body. "You're not so bad yourself," he replied, stopping to pull her into his arms for a long, sweet kiss.

As the path grew steeper, they quieted, focusing on the climb. The pine-scented air was cool and refreshing. From time to time a chipmunk or marmot would scramble across the path, and birds sang their cheerful songs high up in the trees.

Ruby stopped suddenly as they rounded a curve, so that Evan nearly collided into her. "Look," she whispered, putting her hand on his arm. "There."

He focused on a clump of small trees a few feet to their right, at first seeing nothing but shadow and light. Then something moved, a flicker of white, and he saw them—a doe and her spindle-legged fawn, the baby's coat still dappled with white spots. The mother lifted her head toward them, stiffening, though the fawn continued to nibble delicately at some wildflowers.

He started to say something but stopped when Ruby shook her head, her grip tightening on his arm. They stayed as still as the deer, barely breathing. After a while, the doe lowered her head, gently nudging her baby with her nose. Then she dipped her head farther and nibbled the flowers alongside her fawn.

There was a sudden crack of branches somewhere nearby, and in a flash, the pair had vanished into the pine forest.

Ruby blew out a soft sigh. "So majestic," she breathed. "Such grace."

Evan nodded, startled at how moved he'd been by the simple scene, made all the more poignant because he had Ruby to share it with. Though he would have had a good time walking through a garbage dump if Ruby was with him, he was surprised to discover how much he was enjoying himself on the hike. Maybe there was more to life than traveling from city to city, living out of a suitcase, working by day and clubbing at night.

When they arrived at the summit, they were greeted by a stunning view of downtown Portland to the west and Mount Hood to the northeast, just peeking through the trees. Evan took the small pack from his back. Sitting against a broad tree trunk, they shared their meal. Evan couldn't remember when he'd felt happier.

Later that afternoon when they pulled up at the BDSM Connections warehouse, a man and woman were already waiting by the front door.

The guy was big and tall, dressed in black leather and boots, his graying hair pulled back in a ponytail. The woman, at least a foot shorter than her partner, wore a low-cut black gown that barely contained her large breasts. Her arms were sleeved with tattoos from shoulder to wrist.

"Bob?" the guy queried as they approached.

"I'm Evan Stewart," Evan said, extending his hand. "I work with Bob. He'll be along later."

"George Hanson," the man said, catching Evan's hand in his beefy paw and squeezing so hard Evan thought he felt some bones crack. "And this is my Mistress, Simone Goddard."

"Nice to meet you both," Evan said, pulling his hand away as soon as it was politely possible. "This is my"—he hesitated a fraction of a second before settling on—"friend, Ruby Beckett. We'll stick around during the branding in case you need anything."

"Great. Thanks."

Just as Evan unlocked the warehouse, another car pulled into the lot. A tall, willowy woman in black leather pants stepped out of the car. She had very short white-blond hair and pale skin, her lips painted a deep red that matched her red silk blouse. She popped her trunk and pulled out a large black cauldron. Setting it on the ground, she hauled out a large gear bag.

Evan and George went to help her. "This is Goddess Athena," George said by way of introduction. "She's our branding expert."

Evan introduced himself, and they returned to the warehouse, Evan carrying the cauldron, George hefting the gear bag. As they entered the space, Evan said, "Who's getting branded today? You, George?"

George glanced at his Mistress with a lugubrious frown. "Not today. Mistress says I'm not yet ready." He touched the black choker he wore around his neck. "But someday soon I hope to be worthy."

"Slave George tends to bite off more than he can chew," Simone said. "And I'm not just talking about his belly." She patted George's substantial gut, her smile affectionate. "He *thinks* he wants to wear my brand, but he passed out cold when he got the Prince Albert, so I think we'll wait awhile on that."

"How many folks are you expecting for the event?" Evan asked.

"About thirty," Simone said. She glanced toward the front doors. "Our guests of honor should have been here by now. Maybe they got held up in traffic."

Evan and Ruby put two rows of chairs in front of a small staging area while Simone and George helped Athena set up her gear. Athena poured a small bag of charcoal into the cauldron. George got the coals lit while Simone emptied a bag of ice into a bucket that she placed alongside the cauldron. Athena produced a small folding table from her large bag and set up her branding gear.

People began to arrive and take their seats in front of the impromptu stage, chatting excitedly. Simone had set flyers on two seats in the front row to reserve them.

The fire had gone out in the cauldron, the coals now glowing red-hot. Just as Athena placed the branding iron on top of the embers, a couple Evan guessed to be in their forties entered the warehouse, the man athletically built, his partner slender but curvaceous, her eyes heavily made up with eyeliner and mascara. The man had a collar around his neck, a leash attached to it, and the woman held the other end of the leash.

"Ah, Jade, there you are," Simone said, coming over to the couple and taking the woman's hands in hers.

"I'm sorry we're late," the woman called Jade said as she unclipped the leash from the man's collar. "Billy's covering for another doctor who was supposed to be on call this weekend. He had to do a quick run to the hospital to see a couple of patients. Hopefully we can get through this without his being interrupted," she added with a grin.

"Let's hope so," Simone agreed. "Otherwise, I might just let George have his wish." George, standing nearby, looked suddenly alarmed.

~*~

Ruby and Evan slipped into two empty seats on the end of the back row as the branding expert chatted quietly with the Jade and Billy. After a few minutes, the couple took their seats in the front row.

Athena gave a short lecture to the group about the history of ritual branding in BDSM, as well as the mechanics of conducting a safe branding. Then she called up the couple again. At a nod from Jade, Billy removed his shoes, shirt and pants, leaving only his black bikini briefs in place. At a tap on his shoulder, Billy sank gracefully to his knees beside his Mistress.

Jade turned to the group. "A collar can be removed. Chains and cuffs can be unlocked. But branding by hot iron is forever. It's a powerful expression of ownership. My slave and I gave it a lot of thought and discussion before making our decision."

You could have heard a pin drop in the room. Ruby shivered at the thought of that hot brand scalding her flesh, leaving a mark even more permanent than a tattoo. She glanced at Evan, who smiled at her. He reached for her hand and gently squeezed it. "You okay?" he whispered. "We don't have to watch this."

"No, I want to," Ruby said, though butterflies were flitting wildly in her stomach, as if she were the one waiting to receive the burning mark on her flesh.

Jade turned to Billy. "Slave Billy, do you consent to have my brand placed permanently on your body, forever marking you as my property and my treasure?"

"Yes, Mistress," Billy said in a deep voice. "Willingly."

"My mark will be a lasting symbol of our bond to each other," Jade said, her eyes shining as she looked down at her slave.

"I love you, Mistress Jade," Billy said, staring up at her.

"I love you, Billy." She held out her hand, and Billy took it, getting to his feet.

Jade turned to Athena. "We're ready."

Athena handed Jade a bit gag. "Bite down on that," Jade said as she placed it in Billy's mouth. "It will help you handle the pain." Then she pulled down Billy's underwear, taking it from him as he stepped out of it. He turned away so his back was to the audience. Jade stood to his side, taking his hand in hers.

Athena, meanwhile, put on a thick leather glove to protect her hand from the heat. Reaching into the cauldron, she lifted out the branding iron. The brand glowed red and appeared to be the initials MJ.

Ruby's mouth had gone dry and her heart was pounding as she watched the woman bring the brand slowly and carefully to Billy's right butt cheek. Ruby gasped as the brand touched his flesh. Smoke rose around the brand and there was a sizzling sound. Suddenly dizzy, she leaned gratefully into Evan as he put his arm around her.

Billy groaned around his gag, but remained perfectly still. After about ten seconds, which seemed more like thirty minutes, Athena lifted the brand away. As she set it back into the caldron, Jade grabbed a handful of ice from the nearby bucket and rubbed it over the burn on Billy's bottom.

"Are you okay, sweetheart?" she said, using her other hand to pull away the gag.

"Yes, Mistress," Billy replied in a strained voice, but when he turned his face to hers, Ruby could see that he was smiling.

Athena stepped between them to apply Aloe Vera gel to the wound, which she then covered with what looked like Saran wrap. When she was done, Jade took Billy in her arms and they kissed passionately, while the small audience erupted into cheers and applause.

~*~

They were just leaving the warehouse when Evan's phone dinged. He fished it out of his pocket and read the text. He turned to Ruby. "Liam wants us to stop at a bakery on NE Broadway and pick up some dessert on our way back to their place. They're having another couple over for dinner, and of course, we're invited." He glanced at the screen again. "Matt and Bonnie Wilson. Do you know them?"

"I know of them, though I haven't met them yet," Ruby said. "Matt is Liam's best friend, and Bonnie and Allie are close."

Ruby googled the bakery location as Evan pulled out of the warehouse parking lot. Once they were on their way, Evan said, "So, what did you think of that branding ceremony? It was pretty intense, huh?"

"It sure was," Ruby agreed. "I never would have thought that was something I'd want, but the way they did it—like a kind of wedding ceremony almost—it was really moving."

"Would you ever do that—let someone brand you?" An image of Ruby naked and waiting for a red-hot branding iron to sear her flesh with his mark leaped into his mind's eye.

She didn't answer immediately. Then she said, "I don't know. Maybe, if I was with someone I loved and trusted. Maybe with someone like you," she added softly.

Evan glanced over at Ruby, startled at the look of love in her eyes. He looked back at the road, her words lodging like a hot, sweet arrow in his heart, even as the old tapes in his brain instantly started to whir. *Watch out for the L word. When it comes up, it's time to hit the road.*

Evan had never cared that much about sweets, but you'd have thought Ruby was looking at sex toys, the way she got so excited over the many cupcakes, pastries and cookies on display in the glass cabinets.

"Let's get the chocolate éclairs," she finally said.

"Great," Evan agreed. He got the young woman's attention behind the counter. "We'd like a dozen chocolate éclairs, please."

"For here or to go?" the woman asked, her expression deadpan.

"Uh, to go," Evan said with a glance at Ruby, who was grinning at him.

As the woman boxed up the éclairs, Ruby said, "I love chocolate éclairs. A dozen should be perfect. But Evan"—she looked at him, her expression serious—"what about everyone else?"

Evan chuckled, shaking his head. "Maybe her question about here or to go wasn't as crazy as I thought."

When they pulled up at the house, there was a late-model Lexus parked in the driveway. As they entered the front hall, Liam appeared, another guy just behind him. He was tall and imposing, with a broad chest, short blond hair and a neatly trimmed beard, his face open and friendly.

"Hey, guys. I thought I heard you come in," Liam said as he

approached them.

Ruby held out the large bakery box tied with red string. "We got chocolate éclairs."

"Excellent," Liam said. He turned to his friend, who had come up beside him. "This is my best buddy since forever, Matt Wilson. He travels a lot for work or you would probably have met him sooner. Matt, meet Ruby Beckett and Evan Stewart."

After they exchanged greetings, Matt said, "My wife, Bonnie, is in the kitchen helping Allie with the dinner preparations."

"He means Allie is helping Bonnie," Liam said. "Bonnie is a fabulous cook. She brought over my favorite dish—this spicy Cuban beef with corn bread topping that I practically lived on when I was recovering from my car accident."

They made their way to the kitchen. Matt's wife was a dark-eyed, voluptuous beauty. She wore a black leather slave collar that dipped into a V toward her cleavage, which was on display in a figure-hugging, low cut dress.

"It's great to finally meet you two," Bonnie said with a warm smile, giving them both big hugs. "I heard you attended a branding ceremony this afternoon."

"Yeah," Allie said eagerly. "Tell us all about it."

~*~

The conversation was lively during the delicious meal. Ruby sat next to Bonnie, and their conversation turned toward piercings. "I love that little diamond in your nose," Bonnie said, touching it lightly with her fingertip. "When did you get that?"

"I got the piercing in Nepal," Ruby replied. "I was only nineteen. It was my first big trip after I dropped out of college. A bunch of girls were going to this old tattoo parlor, and I went along with them. I didn't get a tattoo that day, but the old woman behind the counter had such a pretty diamond in her nose, and I was admiring it, and she told me her sister in the back room could do it for me really cheap—ten American dollars, and that included the diamond," Ruby recalled with a laugh.

"I'm guessing it wasn't a real diamond?" Bonnie said.

"A good guess." Ruby grinned. "I don't even think it was cubic zirconia. It was just a piece of cut glass. The piercing got infected, and I had to take out the so-called diamond. I actually got it re-pierced just a couple of years ago." She touched the small diamond she now wore.

"It's really pretty," Bonnie said. "I just got pierced recently," she added with a mischievous grin.

"Is it my turn to guess where?" Ruby asked with a smile.

"No guessing necessary." Without the slightest qualm, Bonnie slipped the straps of her dress from her shoulders, revealing her bare, full breasts. Her large nipples were circled by delicate gold filigree hoops studded with gemstones, held in place with a gold bar with a diamond on each end.

"Oh, how beautiful," Ruby enthused sincerely. "I've never seen such pretty nipple rings.

"They're from Australia," Bonnie said. "Matt just brought them home for me."

Matt, who sat directly across from Ruby and Bonnie, lifted his eyebrows at his wife's display, but then he smiled. "Showing off your birthday present, huh?" he said, chuckling.

Evan, who sat on Ruby's other side, leaned forward, craning for a better look. His eyes bugged out, his mouth falling open as he stared at Bonnie's gorgeous, bare breasts.

Ruby couldn't help but laugh. "You look like one of those 1940's cartoon characters whose eyes spring out on coils when a hot tomato strolls by," she teased him.

When Bonnie pulled her straps back into place, covering herself once more, Evan finally managed to close his mouth. A sheepish expression moved over his face as he glanced at Ruby. "You can't blame a guy for looking."

"Yeah, give him a break," Liam said with a laugh. "Most every guy who knows Bonnie is half in love with her, myself included."

"And more than a few women," Allie added fondly. "Because Bonnie is not only sexy and gorgeous, she's about the nicest person you'll ever meet in your life."

"Stop it, you guys," Bonnie protested, blushing prettily. "You're embarrassing me. I'm just your garden variety exhibitionistic submissive."

"No, you're way more than that, Bonnie," Allie said seriously. Turning to Ruby, she added, "It's because of Bonnie that Liam and I are even together."

"No kidding?" Ruby said. "I want to hear all about it."

Liam, Bonnie, Matt and Allie all pitched in with details of the romantic story of Liam and Allie's first face-to-face meeting, and as they were talking, Evan took Ruby's hand underneath the table and gave it a gentle squeeze. She leaned into him, enjoying the feeling of being part of a couple.

Matt lifted his water glass and said, "I want to make a toast to my darling wife."

"To Bonnie," Liam chimed in, clinking his glass against Matt's.

"Here, here," Evan added, lifting his glass, as Bonnie blushed again.

When it had quieted, Matt looked around the table. "As you all know, my sweet slave girl loves the chance to prove her obedience to her Master in any way that pleases me. Isn't that right, Bonnie?"

"Yes, Sir," Bonnie breathed, her eyes shining.

"And," Matt continued, "seeing as she just celebrated her birthday last week, I thought it might be fun to continue the celebration down in the dungeon."

"Absolutely," Liam said. "What did you have in mind?"

"I thought we'd truss her up and let her be the focus of everyone's attention. For those of you who haven't yet had the pleasure to play with slave Bonnie," he added, nodding toward Ruby and Evan, "Bonnie is a pain slut, and she can take quite a lot. Her safeword is apple, just in case things get too intense, but I've only known Bonnie to use it once, and that was with a guy who wasn't paying attention to her distress cues. I've heard only good things about you two, so I'm sure that won't be an issue tonight. She's also a pleasure seeker and highly sexed. The only rule," he added, fixing his gaze on Bonnie, his eyes hooding, "is that she doesn't come until I say so."

"And don't forget the house rule," Liam added. "All sub girls are required to strip naked before entering the dungeon." He turned his gaze to Evan. "That work for you, buddy?"

"Like a charm," Evan replied. Under the table, he slid his hand sexily along Ruby's thigh, and she shivered with pleasant anticipation.

They cleared the dishes and put away the leftovers, the work done quickly with so many helping hands. At the bottom of the basement stairs, the girls all shucked off their clothing. Ruby and Allie were directed to kneel up at attention, hands behind their heads while they waited for play to begin. Excitement zipped along Ruby's nerve endings, her pussy moistening as they watched the guys bind the eager, compliant Bonnie.

Liam brought over a high, padded stool, and Matt helped Bonnie up onto it. They placed cuffs on her wrists and ankles. Liam clipped her wrists to chains that dangled from the overhead beams, while Evan secured her legs to the overhead chains. Matt adjusted the chains until her legs were extended straight out in a V parallel to the ground. She was perched on the edge of the stool, her smooth, bare pussy on full display. Finally, they placed a blindfold over Bonnie's eyes.

"Lucky birthday girl," Allie said as they watched the men work.

"Lucky us, too," Ruby said. "I'm sure we're in for a great scene."

The guys were talking quietly among themselves, and then Matt turned to them. "Girls, your job is to comfort, distract and soothe slave Bonnie while we take turns torturing and using her as it pleases us. I know you'll have no problem with the assignment, Allie. What about you, Ruby? You cool with this?"

"Absolutely, Sir," Ruby said, her nipples aching with anticipation. While she didn't consider herself particularly bisexual, she loved women and was eager and willing to touch and please them in the context of a BDSM scene. Allie, she suspected, shared a similar view toward girl/girl play, and clearly she and Bonnie were close friends with a lot of experience together in the scene.

"Good." Matt gestured for the girls to get to their feet. "Allie, you kneel between Bonnie's legs. Ruby, you can stand behind her. I'm going to start things off with something intense to get my girl in the proper headspace."

As Allie and Ruby assumed their positions, Matt went over to the whip wall and returned with a short-handled single tail whip. Liam and Evan stood together watching as Matt took his position just to the side of Bonnie's extended right leg.

"It's been a while since my slave had a proper foot whipping," he announced, flicking the whip lightly against his thigh.

Bonnie drew in a sharp breath, her entire body tensing. Allie stroked Bonnie's thighs, while Ruby placed her hands lightly on Bonnie's shoulders.

Bonnie leaned her head back. "He's such a sadist," she whispered. "Foot whippings are my least favorite. They hurt so fucking much."

"So, it can only get better from there, right?" Ruby murmured back, kneading Bonnie's taut shoulder muscles.

"Ten on each sole," Matt said. He flicked the single tail in the air, making Bonnie flinch.

"Yes, Sir," she said in a surprisingly steady voice. "Thank you, Sir."

"You're welcome, slave girl."

Bonnie yelped as the first stroke snaked over the sole of her right foot, her entire body tensing.

"Breathe," Ruby whispered into her ear as she continued the shoulder massage.

"Ah," Bonnie cried as Matt struck her three more times in rapid succession.

"Distract her, sub Allie," Liam called from the sidelines. "You know what to do."

"Yes, Sir," Allie said. She dipped her head and lowered her face to Bonnie's shaven sex.

"Oh, yes, yes," Bonnie breathed as Allie lapped at her labia.

Ruby brought her hands around Bonnie's torso and cupped her heavy breasts. She met Evan's eyes. He was watching them intently, the bulge in his jeans leaving no question as to his level of arousal.

Matt continued to lash Bonnie's right foot, counting softly as he did so.

Throughout the whipping, Bonnie alternated between cries of pleasure and yelps of pain.

When Matt moved to the left foot, Bonnie began to whimper. Still standing behind her, Ruby moved her hands so she could roll Bonnie's nipples between her fingers. They hardened and distended beneath her touch.

Allie, still crouched between Bonnie's legs, continued to elicit breathy cries of pleasure, while Matt's cruel whip pulled gasps and whimpers of obvious pain from his slave girl's lips.

"Ten," he finally said, taking a step back. "You did good, sweetheart. You should see the beautiful marks."

"Thank you, Sir," Bonnie breathed, her voice pitched high as Allie continued to tease and suckle her sex. "Oh, oh, oh…"

Matt put his hand on Allie's shoulder. "That's enough, Allie. She hasn't earned the right to come. Not yet."

Allie sat back on her haunches and wiped her mouth with the back of her hand. Her eyes were bright, her own pink nipples erect at the centers of her small, high breasts.

Liam appeared beside Matt, a tube of salve in his hand. Matt took the tube as Liam lifted Allie to her feet and took her into his arms. "Maybe I should introduce you to feet whipping, hmm?" he asked.

"No, thank you, Sir Liam," she replied quickly.

"I wasn't really asking your permission, sub girl," he retorted, a wicked gleam in his eye. "But first things first. Tonight is Bonnie's night."

He let Allie go. At a tap to her shoulder, she sank down to her knees.

Matt, done smoothing the healing cream over Bonnie's tortured soles, glanced toward Liam. "Bonnie's breasts could use a good work-over. Care do to the honors with the single tail while Evan flogs her back?" He glanced back at Evan. "That work for you?"

"You bet," Evan agreed. "But what about the other girls?"

"Patience is a good virtue to cultivate," Matt said. He nodded toward Ruby. "Go and join your sister sub, Ruby." As she did so, he added, "The two of you will kneel up at attention, side by side, and watch this lucky slave girl take a full body whipping. Spread your thighs wide and touch yourselves while you watch, but don't you dare come, either one of you, unless one of us orders you to."

"Yes, Sir," Allie and Ruby said in unison. They grinned at one another as they assumed their positions.

The guys released Bonnie's legs from the chains, though they left her arms tethered overhead. Liam whisked away the stool as the other two helped Bonnie, still blindfolded, stand upright. Evan accepted a large, multi-tressed flogger from Liam and moved behind Bonnie, while Liam took his place in front of her, the single tail whip in his hand.

Bonnie gasped when the whip flicked against her right breast. At the same time, Evan struck her between the shoulders with the flogger, the leather slapping sexily against her flesh.

Ruby stroked her sopping-wet cunt as she watched. Allie, beside her, did the same, and the scent of their joint arousal lightly perfumed the air.

Liam painted myriad tiny red welts all over Bonnie's round breasts while Evan struck her forcefully with the heavy flogger, reddening the skin on her shoulders and back. Matt, standing nearby to oversee the scene, had opened the fly of his jeans, and his hand was buried in his underwear. He watched the action hungrily as he stroked himself.

Bonnie wriggled in her chains and cried out breathily as the two men whipped her. Her color was high, her skin sheened with sweat.

Ruby was thrilled to her bones by the sexy scene. She would have loved to be the one tethered there, enduring what appeared to be quite an intense double whipping. If she weren't careful, she'd end up coming. She forced her fingers to slow their erotic dance, though she kept her hand at her sex as directed.

When Bonnie began to shudder, Matt said, "That's enough, guys. She's on the edge now. Just a puff will send her over." Both men lowered their whips and took a step back. Bonnie, panting and trembling, let her head fall back.

Matt looked over at Allie and Ruby. Allie was breathing rapidly, her fingers still moving between her spread thighs. Ruby, over-stimulated, had slid a finger into her tight heat, but didn't dare do more, too close to the edge of orgasm to risk it.

His smile was cruel. "The girls are all three pretty hot and bothered, both literally and figuratively speaking. What say we string them up on the water wall and cool them down a bit?"

"Excellent idea," Liam said enthusiastically.

Evan just smiled, his eyes fixed on Ruby.

The guys removed Bonnie's blindfold and released her from the cuffs and chains. Matt lifted his wife into his arms and carried her toward the water play area. Liam and Evan helped the girls to their feet and walked with them to the water wall.

Ruby shivered with anticipation as the men secured them to the wall, arms and legs spread wide. The guys put on the rubber coverall aprons and each took a water hose from the wall. Matt and Evan positioned themselves in front of the girls while Liam adjusted the water temperature.

When he took his place in front of Allie, he gave the other guys a nod. They all three pressed the triggers on their hose nozzles. A strong stream of warm water splashed between Ruby's legs. The sensation was instant and intense, and it wasn't long before Ruby shuddered, an impending orgasm hurtling upward through her body.

"Oh god," she gasped.

Allie and Bonnie were reacting with similar intensity, moaning and gasping as the steady stream of water provided direct, intense stimulation to their swollen sexes.

"Oh, oh, oh," Bonnie chanted, while Allie mewled, her entire body shaking.

"Now, girls," Liam cried. "Come for your Masters."

With a relieved sigh, Ruby let the climax crash over and through her, dragging her along in its tumultuous wake. She lost consciousness for a moment or two, wrapped in the arms of the powerful orgasm.

When she came to herself, Evan was beside her. He released her legs and then her arms from the wall. He caught her as she sagged, wrapping her in a large towel. He pulled her close into his arms, nuzzling his face against her neck.

"You're not done quite yet, sub girls," Liam said. "It's time to thank your Masters properly."

~*~

They led the women back into the main part of the dungeon. Both Allie and Bonnie lowered themselves gracefully to their knees. After a second, Ruby followed suit.

"I was thinking a nice blow job might be in order," Liam said, addressing both Matt and Evan. "That sound good to you guys?"

"Sounds great," Matt replied enthusiastically. "And let's add a little spice with a game Liam and I call musical subs."

"Musical subs?" Evan queried.

"Yeah," Liam said. "Remember that game in elementary school called musical chairs? It's like that, except instead of music, whenever one of us guys says to switch, the girls have to worship a different Master's cock."

Evan looked at Ruby. The other four knew each other well, and obviously had scened together often. Ruby and he had no such understanding when it came to playing with others. "Uh, that sounds okay to me," he ventured. "What about you, Ruby? Does that work for you?"

"Yes, Sir," she said promptly. The other two women were smiling broadly.

Liam and Matt were already stripping out of their clothing. Evan hesitated, surprised and confused by his feelings at that moment. Normally he'd leap at the chance to have three different lovely, sexy women take turns worshipping his cock. But if he were completely honest with himself, he would actually rather have taken Ruby up to their bedroom right then so he could make slow, sweet love to her in privacy.

But he didn't want to spoil the moment by acting like a jerk, so Evan went along with the rest of them. He unbuttoned his shirt and let it fall from his shoulders. His eyes on Ruby, he kicked off his shoes and pulled down his jeans and boxers.

The guys stood in front of their respective partners. Evan closed his eyes, sighing with pleasure as Ruby's sweet, hot mouth closed over his shaft. It felt so good, and his erection, which had flagged a little during the conversation, instantly hardened into a bar of steel. He was just reaching for her, his fingers eager to twist into her thick, soft hair, when Matt called out, "Switch."

The girls scooted around until Ruby was in front of Liam, Allie in front of Matt, Bonnie in front of Evan. Smiling up at him, Bonnie took his cock deep into her throat, not stopping until her nose was pressed against his pubic bone. She did something awesome with her throat muscles, and Evan couldn't deny it felt fantastic. But when he glanced at Ruby, who had taken Liam's shaft into her mouth as she cradled his balls, something twisted in his gut, and he pulled reflexively back from Bonnie.

Bonnie, not put off, just moved along with him, recapturing him with her mouth and sucking him in deep again as she stroked his balls. Evan closed his eyes, determined not to spoil things for the others, but the image that instantly rose in his mind's eyes was the lovely, dark-eyed Ruby.

"Switch," Liam called, and the girls at once repositioned themselves.

Allie wasn't quite as ferocious in her attentions, but she was just as skilled. Her touch was lighter, her tongue teasing along Evan's shaft until he actually thrust forward, reaching for her head to pull her onto his shaft. It felt incredible, and it wasn't long before a climax was gathering itself in his loins.

He didn't want to come in Allie's mouth, however. And more to the point, he didn't want another guy coming in Ruby's mouth. "Switch," he gasped, pulling back from Allie before he shot his load.

And there was his lovely girl, kneeling once more before him. She looked up at him with adoration in her eyes, and he stared back, his heart actually hurting in his chest with an emotion he wasn't quite ready to name. All he knew was that he was desperate for this woman. He was dizzy with lust, his body filled with light and heat as she expertly and lovingly worshipped his cock and balls.

He reached for her, entwining his fingers in her hair as he thrust into her mouth. Neither of those guys better call for a switch, because he had no intention of letting go of his girl. He moaned, the sound low and feral, as a powerful orgasm hurtled up from his balls and along his shaft, exploding against her tongue.

Ruby held on, kissing and milking him with her perfect mouth until he sagged with pleasure. Oblivious of the others, he sank to his knees in front of Ruby and pulled her into his arms.

"Ruby," he murmured into her hair, holding her name in his mouth like a prize as he held her close. He felt undone, more vulnerable and exposed than he'd ever felt in his life. "You," he whispered. "All I want is you, you, you."

Holy shit. He was in deep.

He pulled away from Ruby's embrace, his eyes opening as his awareness of their surroundings returned. Both Matt and Liam had apparently finished, as they were both standing with their wives in their arms.

Embarrassed to be kneeling, Evan, too, rose to his feet. He held out his hands, pulling Ruby up and into his arms. He closed his eyes again, hiding his confusion and discomfiture by nuzzling again against Ruby's hair.

What the hell was happening to him?

CHAPTER 13

After the dungeon play the night before, they'd all gone back upstairs for chocolate éclairs, coffee and brandy. Sometime around midnight, Evan and Ruby had said their good nights, leaving the other two couples to continue their visit.

They'd washed up quickly and tumbled into bed. Evan had been strangely quiet, but Ruby chalked it up to exhaustion. She'd curled around him, falling asleep almost the instant her head made contact with his warm, firm chest.

The next morning they awoke around nine. All was quiet on the ground floor, Allie and Liam apparently still asleep. While Evan made the coffee, Ruby unloaded the dishwasher and cleaned up what dishes and glasses were left over from the night before.

As they sat together at the table sipping their coffee, Evan said, "Hopefully Bob won't have any sudden emergencies today. Maybe I'll just *forget* to turn on my phone," he added with a grin. "Should we try the touristy thing today?"

"Sounds great," Ruby agreed. "And we can get breakfast along the way." They left a note for their hosts, letting them know of their plans, and headed out.

They went to a museum and then to the zoo. It was fun to do

vanilla couple things together. Ruby couldn't remember the last time she'd felt so comfortable with a guy, not only in the bedroom, but out of it.

While Evan seemed to enjoy himself, he remained quieter than usual. Ruby wondered if something was wrong, but didn't want to push him. After all, he was allowed to be quiet from time to time, and she was just happy to be with him.

In the afternoon, they ordered bento boxes from a Japanese food truck—Ruby got the honey lemongrass pork with yakisoba noodles and Evan got the spicy ginger beef—and took them to a nearby park. They sat under a tree near a small lake to eat their lunch. It was a beautiful, sunny day, and children ran and played nearby.

After they'd eaten, Ruby leaned back against the tree with a contented sigh. Evan was staring out at the water, a faraway look in his beautiful gray-green eyes.

"A penny for your thoughts," Ruby said lightly.

"What?" Evan turned to regard her.

"I said, a penny for your thoughts. You seem to be off somewhere in your head today. Is everything okay?"

"Uh, yeah. Sure. Just thinking about this week, I guess. The grand opening is this coming Saturday. I have a possible job opportunity in New Orleans after this. Bob had also said he's got something brewing in London, but he wasn't ready to discuss details yet."

"You're so like me," Ruby said with a smile. "We go where the wind blows—where it seems right. I can't imagine ever settling down in one place. At least not for a while—not until I've expended my wanderlust."

"Same here," Evan said. He smiled, but somehow it didn't reach his eyes.

Ruby's phone chimed in her bag. She rummaged inside and pulled it out to see. It was an email from Alan Chandler, a good friend she'd made when working for *Volunteers Around the World*, a group that specialized in literacy programs.

The subject read: *Help! Can you drop everything and come to Mexico City!*

Both intrigued and worried, Ruby clicked on the email.

Hi Ruby,

I hope you're doing well. I heard you were back in the States for a while. I am in something of a jam, as my father was just moved to hospice care (he has stage four lung cancer and we're at the end of a long, difficult road) and my mother is totally cracking up. I am scheduled to teach a new group of volunteers for the literacy program in rural Mexico, and I'm having a hell of a time finding a replacement.

I promised Ernesto I'd teach the Americans that are coming down for the training next week, but there's no way I'm going to make it. You've worked for so many of the programs that I bet you could teach the basics in your sleep. Is there any way you could pop down to Mexico City by Tuesday? I already checked with Ernesto, and he's cool with it.

Class starts first thing Wednesday morning. I would never impose like this if it wasn't an emergency. VAW can cover the plane ticket, and Ernesto says he can get you a teaching stipend as well. It's the usual five-day training intensive. You just need to follow the teacher's manual. It's a piece of cake.

Let me know, sweet girl. I'll be forever in your debt. I'd love to pay you back properly one day soon (wink, wink).

Hugs, Alan

"Everything okay?" Evan asked. "You look worried."

"A good friend is reaching out. His dad is dying, and he needs me to cover a training down in Mexico City."

"Mexico City?" Evan repeated.

"Yeah." Ruby handed Evan the phone.

As he read the email, his eyebrows furrowed, his mouth curving down in a frown. "Tuesday, huh," he said, handing back the phone. "That's only two days from now. You'd miss the grand opening."

"Yeah." Ruby sighed. "I really wanted to be there, too."

"Sounds like you've already made up your mind," Evan said tersely.

"Huh?"

"You said, 'I really wanted to be there.' That tells me you've already decided to go."

"Oh." Ruby looked at Evan, but he'd averted his face, staring out at the lake again. Did he expect her to refuse a friend in need?

Maybe she wasn't the only possibility on Alan's list. Surely there were other people he could tap? But he'd asked her, and clearly, he needed her.

Alan and she had dated for a while when they'd first met some years before. She sensed he would have been happy to pick up where they'd left off, even though he lived with a woman when he wasn't traveling for the job, but it wasn't in the cards, at least not in Ruby's cards.

Still, they had remained good friends, and they'd done a lot of good work together over the years. The literacy program was a worthwhile effort that had helped a lot of poor Mexican children catch up so they could enroll in school and have a chance for a better life.

But it would mean leaving Evan sooner than she'd planned.

"Do you think I should tell him I can't do it?" Ruby asked. She held her breath, not sure if she wanted Evan to say yes or no.

Their time together had been wonderful, and she felt closer to him than she had to any man in her life. But it had also been a whirlwind of intensity and passion. She'd been so caught up in their tempestuous romance that she hadn't really taken a moment to breathe. Maybe this offer had come at exactly the right time. It would be the break they both needed—a chance to take a step back and assess just what it was they shared between them.

Evan looked sharply at her, a range of emotions moving over his face that seemed to encompass anger, fear, desire, longing and sadness in equal measure. But when he spoke, his voice was light. "No, you should go. Your good friend needs you." He put a slight emphasis on the words *good friend*, his tone a little snarky.

Maybe she'd only imagined that. She was reading too much into Evan's expression and his tone. He was just having an off day. He was allowed. She would take him at face value.

"Yeah," she agreed. "You're right. I should do it."

He drew in a sudden breath, as if he hadn't expected the words.

She placed her hand on his arm. "We've been pretty intense these past nine days together. Maybe it's a good idea for us both to take a little time apart."

He pulled his arm away and got to his feet. "Absolutely," he said stridently. "I was just thinking the same thing."

~*~

Why was he being such a dick? He was acting like a petulant jerk, but he couldn't seem to stop himself. He had been looking forward to their being together during the grand opening of the BDSM Connections Event Center. True, he hadn't really thought about what would happen after next weekend, but he had expected to be the one to make the decision.

Now, it had been wrested away from him. She was leaving in two days, and who knew where he'd be in a week's time? He could stick around Portland for a while, he supposed—maybe stay with Bob or at a hotel. But he had never done anything like that in his life. Evan Stewart didn't wait around pining for some girl. He was the one who moved on, like the guys in the old Westerns on TV, riding off into the sunset.

And who was to say she'd even come back from Mexico? For all he knew, she might be off and running on her next volunteer adventure with that dude, Alan, who Evan had gotten the sense was more than just a friend, no matter how Ruby couched it. *"Wink, wink."* It made him want to puke.

Maybe it was for the best. After all, there was no way they could sustain the kind of intensity and passion they'd shared over these past days together. Maybe it was good to cut things off at the pinnacle, instead of waiting for the relationship to fizzle out, as they invariably did.

Meanwhile, he wouldn't ruin things by acting like a teenage boy. He would make the best of the time they had left. "The day is still young. Let's go to check out that street fair you were talking about earlier."

~*~

Evan headed out early Monday morning to meet the workmen who were coming to fix a leak in the roof of the warehouse. Allie and Liam had been out when they'd returned home the evening before, and this was the first chance Ruby had had to tell Allie of the new plans.

"Just like that?" Allie asked, frowning. "You're leaving tomorrow?"

They were already hard at work, finishing the last of the canes for the grand opening sale.

"I know it's really sudden," Ruby said. She explained Alan's predicament. "This is how my life works. Somehow, the next thing always appears at the right time. I love working with the children. I might even stay on, as Alan suggested."

Allie shook her head, her face scrunching in disapproval. "What about Evan? What about the incredible connection between the two of you? And now you're just going to fly away, and that's that?"

Ruby blew out an exasperated breath. "It's only for five days, Allie. I didn't make any further commitment, though they're always in need of volunteers. And anyway, Evan's heading off who knows where as soon as his job is over next weekend. What's a few days early in the scheme of things?"

Allie's expression was outraged, and she opened her mouth to continue her protest, but Ruby stopped her by laying a hand gently on her arm. "Listen, my dearest friend. I know you view the world through your romantic rose-colored love glasses, but not everyone is like Liam and you—destined to be together from the start. Evan's actually in favor of me going. I asked him what he thought when I showed him the email. He's the one who said I should go, before I even fully made up my mind."

"That's just his defense mechanism kicking in."

"Huh?"

"From what you've told me, he's not the kind of guy who would beg a girl to stay, but that doesn't mean he doesn't want you to. Or that it isn't a mistake to just take off like this. What're you afraid of, anyway? Are you afraid that maybe Evan *is* the love of your life, and that admitting it might somehow clip your wings and turn you into some kind of housewife drudge who waits at home washing dishes and scrubbing floors while her man goes to his eight to five job?"

Ruby laughed at the absurdity of Allie's remarks, though she couldn't deny some element of truth hidden beneath them. That was probably one reason she and Evan got along so well. Neither of them wanted any strings attached to their affection. Neither could tolerate the slightest hint of obligation or duty, which would contaminate the pure, sweet joy of being together in the moment.

She shrugged, not willing to continue the argument. "If he is the love of my life, as you say, the universe will let me know. Meanwhile, I have a good friend who needs me, and I'm giving less than a week of my time to help him out. If my leaving a few days before I had planned means Evan disappears off the face of the earth, then clearly, we weren't meant to be."

Allie grunted, but didn't say anything more on the subject. They worked together in silence for a while, and then Allie said, "I'm going to miss you, Ruby. I've really loved reconnecting like this. I hope it's not another decade before we get together again."

"Definitely not," Ruby said staunchly. "I love Portland, and I love the life you've built for yourself here. I'll definitely be back, sooner than later, I promise."

~*~

Allie arranged a dinner out on Monday night, which included Taggart and Rylee. Evan would have rather spent the time alone with Ruby, but he recognized it wouldn't be fair to claim all her attention. He did manage to get out of his head long enough to enjoy the meal and the company. He had no intention of behaving like a grumpy, possessive lover who was about to be jilted.

Nevertheless, he was gratified and deeply relieved when Ruby declined their hosts' invitation to join them at Club Paradise, a private BDSM club both couples belonged to. "Evan and I need some alone time tonight," Ruby said softly to Allie, who nodded her understanding.

When they returned to the house, Evan suggested a last session in the dungeon. He planned to give her a night she wouldn't soon forget.

They both stripped naked at the door of the dungeon. Evan had Ruby stand at attention, her hands locked behind her head. He moved slowly around her, using a heavy flogger on her back, shoulders, ass, thighs and breasts until she was panting, her skin rosy pink, her eyes bright with lust.

Setting down the flogger, he took her face in his hands and kissed her passionately until she was moaning against his mouth. His cock and balls ached with the need to fuck her, but the evening was still young.

"I've never caned that lovely ass," he noted. "I'd love to leave you some marks to remember me by. Would that please you?"

"Yes, Sir. Yes, please," Ruby said eagerly.

Evan had her lie down on the padded bondage horse, her torso draped along the top, her legs resting on the ledges on either side, her lovely ass and cunt on full display.

He tapped lightly against her bottom with the long rattan cane, further warming her skin. All negative thoughts flowed away as he allowed himself to fully enter the moment, entirely focused on what he was doing.

Power coursed through his blood like an aphrodisiac as the cane cracked against her flesh, eliciting a lovely, breathy yelp. A white welt appeared, quickly darkening to pink. He painted three more welts on her perfect ass. Each whistling, whippy blow was punctuated by another sweet cry of erotic pain.

When he couldn't stand it another second, he dropped the cane and pulled her toward him along the bench so her ass hung just off the end. He spit on his hand and fisted his cock, guiding it between her legs into her soft, moist heat.

She groaned as he entered her. He gripped her hips as he pulled her back onto his shaft. Her ass was hot to the touch, the welts an angry, dark red. The sadist in him thrilled to the realization that he'd put those marks on her willing flesh. She suffered for him, and he reveled in her suffering.

"Yes, yes, yes, yes," she chanted as he thrust and swiveled inside the tight grip of her sweet cunt. He reached beneath her, his fingers seeking the slick, wet folds and the hard nubbin of her clit. He rubbed hard and fast as he fucked her, and her words spiraled upward into an incoherent cry. They climaxed together, her body spasming and shuddering against him as he ejaculated deep inside her.

When she stilled and he caught his breath, he pulled out of her and helped her up from the bench. He lifted her into his arms and carried her to the recovery couch. He lay her gently on her stomach and proceeded to smooth salve over her welts.

Their clothes in hand, they returned upstairs to the empty house and continued up to the second floor. Evan drew a bath, adding scented oil to the steamy water. They climbed in together, Evan behind Ruby, his legs stretched out on either side of her.

Words that had been forming ever since her decision to go again tried to rise in his throat. *Don't go. Not yet.* But he refused to let them out of his mouth. Wasn't it only the day before that he'd been freaked out at how close they were getting—how fast they were moving? It was only because he hadn't been the one to make the decision to go first that he felt off kilter.

And wasn't that part of Ruby's unusual charm? Unlike every woman he'd been with since Marissa, Ruby didn't cling. She had never made demands on him, never wrapped possessive tentacles around him, threatening to drag him under. He should be grateful and glad that things would end so simply and so cleanly, without any hysteria or female drama.

And Bob had given him a list of a thousand last-minute urgent tasks to get ready for the grand opening. This way, he was free to fully focus on his work.

He wrapped his arms around the lovely, petite girl leaning against him and nuzzled his face in her soft hair. "Ruby," he whispered, a sudden spasm of longing piercing his heart like an arrow.

She twisted out of his embrace and turned in the water so she was facing him. She cradled his face in her hands and then kissed his mouth lightly. "Let's go to bed."

~*~

They dried each other with big, fluffy towels and then brushed their teeth, standing side by side at the single sink, watching each other in the mirror. When Ruby was done, she set her toothbrush in the cup set there for the purpose and turned around to see her marks.

"Ooh," she breathed, meeting Evan's eye in the mirror. "Those are awesome." Some of the welts were already fading, but there were a few darker ones that would remain for several days—a sweet reminder of their last night together.

"Glad you like them. I had fun giving them to you." Evan smeared another layer of Arnica over the welts, and then they went together to the bed. Ruby set her phone alarm for five o'clock, as she had an early flight out. It was already past eleven, but she could sleep on the plane.

"Just lie back and relax," she said to Evan. "I want to give you a full body massage."

He lay on his stomach and she straddled his thighs. She started slowly, working from his lower back upward, carefully pressing her fingers along either side of his spine. His shoulders were tight, and she spent a long time kneading the knotted muscles until they yielded at last, loosening and easing under her touch. She moved down his back again, massaging each section until it was soft and pliant beneath her fingers.

Then she climbed off him so she could focus on his long, muscular legs. She worked the thighs first and then moved down to the calves. Finally, she focused on his feet, pressing the padded ball, arch and heel of each foot and then pulling gently at each toe as the last of his tension slid away beneath her touch.

"Evan?" she said softly, thinking to turn him over and straddle his lovely cock for a good-night fuck before they slept.

He was still, his breathing deep and even.

"Evan?" she said a little louder, shifting so she could see his face. His eyes were closed. "I want to make love to you before we sleep."

He didn't move, save for a soft snore between parted lips.

With a rueful chuckle, Ruby snuggled up against him and closed her eyes.

She woke some time later. The room was pitch dark. A heavy but comfortable weight was on top of her, something hard nudging between her legs. As she came more fully conscious, she wrapped her arms around Evan's back and arched her hips upward, eagerly taking him inside her.

They made love without speaking, Ruby still half-caught in a dream. Evan's hard, thick cock moved perfectly inside her, sending several sweet, powerful climaxes radiating through her body. He stroked her face as he fucked her, as if memorizing it with his fingers.

He came with a quiet cry, his body heating suddenly on top of hers as he held her tight. Then he slid from her, lowering himself until his face was between her legs. He licked her clit, which was swollen and throbbing from the lovemaking.

She moaned, shifting slightly to get away from the overstimulation of his tongue against her. But he held her fast, his hands on her inner thighs. He licked and suckled until she stopped resisting him. His warm, insistent tongue lapped over her, the intensity of the pleasure mounting until it burst out of her in a powerful series of orgasms strung together like beads that he pulled from her, one by one by one...

She was only dimly aware as he pulled himself up beside her in the dark. As he took her into his arms, she slid helplessly back into a deep, dreamless sleep...

~*~

Evan was awake when Ruby's phone alarm started to chirp. She didn't react, still dead to the world. She looked so peaceful lying there. Her dark hair lay in a riot around her face, her long lashes brushing her soft cheeks. He hated to wake her, and even toyed with the sudden, evil idea of turning off the alarm and going back to sleep. If she missed the flight, oh well...

But no, he wouldn't do such an immature thing. She had a plane to catch, and he'd promised to get her to the airport. He reached for her phone and turned off the alarm. Then he shook her gently. "Ruby. Ruby, wake up. It's time to get up. Your alarm went off."

She opened her eyes, a smile moving over her pretty mouth as she focused on his face. "Evan. I was just having the best dream."

He grinned. "You can tell me all about it on the way to the airport. Now, get that pretty little butt in gear. You've got a plane to catch."

When they came downstairs, to their surprise, Liam and Allie were in the kitchen, the coffee brewed, blueberry muffins on the table, bacon sizzling in the frying pan.

"Hey, you guys didn't have to get up," Ruby said, smiling at them.

"We wanted to," Allie, still in her robe, said from the stove. "You need a good breakfast before you travel." She dumped a mound of scrambled eggs onto a plate and approached the table.

Evan caught Liam's eye. He was already seated, a cup of coffee in front of him. He was shirtless, his hair mussed, his expression bleary. Evan grinned, and Liam smiled sleepily back. Clearly, their getting up early hadn't been *his* idea.

"We've got a little time," Evan said, sliding onto a chair and reaching for the coffee pot. "This was really thoughtful of you, Allie. You guys have been amazing hosts."

"You really have," Ruby agreed enthusiastically as she took a muffin and put it on her plate. "If you guys ever got tired of your day jobs, you could open a BDSM bed-and-breakfast. How many B&B's have a fully equipped dungeon?"

Liam piled his plate with bacon and eggs. He handed the egg platter to Evan, who shook his head. "I don't have much of an appetite in the morning," he explained. The truth was, his stomach was in knots. He doubted he'd be able to get any food past the lump in his throat. "Coffee's great, though."

Ruby ate two muffins and several pieces of bacon. Evan smiled as he watched her. He loved that she wasn't always obsessing about her weight, as so many women seemed to. Was there anything about her that he didn't love?

Well, yes. There was a rather huge thing. She was leaving him in a couple of hours, and she wasn't the least bit teary or apologetic about it. As sweet and loving as she'd been since the moment he'd met her, she seemed perfectly content to let it end. What was wrong with her? She was behaving just like…just like *he* always did…

They said their goodbyes to their hosts and headed out to Evan's rental, Ruby's overnight bag and huge backpack in tow. Allie and Liam had assured Evan he was welcome to stay at their place as long as he needed, but Evan doubted he'd take them up on it. That bed would be entirely too large and empty, now that Ruby would no longer be in it. Better to make a clean break, just like always.

They were quiet on the drive to the airport. There was little traffic, and they made it in record time. At the airport, everything went smoothly, and before Evan knew it, Ruby was checked in and standing at the security gate for international flights.

"Well, here we are," Evan said, his tone over-bright.

Ruby looked up at him, her large, dark eyes suddenly pooling with tears. "I'm going to miss you, Evan Stewart," she said, reaching up to pull him into an embrace.

He held her tightly, blinking back tears of his own. He was the first to pull away. He'd never liked long goodbyes. "Have a safe flight, Ruby. If you think of it, text me that you arrived safely."

Now, why had he said that? That implied some kind of ownership—some kind of ongoing connection that he had no right to assume.

But Ruby just smiled and nodded. "I will," she said softly. "Thanks for *everything*. You're an amazing man, Evan."

"Back at ya, babe," he said stupidly, aware even as the words tumbled from his mouth that he sounded like an idiot. He started to say something else, but Ruby had turned away, already caught up in the snaking line moving toward the security gate.

CHAPTER 14

Ernesto, the Mexico coordinator for Volunteers Around the World, was waiting at the gate when Ruby arrived at the airport in Mexico City. "*Hola, amiga*," he cried happily as she came through customs. He was a big, burly man with a mop of graying curly hair and a full beard. He caught her in a bear hug as she reached him.

"It's so good to see you," Ruby said, falling naturally into Spanish. "It's been too long. How are Maria and the kids?"

Ernesto insisted on carrying Ruby's bags. They caught up on each other's lives as they made their way out of the crowded airport, though Ruby left out any discussion of her BDSM lifestyle, which would probably have given her old friend a heart attack.

They stopped at a phone kiosk to buy a SIM card for Ruby's phone and then made their way outside to a beat-up Chevy that was idling by the curb. A man with the dark, blue-black hair and chiseled features of an indigenous Mexican looked up with a nod and a smile as they approached. He popped the trunk, and Ernesto loaded Ruby's things.

Ernesto climbed in beside the driver as Ruby sank gratefully into the backseat, tired from the long day of travel.

"This is Carlos," Ernesto said, looking from Ruby to the man beside him. "He's the maintenance man for our building and an excellent driver."

"It's nice to meet you, Carlos," Ruby said with a smile. "Thanks for coming to get me."

"My pleasure, *señorita*," Carlos replied, his eyes crinkling good-naturedly.

As they pulled away from the curb and inched their way into the traffic, Ruby popped the new SIM card into her phone and then shot a quick text to Allie to let her know she'd arrived safely.

Allie responded back immediately. *"Thanks for letting me know. We miss you already!"*

She sent back a heart emoticon and then started a text message to Evan. *"Arrived safely. I miss you so fucking much already."*

Wait a minute. What was she doing?

She deleted the second sentence.

Before she could hit send, Ernesto twisted back to update her on all the latest scandals and emergencies that plagued their nonprofit program. Ruby did her best to engage in the conversation, trying to put Evan out of her mind.

She failed.

Leaving him had been harder than she'd expected. She wasn't one to linger when it was time to go. So why was it so hard now?

He'd been reserved on the ride to the airport, barely glancing at her or speaking to her. She understood he hadn't wanted her to leave. She'd seen the look of raw longing and pain that had spasmed across his features as they'd said goodbye. If he'd said something—anything... But he hadn't asked her to stay.

Recalling it now, her heart contracted with longing and remorse.

What the hell am I doing here?

Why had she agreed to cover for Alan? Surely he could have found someone else? Why had she left Evan when they still could have had nearly a week together?

If he'd asked her to stay, would she have?

Okay, hold on. This isn't like you, second-guessing yourself.

Whatever amazing connection they'd shared over the past ten days, it was over now. She still had a few of the marks from the delicious caning he'd given her, but those would be gone soon, leaving only her memories. What was done, was done. She'd made a choice, and she would need to live with its consequences. By the time she finished this teaching assignment, he'd have left Portland for who knew where.

What she needed was a fresh start. She'd been bumming around in the US for long enough. She'd always wanted to go to Australia and New Zealand. Maybe that would be her next adventure.

When Ernesto finally faced front again, Ruby looked down at the unsent message on her phone. She typed a little more. *"Arrived safely in Mexico City. Miss you already."*

Before she continued to overthink it, she hit the send button. Why shouldn't she admit she missed him? Because the truth was, though it had only been twelve hours or so since they'd parted, she missed him with every particle of her being.

They pulled into the VAW headquarters, a crumbling two-story apartment building in the Tabacalera district that had been transformed into a teaching center and hostel. Carlos drove off with a wave, and Ernesto took Ruby to the small bedroom where she'd be staying. It was one of the nicer rooms with its own WC, though the communal shower was the down the hall.

"Maria is waiting for me," Ernesto said, "but Isabella and Gordon are around here somewhere. They want to take you to dinner."

"Terrific," Ruby said. "I can't wait to see them again."

The couple oversaw the various volunteer programs VAW conducted all around Mexico, while Ernesto handled the recruiting and non-profit funding. Ruby especially liked Isabella, a sweet, soft-spoken woman with a will of steel. If something needed doing, Isabella was the one to get it done.

Ernesto's mention of dinner made Ruby's stomach growl, the breakfast back in Portland a distant memory. She had subsisted on pretzels and crappy coffee for most of the day. "And dinner sounds great. I could really go for some *chilaquiles verdes.*"

As Ruby put away her few things and washed up, she tried not to obsess over Evan's lack of response to her text. She shoved her phone into her bag, ordering herself to forget about it.

The evening passed quickly as Ruby caught up with her friends, ate great food and drank too much tequila. When she finally pulled her phone from her bag to steal a surreptitious look, she saw that the battery had died, which made her feel better regarding its silence.

When she got back to her room, she plugged in the phone and powered it up. Her heart jolted pleasantly as she looked at the screen. There was a text from Evan, and her finger actually trembled slightly as she clicked it open.

"Glad you arrived safe. Be well."

Not exactly a declaration of undying love, but better than nothing.

~*~

The key was to stay busy. He took care of all Bob's last minute issues and helped the various vendors get their displays ready. While he was working, he actually managed to put her out of his mind for whole minutes at a time.

Despite their kind offer to let him stay, Evan had moved out of the Byrne house and into a spare room in Bob's place for the duration of the week. Though he told himself it would be easier this way, since Bob and he had a lot to do, the truth was he didn't want to stay in that bed with Ruby no longer beside him.

He sent the Byrnes one of Taggart's gorgeous hand-braided bullwhips as thanks for their generous hospitality. As he signed the note he included with it, he nearly added Ruby's name, but caught himself in time.

She hadn't called, and taking her cue, he hadn't either. Instead, she sent him breezy texts from Mexico, as if they were just pals who had shared a fun week. He responded in kind, keeping it neutral.

On Wednesday, Bob discussed in detail with Evan his latest potential project overseas. "My BDSM Connections personals and product sites are really taking off in Europe and Great Britain, and I want to set up a BDSM Connections Event Center in London. There's this fantastic private BDSM club coming up for sale. I know the couple that's selling it. They've given me first dibs, if I'm interested. It's got a fully equipped dungeon, plus rooms for munches, demonstrations and play parties."

"That sounds like an ideal setup. You've got an excellent model in place now," Evan said enthusiastically.

"Yeah," Bob agreed with a wide grin. "I've got a lot going on in the States right now, but if you were available and willing, I'd love to send you over there in a week or so to check out the club in person. Because there's a fully equipped dungeon that's already licensed for BDSM play, I'm thinking we might want to actually run it as a nightly club, which would require a full-time presence. A couple of months should be enough time to get it up and running to our specifications, especially if you had someone working with you. After that, we'll put someone local in as manager."

When Bob mentioned the sum of money he'd pay Evan, it was a no-brainer, especially when he added in a bonus incentive if things were in place in less than two months. If the place already had a good presence, it should be doable.

"...especially if you had someone working with you..."

Ruby would be the perfect partner to help him get the project off the ground. She was experienced and comfortable in the scene and wouldn't have an issue with picking up and moving overseas for a few months.

The thought had leaped into his mind before he could censor it, but once it was lodged in his brain, it refused to budge. Just to test out its validity, Evan asked casually, "Did you have someone in mind as my partner or...?" He let the sentence trail off.

"Actually, before she disappeared, I'd been thinking of that sweet little number you've been spending a lot of time with," Bob said with a wink. "She's some kind of world traveler, right? There was definite chemistry between the two of you. I had been hoping she'd be here for the grand opening so you could do a repeat flogging demo together."

You and me both, buddy.

"She had to help out a friend in Mexico City," Evan said aloud, keeping his voice light. "She might be back in Portland soon, but not in time for the grand opening."

Now, why had he said that? He had no idea if she'd be back or not.

Wait a second. *Why* did he have no idea? Why the hell hadn't he tried to pin her down? Why had he just let her waltz out of his life?

Because Evan Stewart doesn't...

"Fuck that," he said aloud. Who cared what the *old* Evan used to do? Everything had changed since Ruby had exploded into his life.

"What's that?" Bob, who had turned away to look at something on his phone, shot him a funny look.

"Nothing. Sorry. Just talking to myself." He forced a smile. "So, when do you need an answer?"

"Mull it over for a few days. Get in touch with Ruby if you think she'd be interested. We'll talk after the grand opening."

Bob liked to spend his evenings at Hardcore, and to distract himself, Evan had tagged along a few times. When he was there, he enjoyed the casual BDSM play well enough, but Ruby's lovely face and gorgeous body kept insinuating themselves into his mind and heart. More than once, a play partner had asked if he was okay. He'd apologized, aware he hadn't been giving them the attention they deserved, and done his best to stay focused.

On Thursday, Evan flew to San Francisco for the day to meet with the latest tenants he'd found to stay in his house for the next few months. As he stood on the old wraparound porch, an image of Ruby suddenly leaped into his mind, though that wasn't unusual, since it happened about six hundred times a day. She'd love the old house with its cozy rooms and the wildflower gardens in back and front. If they ever decided to settle down for a while, San Francisco was as good a place as any. They could walk to nearby coffee bars and local hangouts, or take a streetcar into the city.

Settle down?

"Okay, Stewart," he muttered to himself. "You're definitely losing what little is left of your mind."

Though Ruby and he continued to keep in touch, texting once or twice a day, they kept it light. He composed much more elaborate texts and emails in his head, but managed to pull himself back from the brink each time.

He wanted to tell her about the London opportunity, but something held him back. If she had already moved on in her mind, he didn't want to come across as begging her to come back to him. If there was a way to work it casually into a conversation, he might consider it. But this way, as long as he didn't ask her directly, her joining him in London remained a possibility, however unlikely. If he asked outright and she refused... No. He would wait until the time was right. And if the time never seemed right, then that was what was meant to be.

Saturday night arrived at last. The vendors were in place at the various booths, the toys he'd tried out with Ruby set up and ready for action. If only she could have been there to help him demonstrate the wares...

Stop it, he ordered himself. He'd traveled that path of thought way too often over the past few days. No point in rehashing it now. He had a lot of work to do to make sure everything went smoothly.

They'd set up scene stations in the dungeon area, and Matt, Bonnie, Allie and Liam had all volunteered to oversee the play. Taggart did several whip and flogging demonstrations, his lovely partner volunteering as the subject of his attentions. Evan's heart ached as he watched them, and he turned away.

Ruby texted him around nine, wishing him success with the grand opening. *"I wish I was there with you. It would have been fun."*

So, why aren't you, damn it?

Strike that. No pressure. Everything was cool.

Except that it wasn't.

The turnout for the event was excellent, the place packed nearly to capacity. People had arrived with their wallets, and by the end of the night, most of the gear and toys Bob had bought for resale had been sold, along with much of the inventory in the various independent booths.

When the party finally ended and the doors closed at midnight, Bob pronounced the grand opening a resounding success. "I already have signups for every weekend for the next two months, plus a few events scheduled during the week. The new manager will be coming on board next week." He looked around the large space with satisfaction. "Let's leave this mess until the morning."

As Evan nodded his agreement, Bob added, "I'm too keyed up to go to bed. What say we head over to Hardcore to celebrate? The place should be hopping about now."

"I can't keep up with you, Bob," Evan said with a laugh. "You run rings around me."

Bob beamed at the compliment.

"I'll handle cleanup in the morning," Evan added. "I'll be sure to tiptoe out so you can sleep in."

"Unless I get lucky and don't come home at all," Bob said with a wink.

The next morning, Evan woke before eight and was unable to fall back asleep. He grabbed his phone and stared at the screen. Nothing.

"Everything went great last night," he typed. *"How are things in volunteer land?"*

He held the phone in his hand a while longer, willing her to reply, but the screen remained blank. It was two hours later in Mexico City. She was probably already teaching.

Setting the phone back on the nightstand, he got up and showered and shaved. When he walked past Bob's ajar door, he couldn't help but grin. The bed was made, no sign that Bob had ever come home. *Good for you*, Evan thought. *At least someone got lucky.*

Evan had bagged all the garbage and debris left over from the event and was just about done sweeping when Taggart appeared at the warehouse door. He had a cardboard tray with two cups of coffee in one hand, a bakery bag in the other. "Hey there. I was hoping I'd find you here. I brought you coffee. Allie told me how you like it."

"Hey, Taggart," Evan called back, setting down his broom. He had always liked the big, gruff man, ever since they'd met on the BDSM convention circuit, where Taggart used to regularly sell his amazing impact toys, before his online business took off. Evan headed toward him and accepted a cup of coffee. "Thanks, that was thoughtful of you."

Taggart held up the grease-stained white bag he had in his other hand. "I also picked up these awesome egg sandwiches from my favorite food truck. Fried eggs with ham, avocado and cheese and a good dose of hot sauce on toasted sourdough. You got time to take a break?"

Evan, who hadn't bothered with breakfast, realized he was hungry. "Sure. That sounds great. Let's go out back to the picnic table."

As they walked to the back door, Taggart said, "So, things went good last night, huh? I practically sold out of my inventory. I already have two full time guys working with me. I'm going to have to hire more if things keep up at this pace."

"Yeah, sales were brisk all around," Evan agreed. "People really enjoyed the live demos with the equipment. The whole event was a success. Bob's pleased."

The morning was still cool, the sun glimmering through the trees in a clear blue sky. As they sat on opposite sides of the picnic table, Taggart said, "It was good to finally see you last night. We missed you at dinner on Wednesday. And we missed you again Friday night at Bonnie and Matt's house. If I didn't know better, I'd think you were avoiding us." He flashed a grin. "Is Bob really that hard a taskmaster that he had you working nights?"

Evan shrugged, looking away. It was true, he had passed on the various invitations that came in from Ruby's friends once she'd gone. As nice as they all were, he would have felt like a fifth wheel if he'd hung out with the couples. It would have made Ruby's absence all the more difficult to handle. "There were lots of last minute things to attend to. You know how it is."

"Uh huh." Taggart didn't sound convinced. He handed a sandwich across the table. "You look like shit, Evan."

Evan barked a laugh as he took the sandwich. "Gee, thanks."

"I'm serious, dude. I've seen that look before."

"Oh, yeah? And just where have you seen this look, whatever it is?" He kept his tone light, but he couldn't quite meet Taggart's discerning gaze.

"In the mirror. Before Rylee kicked some sense into me."

Now Evan looked back, curious. "What're you talking about?"

"Before she burst into my life, I lived alone and scened with strangers on the road, or at anonymous clubs. I used my work to isolate myself. I kept anyone who might actually see past the armor of my defenses at arm's length. If a woman pushed too hard, or threatened to get too close, I kicked her to the curb. Sound familiar?"

"What?" Evan said, pretending not to understand.

"*You*, my friend," Taggart said firmly. "I was a lot like *you*. Now, I'm not saying we're identical or had the same life experience or anything like that. But from the outside looking in, you sure as hell look familiar."

Evan's face heated. Instead of answering, he took a bite of the breakfast sandwich. "Hey, this is really good."

"Let me ask you something," Taggart persisted, apparently not to be deterred. "When was the last time you had a relationship—one that lasted longer than the time it took to finish a gig and move on?"

"Whoa, what is this? Why're you giving me the third degree, dude?" Evan countered. He held up his sandwich. Taggart had yet to touch his. "You gonna eat your breakfast, or what?" He took another large bite and followed it with a swig of coffee.

Taggart shook his head, a half smile quirking his mouth. "Okay, you don't have to answer if you don't want. I'll put the focus back on me. Before Rylee, I liked to think of myself as footloose and fancy-free, as the old saying goes. I'd pick up hot girls at clubs, share a spicy scene, and move on. But the truth, one I had a hard time accepting, was that I was hiding my heart because I was a chicken shit who was afraid of getting hurt. Even with Rylee, I did my damnedest to fuck things up."

"Yeah?" Evan said, interested in spite of himself, as well as touched that Taggart would open up like that with him.

"Yeah," Taggart said emphatically. "I was so fucked up that I actually tried to break up with her. To throw away the best thing that ever happened to me."

"No kidding." Evan thought of the pretty, athletic girl who clearly adored Taggart. "So, what happened?"

"She tore me a new one, that's what," Taggart said with a laugh. "She called me on my shit. She made me see that being loved, and loving someone back, wasn't only okay, but a wonderful thing. She helped me accept that I was worthy of love, no matter how fucked up I thought I was."

His words pierced Evan's heart like a sharp dagger. Maybe that's why Ruby had left. Maybe he hadn't done a good enough job of letting her know how much she meant to him.

How much did she mean to him?

Taggart's confession threw a bright light on the secret Evan had been keeping from himself.

Holy shit.

He was in love with Ruby Beckett.

He'd been in love with her from the second he'd met her.

And he'd never told her.

What was he so fucking afraid of?

Aloud, he said, "I'm really happy for you guys. But what's this got to do with me?"

"Ruby Beckett, that's what."

Evan drew in a sharp breath. Even hearing her name hurt.

"You miss her, don't you?" Taggart asked, his voice suddenly gentle.

To Evan's horror, tears filled his eyes, one of them slipping down his cheek. He brushed it quickly away. "Fuck, yeah," he admitted.

"So what're you going to do about it?"

"Huh?"

"She went to Mexico, right? Some kind of volunteer gig?"

"Yeah. Some dude had a family emergency and begged her to step in for him."

"For how long?"

"Five days."

"Five days," Taggart repeated. "So, she left on Tuesday, and today's Sunday..." He looked up at the ceiling, apparently doing calculations in his head. "So she should be done today, right?"

"Yeah, but we hadn't talked about the future at all. She's a traveling gypsy, just like me. For all I know, she's already got another gig lined up in some other part of the world."

Taggart shook his head. "Listen to me, Evan. Don't do what I almost did. Don't fuck this up. There was something between the two of you that is rare and wonderful. Something that needs to be nurtured, not tossed away the second you face a little bump in the road. We all saw it. Even if the two of you are too stupid to admit it, you're crazy in love with each other."

"What, are you guys sitting around discussing me and Ruby?" Evan tried to laugh, but it came out as more of a bark.

"You bet your ass we are, buddy. Because we all know real love when we see it, and we've all had our issues getting there. A love like this comes along maybe once in a lifetime if you're lucky."

Love.

The word lodged deep in his heart, sending a sharp, sweet pain of longing through his being.

He looked up at Taggart, no longer trying to hide the tears that had welled again in his eyes. "But what do I do? She's gone now. I let her go."

"I'll tell you exactly what you're going to do. You're going to get your ass on a plane and you're going to fly down to Mexico City. You're going to find Ruby Beckett, and you're going to tell her you love her. If she has a problem with that, you will tell her to cut the shit and face the truth, just like Rylee did me."

CHAPTER 15

As the days passed, Ruby tried to keep Evan from constantly infiltrating her thoughts, but she never quite managed it. Like a cat, he had a habit of slinking back and curling up in the warm corners of her mind, no matter how she tried to distract herself with teaching and revisiting her favorite haunts in the city with her old friends.

She finished the last day of training at two o'clock on Sunday. She had decided not to stay on as a volunteer for the literacy program. She hadn't made any plans for the next great adventure because she'd been waiting…hoping…

Why hadn't he asked her, not once, what her plans were after the teaching assignment was over? Didn't he care enough to even find out what she might be doing?

But then, why hadn't she asked him about his plans? Early on, he'd said he'd be leaving after the grand opening. Was he already on a plane heading to his next adventure?

Ruby's cell phone vibrated in her pants pocket, the continuing buzz indicating a phone call. She pulled out the phone, excited in spite of herself. Maybe he'd just been waiting until Sunday, now that both of them were free.

Yes! That must be it!

But it wasn't Evan calling. Allie's picture was on the screen. Ruby stepped out into the hallway to take the call. "That's good timing," she said by way of greeting, trying to keep the disappointment out of her voice that Allie wasn't Evan. "We're just finishing up here."

"Good. Because you have about three hours to get yourself to the airport."

"Huh? What're you talking about?"

"I bought you a ticket. A direct flight to Portland on Aeromexico. You need to get your ass back here."

"But—" Ruby began.

Allie cut her off. "But nothing. You're in love with Evan Stewart."

It wasn't a question, but rather a declaration. Though Ruby hadn't allowed herself to even think those dangerous words, the truth of them resonated like a tuning fork inside her, the sound pure and filled with longing.

"Yes," she whispered in agreement, tears filling her eyes. "Is he still in Portland?"

"Yes. That's why you need to get back here pronto, before he heads off to who knows where."

"But—"

Again, Allie cut her off. "But nothing. Evan's been mooning around like a lost puppy since you left. Oh, he tried to put up a good front, pretending to smile, going through the motions, but he's a mess. The guy is crazy in love with you, but too stupid to figure it out on his own. It's up to you, Ruby. You need to get back and knock some sense into his head, just like I'm trying to do with you."

"But—" Ruby tried again, to no avail.

"Take it from me, I know firsthand—men can be total jackasses when it comes to admitting they're in love. Don't join him in the donkey ranks, Ruby. You're a strong, courageous woman. So use some of that courage. Get your ass back here and face him. I'll forward your ticket info as soon as we hang up. You pack your things and get your butt to the airport. Now."

Her Mexican hosts weren't happy to see her go, having planned a party for that evening, during which she was pretty sure Isabella was going to press her to stay on. Ruby felt bad for leaving them so abruptly, but when she explained that she had an emergency and had a flight scheduled, they seemed to understand.

On the way to the airport, the cab driver tried to take her on a rather circuitous route through the city. But when she barked directions at him in Spanish, he behaved himself.

She arrived at the terminal with an hour to spare. Even as she was checking in, she kept telling herself this was crazy. Here she was, flying back to confront a man about love. She'd never done anything like it in her life.

What if Allie's plan backfired? What if she was wrong, and Evan had already moved on to the next conquest? After all, he hadn't dropped the slightest hint of this supposed love during their texts over the past five days.

But then again, neither had she.

The thought of seeing Evan again slung her heart sideways. To distract herself while waiting at the gate, she watched with idle curiosity as the passengers disembarked from the plane that would soon take her back to Portland. It was mildly amusing to guess which ones were tourists and which were native, not that it was really difficult. The dark man in the business suit and sunglasses was native. The large, garishly dressed couple who were talking loudly in English were not.

Then a tall, broad shouldered man appeared carrying a small overnight bag. His auburn hair was streaked with gold, cut longish on top and short on the sides. He had a Roman nose and a square jaw. As if drawn to her by her gaze, he turned his beautiful gray-green eyes in her direction and then stood stock-still, so that the middle-aged woman behind him nearly collided into him.

All the air whooshed out of Ruby's lungs, her heart kicking into high gear. *Evan*, she mouthed. There he stood, in the flesh, even more gorgeous than her memories. His face lit up like a Christmas tree as they stared at one another. And then he began to walk again, moving faster and faster until he reached her.

She rose as he approached, still not fully comprehending what was happening. His arms opened as he got to her, and she slipped into his warm, strong embrace, pressing her cheek against his firm chest as he held her close. When his grip loosened, she lifted her face to his. They kissed for a long moment, their tongues touching, the breath sighing between them.

They were startled apart by the loud speaker saying, first in Spanish and then in English, that the flight would be boarding shortly for Portland.

They looked at each other and started to laugh. "What're you doing here?" they asked each other in unison.

"Allie called and…"

"Taggart read me the riot act, and I realized…"

"I think we've been manipulated by those guys," Ruby finally said when they'd sorted out their stories.

"Because they care about us," Evan said with a good-natured laugh. "Apparently we're both total idiots, did you know that?"

Ruby grinned back at him. "I'm beginning to figure that out."

Again the loudspeaker interrupted them, this time calling for anyone who needed extra time to board. "Oh, shit," Ruby said. "What're we going to do? I've got a flight back, and you just got here."

"What do you want to do?" Evan stared down in her eyes, and she could feel the power and passion in his gaze.

"I want to be with you," she whispered.

He put his hands on her shoulders. "I love you, Ruby. I've loved you from the second I saw you. I know that sounds insane but—"

Ruby put her finger to his lips. "I love you, Evan. I should have said it sooner. I should have let you know. I guess I was waiting…"

"I don't know what the hell I was waiting for," Evan interrupted with a laugh. He looked around the crowded airport. "I've never been to Mexico City. Maybe we could stay a few days and sort things out? Have an actual vacation together, just you and me?"

"Yes," Ruby said excitedly. "That's a great idea. Let me just see about this ticket."

They walked together to the credenza by the gate. "I have a ticket for this flight and I already checked in," Ruby explained. "But a family emergency has come up and I need to see if I can reschedule for a later date?"

The young woman lifted her head, her expression grim. "If you've already checked in, it's unlikely," she said ominously. Standing on tiptoes, Ruby noticed the Spanish novel on her desk, one of those bodice-ripping romances with swashbuckling heroes and swooning heroines.

She switched to Spanish, deciding to tell the clerk the truth. The woman listened, her grim expression softening and then lifting into a wide smile. *"Eso es muy romántico,"* she said, now busily tapping on her screen. After a moment, she looked up and continued in Spanish, "I could get you on a flight in two days. I'll be able to waive the two hundred dollar rebooking fee."

"You're wonderful," Ruby said sincerely.

She turned to Evan, translating what the clerk had said about the flight. "Does that work? We can spend two days here and then fly back to Portland?"

"Like a charm," Evan agreed. Turning to the clerk, he flashed a smile. "Can you get a ticket for me, too, señorita?"

Apparently still entranced by their romantic tale, she agreed that she could. As Evan pulled out his wallet, the clerk said in Spanish to Ruby, "He's absolutely gorgeous, girlfriend. Don't ever let that one go."

~*~

The first thing each of them did was text their friends—Evan connecting with Taggart, Ruby with Allie, to let them know they would be staying in Mexico for two days and would forward the return flight information. They shared the replies with each other, laughing.

Allie had texted back, *"What's the emoticon for fist pump?!"* Taggart had replied, *"Good job, dude. Score another one for true love."*

Ruby found a charming boutique hotel off the beaten path. As soon as they entered the room and dropped their bags, Evan started to speak, but Ruby stopped him by pulling him down for a kiss. Her mouth was eager, even urgent, and Evan let himself be swept into the kiss.

He pulled her close. Her mouth was sweet, her skin soft. As he slid his hands along her bare arms, she shivered. He dropped his arms, his fingers seeking the hem of her embroidered sundress. He lifted it, pulling it over her head.

She shook her hair, which spilled in shiny waves over her bare shoulders. Her lacy bra had a clasp in front, and she reached for it, letting her lovely breasts tumble free. At the same time, he reached for her silky panties, tearing them from her body in his eagerness.

She hurled herself again into his arms. Evan ducked his head and kissed her throat, her shoulders, her breasts. She clung to him, breathless, as he slid his tongue over her nipple and drew it into his mouth. His hands on her waist, he guided her to the large bed that took up most of the room.

As he pressed her down onto the mattress, she reached for him, gripping fistfuls of his shirt. He pulled away from her just long enough to kick off his shoes as he yanked his shirt over his head. His eyes on her, he pulled off his jeans and boxers, his fully erect cock springing free.

Ruby reached for him again, her lips parted, her eyes shining. He crouched beside her, placing one hand on her neck, the other between her legs. He could feel the pulse at her throat as he brushed his knuckles lightly against her sex. He kept his eyes on her face as he rubbed his thumb against her clit.

She moaned.

He tightened his grip on her throat as he continued to stroke her.

A shudder wracked her body. "Please," she begged throatily. "Please...fuck me. Fuck me, Sir..."

The Dom in him thrilled to the honorific, but he ignored her pleas, continuing to stroke her perfect cunt. He dipped his fingers into her and drew a long line of silky wetness over her labia. She moaned again, color rising up her chest and spreading into her cheeks.

Then, all at once, she thrust her hands at his chest, knocking him back onto the bed. He barked a startled laugh as she climbed over him.

"I *said* please," she gasped, though her eyes were dancing. She eased herself onto him, enveloping his cock in her velvet, tight heat. As she rocked, he placed his hands on her hips. He tried to keep his eyes open so he could watch her. She was wild and beautiful, her breasts heaving, her hair flying, her cunt tight and wet around his cock.

But as she swiveled over him, the pleasure was too great. His eyelids closed of their own accord, his mouth going slack. A rising climax moved through him in widening ripples as she held onto his shoulders and rocked against him.

"Evan, Evan," she murmured softly as he groaned helplessly and surged up against her. She pressed her knees hard against his thighs, clinging to him as the waves of a juddering orgasm rolled relentlessly over him.

"Ruby," he cried, his voice breaking. "Ruby, my darling, my love. I love you. I love you. I love you..."

~*~

Ruby lay beside Evan in a pleasant stupor. She'd come hard and fast as she'd straddled him, and it had taken the edge off her desperate need of him. There would be time later to continue their lovemaking. But now he was probably hungry after traveling. They could go out for some authentic Mexican food and she could show him around the city a bit.

"Hey, you," she said, turning to focus on the handsome man beside her.

Evan raised himself on one elbow and looked at her. His face was so open and vulnerable in its ease and fulfillment and tenderness that she had to reach up and touch his mouth. This led to his taking her in his arms again, and Ruby forgot her plans for dinner as their lips met...

When Ruby next opened her eyes, it was dark outside. They'd

made love twice more. At one point, Evan used two of Ruby's scarves to tie her down, reminding her with the crack of his hard, perfect palm on her ass that he was still the Master in the bedroom.

She glanced at the clock beside the bed, which indicated it was nine fifteen. "Hey, Evan," she said, giving his shoulder a little shake. "You awake?"

"Mmm," he said sleepily. But after a moment, he lifted his head and focused on her, his mouth splitting into a wide smile. "Wow, you're real." He reached for her, stroking her cheek with his thumb. "I thought for a second I had to be dreaming."

"I'm real, all right," Ruby agreed with a laugh. "And I'm starving. How about you? Want to get something to eat? I know a great little place not that far from here."

~*~

The food was delicious—fresh and spicy, nothing like the TexMex Evan thought of as Mexican. They were seated outside on a large patio near the water. The space was lit by hundreds of tiny Christmas lights strung across poles overhead, and a live band played on a small stage in the corner. While he enjoyed the meal and the atmosphere, he wouldn't have cared if they'd eaten at Taco Bell as long as he was with Ruby.

He told her about the offer Bob had made to get a BDSM Connections Dungeon going in London. "I haven't given him an answer yet. He's got money in the budget to include a partner. He even mentioned you specifically as a possibility."

"Really?" Ruby said, leaning forward. "Tell me more."

They discussed the details, what little Evan knew of them. "He wants us to scope it out and see what's there. If it looks like the right fit, we would jump in with both feet to get it up and running. Organizing a

BDSM dungeon might not be as fulfilling as helping to resettle refugees or teach little children how to read, but it would definitely be something fun and different."

"A new adventure," Ruby agreed enthusiastically. "I knew there was a reason I hadn't figured out my next project. I've never done anything like that, and I can't think of anyone I'd rather do it with. Count me in."

Evan thought back to the airport when those words he hadn't uttered in over a decade leaped of their own accord from his lips.

I love you.

The world hadn't tilted precariously on its axis at his pronouncement. No walls had crumbled, no thunder had cracked, no iron ball and chain had suddenly locked itself onto his ankle.

Reaching across the small table, he placed his hand on Ruby's arm and said it again. "I love you, Ruby."

Her dark eyes shone with an inner light, her lovely mouth lifted into a sweet smile. "I love you, too, Evan."

As they sipped strong coffee and shared a delicious, creamy flan for dessert, Evan contemplated the light, pure feeling that loving Ruby brought to him.

"What?" Ruby said, tilting her head as she regarded him. "You seem lost in thought. What're you thinking?"

By reflex, he started to say, "Nothing important," but he stopped himself. This *was* important. And he wanted to share it with Ruby. "I was thinking," he said instead, "that I've never really been in love before."

Ruby lifted her eyebrows. "But you said you were married. Surely you loved your wife? At least at first?"

"I thought it was love at the time, but looking at it now, now that I'm actually in love, I think I'm figuring out I was at a time and place in my life when I was in love with the idea of being in love more than anything."

Ruby nodded. "That's not unusual, especially when you're a kid. You were, what, nineteen? Twenty?"

Evan nodded. "Looking back at it now, I wasn't really even capable of love back then. I didn't have girlfriends—I took hostages."

"Hostages?" Ruby laughed. "What do you mean?"

"Back then I was super possessive and controlling, and it had nothing to do with being a Dom. It didn't have much to do with love either, not as I would define it now. I think it had everything to do with being insecure. I would essentially take a girl over and completely lose myself in her. I gave and demanded full devotion and constant attention. It had to be kind of overwhelming to them."

"You were a kid," Ruby reminded him.

"Yeah, but I'm no kid now." He shook his head, marveling at the close call. "I can't believe how stupid I was. I almost blew it. I would have let you go, Ruby, if Taggart hadn't stepped in and forced me to look at what I was doing."

"You know, a good friend once said a wise thing to me. She said, 'It takes what it takes,' meaning we go through what we need to in order to get to the next place in our development. That's just life. You need to stop beating yourself up over this stuff. Especially about me, because I did the same thing, Evan."

"Huh? No." Evan put his hand on Ruby's arm, confused. "You were the most wonderful, open, loving person I've ever met in my life. And you took this teaching thing because you were helping out a friend. You're this amazing, free-spirited, altruistic gypsy girl, and instead of being thrilled to my bones that you were with me, I got all pissed that you were leaving *me.*" He gave a small, brittle chuckle. "There it is again, all about me, me, me."

"I get that. You *were* a little bit of a dick," Ruby said, flashing a grin. "But I was, too. I kept waiting for you to say you loved me. Though it wasn't a super conscious thing, I was damned if I was going to say it first. And when Alan asked me to fill in for him, I could have said no. Ernesto could have found someone else. I think a part of me was waiting for you to object, and when you didn't, I took that to mean we weren't meant to be. And while I was down here, I could have been more honest. I could have sent the texts I actually typed, the ones that said how much I missed you and longed for you and needed you and...loved you..." She trailed off, her face suffusing with color.

Evan's heart contracted with surprise and delight. "You wanted to text those things? Really?"

"Yes!" Ruby laughed. "Yes, Evan. I wanted to call you, too, and *tell* you those things. So why the fuck didn't I? I'm thirty-two years old, and I was acting like a teenager, waiting for the guy to call. I'm so used to telling myself and the world that I'm a gypsy and I have to be free that I almost let the best thing to ever happen to me—you—slip away." She laughed. "It's a good thing we have friends like Allie and Taggart, right? Left to our own devices, we'd have totally fucked up this relationship."

"Maybe," Evan said. He put down his napkin and got to his feet. Stepping around the small table, he held out his hand, and Ruby took it, allowing him to pull her upright. Taking her into his arms, he said softly, "I guess it takes what it takes, huh? I want you to know that my heart belongs to you, and only you. That doesn't mean I expect to own you or control you."

"Not even in the bedroom?" Ruby retorted with a mock pout. "Damn."

"Okay, okay," he amended with a laugh. "In the bedroom, I

promise to own and use you as I see fit, sub girl."

"Phew," she said with a laugh.

"But seriously, Ruby. I get it that you have your own ideals and your own dreams. I promise not to take you hostage, except maybe during a fantasy kidnapping."

"Oooh!" Ruby said, hugging herself. "That sounds yummy."

Evan laughed, the tight coil of anxiety and pain he'd carried since her departure now completely unwound inside him. "You're incorrigible, young lady. I think another spanking may be in order."

"Yes, Sir," she agreed eagerly, making him laugh again.

~*~

When they emerged from customs at Portland International two evenings later, Ruby saw Allie first. Liam was beside her, and he waved as they approached.

"Hey, there's Taggart and Rylee too," Evan said, pointing to the couple who stood just behind the other two.

Ruby laughed. "What the heck are they all doing here?"

When they reached their friends, they exchanged hugs, hearty backslaps and kisses. "In case you're wondering why we're all here," Rylee said with a grin, "we couldn't agree on who would come get you. We've all gotten kind of invested in the outcome of this crazy romance of yours."

"About that," Evan said, looking at them each in turn. "Thank you all for what you did." He put his hand on Taggart's shoulder. "Especially you, buddy. Thanks for knocking some sense into my thick head."

Ruby smiled as she watched the two men, her heart warming. She turned to Allie. "And thank you, girlfriend, for reminding me that even gypsies can fall in love."

"I gotta ask," Evan said. "Were you guys in cahoots? Tag, when you were telling me to get on the next plane, did you know Allie had sent Ruby a return ticket?"

Taggart's laugh was hearty. "We acted independently, if you can believe it. But then Rylee and Allie told each other what was going on, and we figured out what we'd done. We were just deciding how to handle it when Ruby texted Allie."

"So it was kismet," Liam said. "You two were destined to reconnect. We just gave a helping hand."

They all piled into Taggart's big truck, which had two bench seats and easily accommodated them all. Taggart, Rylee and Liam sat in front, Allie, Ruby and Evan in back.

"You guys hungry?" Allie asked as they got on the road. "Bonnie and Matt are waiting for us at this great Italian place downtown."

"Starving," Evan and Ruby said in unison, and everyone laughed.

Matt and Bonnie were seated at a large table in the corner of a small, bustling restaurant. The intoxicating scent of garlic, fresh bread and rich tomato sauce permeated the air. As everyone greeted one another and sat down, Bonnie explained, "Wild horses couldn't have kept us away from this reunion. I always was a sucker for true romance."

"More than a sucker," Allie said with a laugh. "Did Ruby tell you what Bonnie did to get Liam and me together?"

"I never got a chance to tell him," Ruby said. "You guys are all into playing Cupid, huh?"

"Lucky for us," Evan added, giving Ruby's hand a squeeze under the table, his smile melting her insides.

As Bonnie recounted the way she'd arranged Allie and Liam's first face-to-face meeting, Matt poured red wine into everyone's glasses. When she was done with her story, he raised his glass and the others followed suit.

"To good friends," he said, beaming at Ruby and Evan. "New and old."

They clinked glasses and sipped at the dry, delicious Cabernet. Then Evan raised his glass. "I'd like to make another toast," he said, his thigh warm against Ruby's. "To true love, the greatest adventure of them   all."

Epilogue — Three Months Later

Ruby sat on the wraparound porch of Evan's charming Victorian house, which was at the top of a steep street in the Mountain View district of San Francisco. It was a remarkably sunny day, the early morning fog burned away. The bay was visible in the distance, and though it was the middle of December, some wildflowers were still blooming in his front garden.

She pulled her shawl closer around her shoulders as a chilly wind blew across the porch and took another sip of hot coffee.

Evan had flown to Los Angeles the night before to meet with a group interested in holding a BDSM convention in the spring. Ruby had chosen to stay behind, eager to continue work on the series of abstract paintings on silk she'd been working on, inspired by the flowers in Evan's garden.

When he arrived home that evening, she planned to be waiting for him in the front hall, naked and on her knees, their favorite flogger balanced across her thighs.

Taking over the BDSM Club in London and getting it up to BDSM Connections standards had been both more fun and more of a challenge than she'd expected. While Evan was great at negotiating contracts and procuring equipment at bargain prices, Ruby had discovered she was good at connecting with local BDSM groups.

She loved Bob's vision of creating not only a BDSM play club, but an events center where like-minded folk in the lifestyle could gather to learn and explore new topics in privacy and safety. She spent a lot of her time during their first two months on the job scoping out the local BDSM scene, connecting with the key players in various groups and organizations and getting them as excited about the prospect of the events center as she was.

When they'd held their grand opening their ninth week in, the turnout had been spectacular. She'd had a great time helping Evan demonstrate the various equipment and toys they'd bought to resell. Bob had flown over for the event. He'd been so delighted that he'd given them both a rather substantial bonus on the spot.

Beyond the simple satisfaction of succeeding in their shared project, Ruby was happier than she'd ever been in her life. As far as she was concerned, it wouldn't have mattered if Evan and she had been working together in a hardware store in Iowa, building fences in Nepal or sailing around the world on some billionaire's yacht—as long as they were doing it together.

She looked again at the email she'd just received from a volunteer group in India she'd heard a lot of great things about, but had never worked with directly. The opportunity was in the Sadhana Forest in Tamil Nadu. The ongoing project revolved around the reforestation of seventy acres of severely eroded land. No particular skills were required, other than a willingness to work hard, a commitment of at least a month, and a taste for adventure.

After spending so much time in the urban sprawl of London and now San Francisco, Ruby was eager to return to the peace and purity of nature. But what about Evan? He was much more of a city boy, no question about that. How would he handle the idea of living in a tent or a shack on the other side of the world, doing backbreaking labor for ten hours a day?

Another chilly breeze wafted over her, the sun suddenly eclipsed by a series of dark, rolling clouds. Ruby got to her feet and went inside. Evan would be home soon, and the thought made her smile.

~*~

Evan opened the front door, Ruby's name on his lips. Then he saw her, the very picture of feminine submission, kneeling naked on the floor at his feet. His cock sprang into an instant, aching erection.

He dropped his briefcase and moved to stand in front of her. She raised her head slowly, a small smile flitting over her lips, the tiny diamond in her nose glinting prettily against her olive skin. "Welcome home, Sir. How may I please you?"

Power and desire surged like fire through Evan's blood. He gripped the fly of his jeans and yanked at the metal buttons that held it closed. Ruby rose on her haunches, the flogger on her knees falling to the floor between them as she reached for his shaft through the fly of his boxers.

He closed his eyes with a satisfied sigh as she took in the length of him. He entwined his fingers in her thick, soft hair as she sucked and stroked him with her perfect mouth and slender fingers.

He wanted to make it last, but it was a losing battle as she worked her skillful magic. Within minutes, he groaned and stiffened, his seed shooting in ribbons down her throat.

She pulled back, letting his still-hard cock fall from her pretty lips, a catlike look of satisfaction on her face.

Evan bent down and picked up the flogger. "Stand up," he commanded. "Back to me, hands behind your head."

He brushed her skin with the tresses, moving rapidly from a caress to stinging, thuddy blows that reddened her skin from shoulder to thigh. She was breathing hard, the sound audible between the swishing strokes of the whip.

He could feel each sting of the lash as if it were kissing his own skin. And when she passed through the pain and moved into that sweet, altered state of submissive peace, he flew alongside her, more in love with her than ever.

Finally, he lowered the flogger and moved to stand in front of his still-flying angel. She opened her eyes slowly, fixing them on his face, her lips softly parted. Without speaking, he lifted her into his arms and carried her up the stairs to the bedroom.

He lowered her gently to the mattress. Stripping quickly out of his clothing, he draped himself over her. Her legs fell open as she lifted her arms to pull him down. He groaned with pleasure as he entered her.

"I love you," they whispered in unison.

Sometime later Evan opened his eyes. Ruby lay beside him, lifted on one elbow, her eyes moving over his face. "What?" he said, coming more fully awake. "Is everything okay?"

She had her cell phone in her hand. "I got an email today. We have a chance to go to India. I've done projects like this before, and while it's hard work, it can be incredibly rewarding. We've been looking for the next adventure, so…" She trailed off, looking both excited and a little anxious.

"India, wow," Evan said. "I've always wanted to go to India. Does it involve BDSM? Are we going to teach some Buddhist monks Shibari knot techniques?"

Ruby laughed. "Who knows, maybe there's a whole unexplored market there. But no"—she held out her cell phone—"it's a little more basic than that."

Evan took the phone. The screen was open to an email with a subject line of, *"Volunteer to re-create the tropical dry evergreen forest indigenous to our area."* Evan scanned the email. As he read the details, excitement bloomed in his chest. Ruby wanted him to do this with her. He had included her in his life with the London project, and now she was including him in hers with this opportunity.

Before he'd met this amazing woman, he would never have considered volunteering for anything not BDSM related and would never have imagined himself digging in the dirt in some obscure location in India. The old Evan would have been in panic mode, his suitcase already packed, his shoes waiting under the bed. But that guy was gone, and Evan didn't miss him one bit. For the first time in his life, he was living fully in the moment, and he was doing it with the woman of his dreams.

He looked at Ruby, his heart aching with love. "When do we go?"

Did you enjoy the story? Indie authors rely heavily on reviews to get the word out. Please take a moment to leave a quick review on Amazon.

And here's a sneak peek at chapter one of *The Compound* – Book 1 of *The Compound* series.

CHAPTER 1

"Offer yourself. Stop holding back. Give it to me!" The flogger struck her body with so much force Alexis was knocked out of position. She stumbled forward into the two men standing just in front of her who were watching the scene with gaping mouths and visible erections.

They both reached for her with hot hands, catching and steadying her. Alexis twisted back to face Arthur as she pulled away from the strangers. She was panting, her skin on fire, her nipples hard as cherry pits. She wrapped her arms around her torso and licked her lips, wishing the men clustered around them would disappear.

"Focus," Arthur snapped, his dark eyes blazing. "Nothing matters but you and me and this." He held up the heavy-tressed leather flogger. "Get back in position. Now."

With a nod, Alexis turned again, facing the men whose eyes moved hungrily over her body, which was covered only by a pair of black silk bikini panties. She grasped her left wrist with her right hand, extending her arms high over her head. She planted her bare feet firmly on the floor, shoulder-width apart.

Arthur came up close behind her and she had to resist a sudden impulse to lean back into him. He reached for her long ponytail, which he lifted and placed over her shoulder and out of the way. Alexis almost smiled—Arthur was always so thoughtful.

The flogger struck her ass, a heavy, thudding thwack that made her tense her muscles in order to stay upright. Stinging ribbons of leather struck her back and shoulders. The burn on her skin was matched by the heat in her cunt, which was stoked by each stinging cut of the lash.

She was close. She could feel it. She was almost there, almost to that point where she could let go and soar, becoming one with the leather, one with the pain, one with the pleasure of pure, sweet submission...

"Jesus, she's so fucking hot. What I wouldn't give to bury my cock in that."

The words distracted her, uttered by one of the gawkers that always surrounded her at every scene. She felt herself being pulled back to earth by the snickers and muttered agreement of the spectators. She could smell their body odor—sweat, stale cigarette smoke and cheap cologne. She opened her eyes, glaring at them, twitching and jerking as the flogger thudded against her.

Another hard blow made her stumble forward, her concentration shattered, her balance off. She jerked away from the greedy hands of the men waiting to catch her and whirled toward Arthur, her anger at herself misdirected toward him. "I can't do this. I can't!"

"You won't," he retorted, frowning, but he put down the flogger and reached for her robe, which he draped around her shoulders.

"Show's over," he said to the men still crowded around them. The group parted as he led Alexis past them toward the juice bar. She perched gingerly on the stool, her ass still stinging from the flogging.

She sipped fresh grapefruit juice over crushed ice, watching Arthur out of the corner of her eye. He had ordered coffee, into which he was stirring several spoons of sugar. He was frowning into the cup.

"What?" she demanded, feeling defensive.

"You know what. That scene back there. When are you going to move past whatever it is that's holding you back?"

"Maybe I can't." Alexis snapped angrily. "Maybe I'm just a player, a masochistic exhibitionist with something to prove."

Arthur looked at her, his kind, hound dog eyes searching hers. "Do you really believe that?"

Alexis shrugged miserably, looking away. "I don't know. I'm starting to think so. I get to a certain point and I just, I don't know, I shut down."

Arthur nodded. "It's not so easy here in this public venue. Maybe we should..."

Alexis shook her head firmly. It wasn't the first time one or the other of them had entertained the idea of meeting at a motel to try their scenes in private. Alexis knew in her bones that would be a bad move for both of them, and she reminded Arthur of this now. "No. You know you would hate yourself if you did something behind Naomi's back. And that would make you hate me, too. I couldn't bear that, Arthur, losing what we have now."

Arthur nodded, unconsciously playing with his wedding ring. His wife of twenty-six years was not at all into the BDSM scene, but understood Arthur's need to explore his dominant side. After years of failed experimentation, and Arthur sneaking around to get his needs met, they'd come to a compromise that he could scene all he wanted at the BDSM clubs, as long as he kept it there, and kept his cock in his pants.

Though twenty-five years Alexis's senior, Arthur was still a handsome man, in a grizzled, rough sort of way, and she found it romantic that he was so obviously still in love with his wife, despite their sexual differences. Alexis never wanted to be the one to come between them, no matter how attracted she might be to her favorite scene partner.

The scene, as much as she hated to admit it, was getting old. But what was left?

Maybe it was because she was about to turn thirty, and she'd recently been taking stock of her life. On the surface she looked like a Manhattan success story—already a junior partner at a top CPA firm, making good money in a job she found both challenging and satisfying. She had a great apartment in a good neighborhood near Central Park, where she jogged each morning before work to keep herself fit and toned.

She'd had several serious relationships in her twenties, the first two vanilla, the last one this past year with a dominant man she thought she might be in love with, but it had fizzled out. She'd met him at this very BDSM club, and had been excited by the promise of a 24/7 D/s relationship, but their ideas of what that entailed hadn't matched.

Alexis longed to connect with what she believed was her inner submissive core, while James, it turned out, was more into the trappings of the scene—like having her wear a collar and meet him naked in the foyer when he got home from work. He wanted her to call him Master, and wake him up with a blow job each morning. He was good with a whip, but somehow always seemed to stop just before she reached that place that she felt, in her bones, would somehow set her free.

She had come to realize it was more of a sexy game for him than anything. She rarely felt that tremor of fear and desire that infused her sexual fantasies with a blaze of erotic heat. She never truly submitted to him, not with her heart and soul, as she dreamed of doing with the right man, if such a man existed. In the end, she realized she had wanted more than he could give. Yet when he'd gone she was lonelier than ever, left to wonder if what she craved was unattainable.

"Earth to Alexis." Arthur was regarding her with a quizzical smile.

"Oh, sorry. I was drifting."

Arthur studied her a moment and then said, "You're sad." It wasn't a question, but a statement, and Alexis nodded, surprised to find a tear rolling down her cheek. She wiped it away, annoyed with herself. She was at the club to have fun, to forget, not to wallow in her misery.

As if sensing her embarrassment, Arthur turned back to his coffee. He lifted the cup and took a long sip. "You know," he said, "I've been thinking for a while now that you need more than you can get at a club like this. You need someone who can break past those barriers you place in your own way."

"Tell me about it," she agreed morosely. "You saw how great things worked out with James."

Arthur smiled kindly. "James isn't the only dominant fish in the sea, my dear. In fact, between you and me, I'm not sure he's dominant at all. He's more of a slap and tickle kind of guy. I never thought he was right for you."

"Ha." Alexis grinned in spite of herself. "Well, thanks for the heads up on that one."

"Like you would have listened to me," he rejoined. "You were sure you'd found 'the one', remember?" He used his fingers to put quotations around the words.

"Yeah," she admitted with a sigh. "I don't know if such a person exists, to tell you the truth. At least not for me. I'm scared to admit it, but I think I'm the problem, and that really sucks, you know?"

"I might have a solution for your problem," Arthur said slowly, turning on his stool to face her. "There's a place I heard about recently, located upstate. It's a BDSM training facility. It's pretty intense, from what I understand. The primary focus is on slave training. Maybe the trainers there could help you get past whatever it is that's holding you back."

Alexis felt a chill move down her spine, part fear, part thrill. Just the words *slave training* sent a tremor of excitement and longing through her entire being. "Tell me more," she urged, leaning toward him. "Is there a website?"

Arthur shook his head. "No website. It's a very private place. Word of mouth only. Off the grid, I guess you'd say. You need a referral. I know someone who knows someone. If you were interested, I could probably get an email address for you to at least start the process."

"It sounds intriguing. But upstate? How far? I don't have a car, you know. Not to mention I work sixty hours a week."

"Well, if you were serious about it, you'd have to take off from work. It's not some part time commitment, Alexis. You live there during the training. We're talking full immersion, 24/7. I believe the initial commitment is a month."

"A *month*? How could I ever take a month off work?" Even as she said this, she knew she could get a month if she wanted. In fact, just the week before, Jenny Olsen, her friend in human resources, had called Alexis into her office, handing her a printout of her accrued vacation time. "I wanted to give you the heads up. You have six unused weeks of vacation time. There's a new policy coming down the pike—starting next year, whatever you don't use, you lose. My advice is to take your time now. You know the senior guys will get priority once word's out about the change."

Arthur raised his eyebrows. "When was the last time you took a vacation? I mean a real vacation, not a long weekend? Tax season is over." He shrugged. "Maybe you should find out more about it before you make a decision. Maybe it's more than you could handle anyway."

"Get me the email address," she snapped. Arthur grinned and she grinned back, aware he'd set her up. The minute he'd suggested it was more than she could handle, she'd bristled, taking the challenge.

Later that night alone in bed, Alexis reached for her trusty vibrator. She squeezed a dollop of lubricant onto the head and nestled the phallus between her labia. Flicking it to a low setting, she closed her eyes, surrendering herself to her favorite fantasies of being bound and controlled by a strong, sexy guy who took her past her limits with his touch, his words, his whip, his kiss...

She is tied with strips of red silk, knotted around her wrists and ankles, pulling her into a human X. Her body is bathed in sweat, her dark hair flying as she twists and moans with each cutting kiss of the single tail he is flicking over her body. She is panting, nearly crying, biting her lip to keep from begging. "Stop, don't stop, never stop..." Dropping the whip at last, he moves to stand in front of her, taking her face in his hands and kissing her lips, slipping his tongue into her mouth while his hard, insistent fingers push into her wetness.

She is on his bed, a large bed with soft sheets. He looms over her, his body hard and strong as he eases his huge cock inside her. "What are you?"

"The place where your cock goes, Sir."

"I own you."

"Yesssss..."

She flicked the vibrator to high and slid it inside herself. The vibrations whirred against her engorged clit, the phallus throbbing inside her. As his hard cock pummeled her to orgasm, Alexis tried to see the man's face in her fantasy, but there was only shadow, and then even that slipped away.

With a sigh, she turned off the toy and eased it from her pussy, dropping it onto the small towel by her bed so she'd remember to wash it in the morning. She closed her eyes and sighed, waiting for sleep to claim her.

But instead of slipping into dreams, her conversation with Arthur kept coming back to her. *The Compound*. It sounded sexy and a little dangerous.

Without realizing what she was doing, Alexis found her fingers had slipped back between her legs, sliding into the wetness still left from the lubricant and her own lust. She rubbed herself, imagining her breasts pressed against rough stone as a whip struck her again and again. Her wrists were cuffed into manacles set into the stone, her legs stretched wide and secured at the ankle.

The man drops his whip at last and presses his hard body against her flayed, stinging back. She feels his hands spreading her ass, and then the press of his impossibly hard cock against her nether entrance. He eases himself inside her, moving slowly, but still she feels as if she's being split in two by his girth. His fingers dig into her hips as he begins to thrust in and out of her ass. "Someday," he murmurs, his lips touching her ear, "I will fuck your cunt. When you prove yourself worthy, when you submit without reservation, when you give of yourself completely."

Alexis moaned aloud, arching her hips, her fingers a flurry as she brought herself to a second orgasm, more powerful than the first. She lay still, a light sweat cooling on her skin, until the rapid tapping of her heart slowly subsided.

She heard a pinging sound on her iPhone and reached for it from the nightstand beside her bed. She had an email from Arthur. The subject read: *The Compound.* The body of the email consisted of an email address along with a note from Arthur that she'd been cleared as a possible applicant.

Just tell them the truth, he'd written, *about what you're looking for, and that you'd like more information about the program offered through The Compound. Don't wuss out, Alexis. This is your chance. Take it. Good luck! Arthur.*

Before she could lose her resolve, Alexis copied the email address and pasted it into a new email.

Dear Mistress Miriam,

My name is Alexis Stewart...

It had been two weeks since she first began her email correspondence with Mistress Miriam. The initial exchange had been conversational in tone, with Alexis being as honest as she could in expressing her needs, experience and goals. She'd been surprised but pleased to learn there was no cost to attend the program.

Alexis had completed a lengthy questionnaire about her experience in the scene, likes, dislikes, goals, hard limits, etc. She'd undergone a complete physical and blood work to prove she was in good health and disease-free. She was impressed when Mistress Miriam told her all staff members at The Compound were held to the same high standards. Alexis had been thrilled when Mistress Miriam told her she appeared to be a good candidate for The Compound. She put in for and was approved for a full month's vacation time at work.

Arthur drove her the two hours from the city. As he pulled up in front of the large main building of what appeared to have once been a horse farm, Alexis experienced the same clutch of excitement and fear as when she'd been shipped off to sleep away camp as a child. Arthur gave her a quick farewell kiss on the cheek. "Good luck, kiddo."

There was still the face-to-face interview to undergo before she was formally accepted into the program. "If by some chance we decide you aren't right for the program," Mistress Miriam had assured her in her last email, "we have a driver who can give you a lift back to the city. No need to make your ride wait."

Alexis grabbed her bag and went up to the large front door. Before she could even lift the heavy brass knocker, the door was opened by a tall young man dressed in only a black thong, a thick leather collar secured at his throat by a padlock. He didn't speak, but only nodded toward her as he reached down to take her suitcase. He led her into a brightly lit office space with large bay windows that looked out over a huge swimming pool and beautiful flower gardens.

An imposing woman in her late thirties stood as they entered, moving from behind her desk to take Alexis's hand in hers. "Welcome, Alexis. I'm Mistress Miriam." Her voice fit her perfectly, low and smooth, with just the hint of a British accent. She was a striking woman, with lustrous dark hair falling in waves to her shoulders and eyes a vivid blue. She wore a tailored red silk jacket that revealed a hint of bare nipple beneath, over red leather pants that looked soft as butter. She radiated confidence and power. She exuded raw sexuality, and for a nearly irresistible second, Alexis had the impulse to lean forward and kiss those full, sensuous lips.

"You may wait outside, Josh," Mistress Miriam said, turning her attention for a moment to the male slave. He nodded and stepped out, closing the door silently behind him.

Mistress Miriam leaned against the edge of the desk and regarded Alexis with a cool gaze. Without any preamble, she said simply, "Take off your clothes, everything except panties."

Though she'd been expecting this, or something like it, Alexis's mouth went suddenly dry. Under Mistress Miriam's cool gaze, she stood and reached for the buttons of her blouse, praying her hands wouldn't shake. Her eyes flicked toward a black leather flogger and a long, thin rattan cane that rested on the desk beside Mistress Miriam. Alexis let the blouse fall from her shoulders as she kicked off her sandals. She unbuckled her belt, opened her pants and slid them down her legs. Finally, taking a breath, she reached back and undid the clasps to her bra.

"Fold your things and place them on the desk," Mistress Miriam instructed. "Then stand at attention, hands behind your head." Alexis reached for her things, placing them on the desk as instructed. Lifting her arms, she locked her fingers behind her head and waited, hoping she didn't look as nervous as she felt.

"Stand up straight," Mistress Miriam snapped. "Breasts out."

Alexis put her shoulders back, thrusting her size C breasts forward, willing away the heat that wanted to climb into her face. She wasn't shy about her body, but something about Mistress Miriam's piercing gaze made her want to cover herself. She forced herself to resist the impulse.

Mistress Miriam stood, moving to stand directly in front of Alexis. "You stated on the questionnaire that you believe you are submissive, but you've had trouble reaching the inner core of that submission. In your essay you questioned if you might only be sexually masochistic, and not really capable of true submission. Do I have that correct, Alexis?"

"Yes, Mistress."

"Are you obedient?"

In the right circumstances, Alexis thought. *With the right man.* Glancing at the gorgeous Mistress Miriam, she suddenly wondered—with the right woman? Aloud she replied, "Yes, Mistress."

Mistress Miriam stepped back. She cupped Alexis's left breast, lifting it and letting it fall. She pinched both Alexis's nipples with her sharp, blood red nails. Alexis pressed her lips together to keep from crying out, her eyes on Mistress Miriam's face, her hands locked obediently behind her head. When Mistress Miriam finally let go, Alexis's nipples were erect and throbbing.

Mistress Miriam put a hand over Alexis's crotch, and Alexis almost stepped back, embarrassed to be touched so intimately by another woman, especially when she knew her panties were damp from the exchange between them so far. She stopped herself in time, determined to prove she was obedient, though she couldn't stop her gasp when Mistress Miriam slipped a finger into her panties.

"If we accept you, this will have to go." Mistress Miriam tugged lightly at Alexis's pubic hair. "We have a specialist in full body waxing. All our trainees must be smooth and completely accessible at all times. Is that a problem?"

"No, Mistress," Alexis replied.

Mistress Miriam returned to the desk, though she didn't sit down. "Which do you prefer, the flogger or the cane?"

"The flogger," Alexis said immediately. It was no contest—she hated to be caned. It held none of the sweet, thuddy sensuousness of a flogging. It just plain fucking hurt.

"Ah. Then we'll use the cane." One side of Mistress Miriam's mouth lifted in a cruel smile.

If she had said the cane, would Mistress Miriam have picked the flogger? Probably. Though then again, probably not. Somehow Alexis sensed she would have known she was lying. How had Mistress Miriam managed to hone in on the one thing Alexis had a hard time with? Was it some kind of sadist's sixth sense? She could take a single tail, she could even handle a bull whip. But the cane—with its stingy bite, and that scary whooshing sound just before it struck the skin—sent a chill down her back just thinking about it.

You got this far, she admonished herself. *Don't screw it up now.*

"Face the chair, bend over and grab the arms. Legs wide, ass out. Oh, and take off those panties."

Alexis pulled her panties down and stepped out of them, adding them to the folded pile of her clothing. Taking a breath, she turned toward the chair. She bent forward and gripped the smooth wooden arms, steadying herself as she spread her legs. Her heart was beating a mile a minute, but she was determined. She could do this. She *would* do this.

She could hear Mistress Miriam moving behind her. When she felt the light tap of the cane against her ass, she stiffened, but managed to remain still. By turning her head, she could just see Mistress Miriam out of the corner of her eye, standing back and to the side.

"Eyes straight ahead," Mistress Miriam snapped, punctuating her words with the first real strike of the cane. Alexis gasped in pain, gripping the chair arms hard as she struggled to maintain her composure. Several more hard whacks followed in quick succession, each one landing just below the last. As the cane moved lower, covering the fleshier part of Alexis's ass, she found herself better able to tolerate the stinging blows.

Until the one that struck just where her ass met her thighs. It was harder than the others, preceded by that sudden, terrifying *whoosh* and then a searing, biting flash of pain that pushed a cry from Alexis's lips.

She lifted her head, her eyes momentarily blinded by tears. *Stop fighting it. Flow with the pain. Become one with it.* She could almost hear Arthur admonishing her, and she tried to do just that, though she'd never really understood the concept, not on a gut level. Another blow caught her on the hip and she gritted her teeth, not sure she could take much more of this.

She looked out the window, thinking maybe she could distract herself enough with the view to at least get through this caning without making a fool of herself by screaming, or worse, turning around and grabbing the fucking thing from Mistress Miriam's hands and breaking it clean in two.

And then she saw him.

The pool had been empty when she'd first entered the office, but now someone was swimming in it— muscular back and powerful shoulders moving through the water and then a head lifting, shaking the water from long auburn hair that glittered like dark, wet gold in the sunlight.

The man moved to the opposite side of the pool and lifted his arms on either side, leaning back against the edge of the pool, revealing his smooth, bronzed chest. His jaw was square, his nose prominent.

He seemed to be staring directly at her.

The cane cut her ass again, and again, but somehow, with her eyes on the handsomest man she'd ever seen in her life, Alexis found herself able to tolerate the blows. She began to breathe more deeply, her tightly-clenched muscles easing as she imagined that the man could see her, even though she knew he probably could not, being out in the sun as he was.

Still, he kept his gaze toward the window, and she kept her gaze on him, drawing strength and courage from his handsome visage, her cunt moistening as she drank in the masculine curves of his body. Would he be her trainer?

Please, please, please, let him be my trainer.

Suddenly Alexis felt Mistress Miriam's cool fingers tracing the welts she had raised along Alexis's ass and thighs. When the hand slid between her legs, Alexis gasped, but maintained her position. She looked again at the Greek god still leaning back against the side of the pool, and imagined it was his hand touching her pussy, probing her entrance, sliding over her clit.

When Mistress Miriam began to rub and tease her, Alexis kept her focus on the man in the pool. The caning, though it had hurt like hell, had aroused Alexis, as all erotic pain did. That arousal, along with the vision of the man in the pool, and the realization that a gorgeous, dominant woman was touching her, all combined to make Alexis tremble and moan, teetering suddenly on the edge of an orgasm.

She felt Mistress Miriam moving closer, her small breasts touching Alexis's bare back. Her perfume was intoxicating, her touch a velvet heat at Alexis's cunt.

"Come for me, Alexis."

She did, keeping her eyes on the handsome man until they fluttered shut in the last throes of a powerful orgasm. She sank to her knees in front of the chair, her body shaking, her heart beating fast, her breath ragged in her throat.

When she finally regained enough control to pull herself upright, she turned to face Mistress Miriam, who was seated once more behind the desk, the cane back in its place beside the flogger.

"You'll do," she said, a small smile playing over her lips. "Sit down and we'll go over the contract."

With a glance at her clothing, Alexis settled gingerly on the edge of the chair, her ass still smarting from the cane. Mistress Miriam pushed a piece of paper over the desk toward her. "This is the contract. Take your time. Read it carefully. It basically gives us full discretion to train you as we see fit. The minimum stay is one month, and by signing the contract, you give up all rights and control. You will become a compound slave, and as such subject to the dictates and control of every Master and

Mistress here. You will be assigned to a specific trainer, who will have primary responsibility for your training.

"Once training is deemed complete, if you're interested, there is a significant market of Dominants interested in procuring trained sex slaves and submissives for their own use. You would be amply compensated, if that's a route you choose, and the fees for placement are handled by the Master who procured you. Otherwise you are free to return to your life. Some slaves choose to remain on The Compound after training, if there's a place for them."

Mistress Miriam smiled. "But I'm getting ahead of myself. First things first. Read the contract. Take your time. Just be aware, once you sign, there's no going back. You are committed to the month, with no recourse to leave the program. I'll give you a few minutes alone. Can I bring you something? Coffee, a cold drink?"

Alexis swallowed, her mind reeling with what she was about to do. "Water would be good," she managed, realizing she was in fact quite thirsty. She picked up the single page, trying to focus on the words. She couldn't resist turning back toward the window, but the man who had been swimming was gone.

She read the terms of the contract, which were as Mistress Miriam had stated. If Alexis signed, she basically agreed to give up all rights to her person for the duration of the one-month training period. Once she signed the contract, she would be expected to comply with every dictate of The Compound staff. She would agree to submit to physical punishment and training, including but not limited to whipping, flogging, caning, bondage, sexual torture and stimulation, orgasm training and control, and sexual interactions of all kinds with her trainer and whoever the trainer deemed appropriate in the course of her training. She thought back to the first night Arthur had brought up the idea, and realized her fantasies, as wild as she had thought them at the time, weren't at all far from the truth.

She lifted the pen Mistress Miriam had left for her, hesitating over the signature line. She didn't have to sign. No one was holding a gun to her head. It wasn't too late—she could still walk away. This was her choice, and hers alone.

Her ass still stinging from the bite of the cane, her cunt still throbbing from the intense orgasm she'd experienced under Mistress Miriam's direction, Alexis asked herself if she was ready for this. Did she have the courage to go through with it? Did she want to?

She thought about the years she'd been alone. Even when she was dating guys or involved in a relationship, she always felt, at her core, alone. Her email discussions with Mistress Miriam had clarified what she'd really always known—she was a submissive who hadn't yet found the right person or situation in which to explore and embrace that submission. Now she was being offered an amazing opportunity, and if she walked away she knew she would regret it for the rest of her life.

The office door opened and Alexis turned, expecting to see Mistress Miriam with her glass of water. Instead it was the man she'd seen in the pool, dressed now in a black button-down shirt rolled to his muscular, tanned forearms, and black jeans. Up close he was even handsomer, his eyes the same coppery color as his hair, his skin kissed by the sun.

"You must be Alexis," he said, handing her the water. His eyes moved over her naked body and the blush she'd managed to keep at bay under Mistress Miriam's scrutiny now bloomed over her chest and cheeks. "Mistress Miriam has been detained for a few moments. I'm Master Paul."

Alexis took the water, electrified as their fingers touched. *Please, please, please let* him *be my trainer.*

She realized she was still holding the pen, the contract as yet unsigned. Setting down the water, she leaned over the paper and scrawled her signature on the indicated line.

There! It was done.

She leaned back in her chair, turning toward Master Paul with a nervous smile. He smiled back, his teeth even and white, his eyes crinkling at the corners suggesting a man who laughed often. "I'll take that." He held out his hand, and Alexis passed over the signed contract.

"Welcome to The Compound." He glanced at his watch. "Master John, your trainer, should be here shortly to meet you."

Made in the USA
Monee, IL
25 May 2022

97023724R00163